Blackthorne's Bride

Shana Galen

Blackthorne's Bride

AVON

An Imprint of HarperCollinsPublishers

AVON BOOKS
An Imprint of HarperCollins*Publishers*
10 East 53rd Street
New York, New York 10022-5299

Copyright © 2007 by Shane Bolks
ISBN: 978-0-7394-8996-3

For Linda Andrus
Your support has been invaluable.

Acknowledgments

Thank you to Evan Fogelman, for your steadfast support; to May Chen, for pushing me to make this my best work yet; to Christina Hergenrader and Courtney Burkholder, for your friendship and insight; and to my husband, for your encouragement and unwavering love.

The FULLBRIGHTs

NO MAN'S BRIDE
Edmund and Cordelia (née Brittany)
Catherine (20), Elizabeth (17)

GOOD GROOM HUNTING
Mavis (née Fullbright) and Joseph Hale
Joseph Jr. (22), John (20), Josephine (18)

BLACKTHORNE'S BRIDE
William, Earl of Castleigh and Ellen (née Todd)
Madeleine (18)

The BRITTANYs

Sir Gareth and Imogen (née Stafford)
Thomas (23), Charles (21), William (20),
Ashley (18), Devlin (17), George (15)

Blackthorne's Bride

Chapter 1

London 1801

Lady Madeleine was going to make the best of this night, even if it killed her.

And it probably would kill her.

Maddie shook her head. That was no way to think. If one expected the worst, one received the worst.

But there simply wasn't anything good about dressing in boys' clothing and running around London in the dead of night. Unless one wanted to be kidnapped.

You're doing it again! Maddie chided herself. She had to start thinking positively.

Very well, then . . . She might not like wearing boys' clothing, but at least it was comfortable.

She didn't like to sneak out at night, but at least she didn't have to carry a parasol in the dark.

And she didn't like to climb into darkened windows, risk the wrath of her horrid uncle, or tempt the cutthroats hiding down every London alleyway, but . . .

Oh, Lord! She was going to be murdered, and there was just nothing good about that!

Maddie tightened her grip on her cousin Catie's arm and hurried to catch her two adventuresome cousins, Ashley and Josie.

Above her, the moon was but a sliver in the dark, starless sky. The tall, terraced houses of Mayfair—white and bedecked with flowers spilling from boxes in the daylight—now loomed menacingly over her. They stared at her from sightless eyes.

Maddie tried to keep her gaze on Ashley's blond hair. The London fog obscured everything except what was right in front of one's face, but Ashley's wheat-blond tresses shimmered silver in the meager light. Ashley turned a corner, and Maddie clutched Catie tighter.

"Hurry," Maddie whispered, not wanting to lose sight of Ashley. But then the fog closed in, thick and heavy, and Maddie had to reach out and feel her way past the building on her right. She lurched to the side and stepped on something furry.

With a squeak—hers or its—she ran on.

Catie and she rounded the corner, and Maddie saw Ashley's bright hair. She was waiting for them. Thank heaven for her luminous cousin. The fog hadn't infiltrated this street as thickly yet, and Maddie was able to see the welcoming houses and the small tree-lined park that made up Berkeley Square.

Home. Almost home.

She wasn't going to die.

"Are you well?" Catie asked, pausing for a moment.

"Perfectly fine," Maddie replied, wishing she weren't shaking so badly. "Why do you ask?"

"You're holding my arm so tightly that I'm going to have a bruise."

Maddie loosened her hold. "Sorry."

"It's all right," Catie said.

Jiminy! If anyone should be consoled, Maddie thought, it was Catie. Her horrible father had locked her in a closet for two days. She herself was only out on the dark, unsafe streets because, though she was scared half out of her mind, she couldn't leave Catie in there.

Up ahead, rising out of the fog like a ghostly galleon from a storybook, floated her father's town house.

Home. Safety. For all of them.

The girls climbed up the bed sheets they had left hanging down the side of the house under Maddie's bedroom window. Maddie collapsed gratefully on the floor when her feet were again on solid ground.

When her stomach had ceased fluttering and her limbs were no longer shaking like saplings in a storm, she rose and fetched nightgowns, cool water, and fresh linens for the others. While the girls washed and changed, Maddie opened her desk drawer and pulled out a stash of almond biscuits she'd been saving for just such an occasion. She passed them out as her cousins gathered on the bed.

"Thank you, Mother," Ashley said as she took her biscuit. Maddie stuck out her tongue. She was used to the other girls teasing her for fussing over them, but she knew they appreciated it.

She wasn't the eldest or the bravest or the most beautiful. Respectively, Catie, Josie, and Ashley fit those roles. Maddie had always been the most privileged. Her father was the Earl of Castleigh— rich and powerful.

But privilege was not something one chose, nor something Maddie enjoyed. She would have much rather been courageous or beautiful or wise. Instead, she was frequently described as kind and tenderhearted. Boring descriptors, especially for a girl of eight, but she figured it was the best she could expect.

She scooted onto her bed next to her cousins, and Ashley elbowed her. "Well, that was fun, wasn't it?"

Maddie wanted to groan. Fun? Her insides still jittered from the so-called adventure, and her hands shook as they tried to hold the almond biscuit.

"You know . . . " Catie said quietly. Maddie thought she looked almost dead from fatigue. "Once we grow up and marry, we won't be able to have adventures like this anymore. Our husbands won't let us."

Now, this was a new idea, and one Maddie rather liked. No more climbing out windows. No more scratchy— er, rather comfortable —boys' clothing or dark city streets.

Josie sat forward. "When I become a pirate, I won't need a husband. I'll have loads of treasure all for myself."

"And I'm going to have lots of adventures," Ashley said. "I won't have time for a husband, especially a mean one."

Everyone knew she was talking about Catie's horrible father. He was even worse at being a husband than a parent.

"But how will you have money for adventures without a husband?" Josie asked. Maddie wondered the same.

"Well, I don't care how poor I am," Catie said confidently. "I'm not going to marry at all. Ever."

Maddie blinked. It was a shocking statement, one she couldn't imagine making herself. Not marry? Her father said it was a woman's job to marry.

Of course, her mother laughed at her father when he said that because her father always assigned women roles they didn't particularly want. Just the other day, when Maddie had tried to give a shilling to a little beggar boy on the street, her father scolded her because little ladies were not to consort with street urchins.

Little ladies weren't supposed to consort with a whole list of other people and things as well: injured puppies, spirited horses, homeless children, the poor and downtrodden.

Maddie didn't understand it. What good was all the wealth her family possessed if they didn't share it?

When she grew up, she intended to help people. And if a husband would stop that, then Catie was right, and Maddie had no need of one either.

Maddie stood. "And I'm not going to marry either. Never. I don't need the money. If you want, Catie, you can come stay with me. You too, Ashley, when you're not on an adventure, and you, Josie, when you're not on your pirate ship."

Catie smiled at her, then sat up straighter. Maddie thought she looked awake and alive again. "I propose that we make a pledge, a promise never to marry. I'm the oldest, so I go first. I, Catherine Anne Fullbright, swear never, ever, ever to marry so long as I live. Now your turn, Maddie."

"I, Madeleine Richael Fullbright, swear never, ever, to marry so long as I live. Now your turn, Josie," Maddie said.

"I, Josephine Linet Hale, swear never, ever, to marry so long as I live. I promise to be a pirate!"

"Now you, Ashley," Catie directed.

"I, Ashley Gweneira Brittany, swear not to marry for as long as I live. But you know what this means, don't you?" She didn't wait for an answer. "We're going to be spinsters."

Maddie didn't like that word. No, not at all.

Then Josie said, "It won't be bad to be unmarried if we're all unmarried," and Maddie felt a little better.

"So we'll make it fun," Catie interjected. "We'll be the Spinster's Club."

"That's right," Josie agreed. "We'll stick together. No men or mean girls allowed."

Catie was the first to sit up, stick out her hand, and Maddie took it gladly. She felt warm and happy, safe in her room with her best friends surrounding her.

Ten Years Later

"Lady Madeleine, I simply must have you. I *must*. May I call you *darling*?"

Maddie gave Sir Alphonse Pennebacker a shove, thrusting him back far enough that she could catch a breath of fresh air before his perfumed stench invaded her nostrils again. "No, you may not call me *darling*. In fact, Sir Alphonse, I asked you not to call on me ever again."

Sir Alphonse smiled. "But, my lady, that is the beauty of our present circumstance. I am here. You are here. We are fated to be together."

"I hardly think fate played a role," Maddie said, scooting along the bookshelf in the Westmans' library. If she could reach the end, she might have a chance to dart out the door and escape Sir Alphonse. "You knew I would attend my cousin's wedding breakfast. My entire family is in attendance."

Maddie inched past a volume of Shakespeare and several books of poetry. A section of essays remained and then she would be free. Well, as free as she could be in a house brimming with her meddlesome family.

"The question," Maddie said, eyeing the essays, "is why you are in attendance."

"Distant relation," Sir Alphonse said with a wave of one lace-bedecked sleeve. He edged closer, and Maddie could not help but stare at the beauty mark above his lip. It was obviously painted on. No less obvious was the copious rouge he used to redden his cheeks.

Maddie moved imperceptibly nearer to the volumes of essays. "Distant relation of whom? The bride or groom?"

The edge of her dress brushed the volumes in question, and Maddie prepared to make her move when Sir Alphonse pounced, cornering her, and suffocating her with the overwhelming stench of roses.

"What does it matter, my dear lady? I am here. You are here. Say yes, my darling. Consent to be my wife."

Maddie tried to force the words out without taking a breath. "I cannot, sir. I do not love you."

He stepped back, hand to his heart as though mortally wounded. Maddie almost felt sorry for him. She would have, had she not seen the same reaction from him seven times before.

"You wound me, my lady. I *love* you."

"No, you do not," Maddie said levelly. "You love my money, and you love my father's title. You do not love me."

"There you are wrong," Sir Alphonse said firmly. "That may be true of your other suitors, but not I. Tell me, my sweet, what can I do to prove my love?"

He leaned closer, and Maddie felt faint from the lack of fresh air. She could not back up any farther. The spine of a book dug into her shoulder.

"Shall I climb a mountain for you? Write you a hundred love songs? Quote poetry to you all night long?"

She swallowed the bile rising in her throat and closed her eyes. "Tell me what color my eyes are, Sir Alphonse, and I will consider your proposal."

There was a long silence. Maddie heard the distant sounds of laughter in Josie's new ballroom and the quiet ticking of the clock in Lord Westman's library.

Finally Sir Alphonse cleared his throat. "My lady, such a question—"

Maddie shook her head, refusing to open her eyes. "Answer me, sir." She almost hoped he'd answer correctly. She had no intention of marrying Sir Alphonse, but just once she would have liked a man to notice something about her.

Something besides her dowry.

He took a deep, raspy breath. "Brown. Brown like your glorious hair. Beautiful, lovely brown."

Maddie opened her eyes. Her very blue eyes. "I'm sorry, Sir Alphonse. Now, if you don't mind—"

"Maddie? Where are you?" The library door Maddie had been eyeing so longingly flew open, and Ashley stood in the opening.

She took in the scene at once and scowled at Maddie's captor. "Sir Alphonse, what are you doing?"

Alphonse jumped back. "Nothing, Miss Brittany. I—I—I—"

Ashley, so beautiful and so self-assured that she intimidated all but the most confident of men, shook her head. "You are monopolizing Lady Madeleine on a day when her family needs her most. Please leave us at once. I have urgent family news to discuss with my cousin."

"Of—Of—Of—"

"Good-bye, Sir Alphonse," Ashley said, pushing him out the door and closing it on his agitated stutters. She turned back to Maddie. "Good God, how can you stand him?"

"I can't." Maddie moved away from the bookcase and toward the window. She threw it open, ostensibly to let in fresh air, but took the opportunity to scan the garden. "But I don't see any reason to treat him rudely."

"Oh, then you want him to keep proposing marriage?"

"No." Maddie saw no sign of the one she sought

and turned back to Ashley. "But I don't want to hurt Sir Alphonse's feelings."

Ashley shook her head. "Maddie, you are rich and your father is powerful. A dozen men a day must propose to you and will keep on doing so if you do not firmly reject them. That is not rudeness. That is sanity."

"You reject suitors your way, and I shall use mine."

"Yours doesn't work."

"Not so far," Maddie mumbled, her gaze roving to the garden again. Where was he? She turned back to Ashley. "Thank you for your help, but if you don't mind, I want to sit here alone for a few moments."

Ashley's pale eyebrows rose above her sea green eyes. "Oh, really?"

Maddie looked down at her dainty, beribboned lavender and ivory slippers. They were a perfect match for her muslin day dress, which was composed of a lavender overdress and ivory underdress. The layers of the outer garment were draped and held in place at the knee by glossy lavender ribbons.

She couldn't have chosen less practical attire for running away. And with the exception of her father, no one but Ashley could hinder her plans. Willing her voice to sound convincing, Maddie said, "I'll join you again in a moment." She looked at Ashley from under her lashes to gauge the effect of her statement.

Jiminy! Ashley still looked skeptical. The clock
on the mantel chimed quarter past the hour, and
Maddie knew she had to remove Ashley quickly.
Mr. Dover was bound to show up in the garden
behind her at any moment.

Standing before Maddie, Ashley narrowed her
eyes. "Madeleine Richael Fullbright, what is going on?"

"Nothing," Maddie said automatically.

Ashley stared at her. "You're lying!" She put
her hands on her hips. "I cannot believe you lied
to me."

Maddie felt as though she were standing on a
narrow strip of beach and the tide had just come
in. Cold, threatening water swirled at her ankles.
She tried to pretend it was warm, scented bath-
water.

"Ashley, might we speak of this later?" she said,
and this time couldn't stop herself from looking
over her shoulder at the garden.

The water surged to her waist, and she almost
fell back from its force. Mr. Dover was skulking
about outside the window.

Maddie swung back around.

"What is it?" Ashley said. "You look like Ham-
let after he saw the ghost of his father."

Maddie felt a hysterical giggle well up inside. If
her father went looking for her now, she'd be the
one who ended up a ghost. She had to go.

Now.

Taking her cousin by the shoulders, Maddie pushed Ashley toward the door. "Thank you for your concern. I'll explain everything later."

But Ashley was not looking at her. She was looking past her, out the window.

The ocean floor dropped out from under Maddie.

"Who is that man?" Ashley pointed a finger, and Maddie didn't have to turn to know what her cousin saw. Mr. Dover was tall, almost too tall for his own body. He always seemed to have too many arms and legs and never knew what to do with them. He was young, not yet thirty, but he wore small spectacles over his brown eyes. At least she thought his eyes were brown. She hadn't looked all that closely.

"Man?" Maddie said with exaggerated innocence. "I don't see a man."

Rigid disapproval on her face, Ashley took her by the shoulders and turned her around. She pointed to the window, where Mr. Dover was indeed peering in. "That man."

"I have no idea," Maddie said.

Mr. Dover broke into a grin and waved at her.

Ashley sighed and released her. "You are a horrible liar, Madeleine Fullbright."

Ashley started for the window, and Maddie reached for her. Her hand closed on thin air. "Ashley!"

Her cousin was already at the windows, pushing another open. She leaned out, resting her palms on the casement, and said, "Hello. Are you looking for Lady Madeleine?"

Mr. Dover removed his hat, a scuffed beaver that looked like it had been run over by a carriage. Knowing how clumsy Dover could be, Maddie rather thought it had.

"Yes, miss." He pulled out a pocket watch. "We have an appointment."

Maddie rolled her eyes. Why didn't the man just announce it in Hanover Square? *Hear ye, hear ye: Lady Madeleine and Mr. Dover elope to Gretna Green!*

"An appointment?" Ashley said, her voice oozing sweetness. "May I ask the nature of this appointment?"

Mr. Dover considered, and Maddie waved her hands wildly behind Ashley's back.

"Lady Madeleine," Ashley said without turning around, "please refrain from making hand signals to Mister . . . ?"

"Dover," he supplied.

Maddie threw her hands down in frustration.

"Ah, Mr. Dover."

Maddie could hear Ashley smiling and knew the elopement was doomed. No man could resist one of Ashley's smiles. She closed her eyes and waited for the rising tide to surge over her head.

"I'd rather not discuss the nature of the appointment with you, miss," Mr. Dover said, and Maddie gratefully clutched hold of this rescue boat. "May I speak with Lady Madeleine?"

"Certainly." Ashley's smile was still in place, but it was tight at the corners. "One moment."

Ashley left the window and advanced on Maddie, who tried to move past her. But Ashley blocked her way, backing her into a corner. "Now, Ashley"—Maddie gave Dover a look pleading for patience—"it's not what you think."

Ashley raised one brow. "How do you know what I think?"

"Good point," Maddie conceded. "Um, what do you think?"

Ashley stomped to Lord Westman's desk, yanked the valise out from under it, and glared at Maddie. "I think you're about to run away with Mr. Dover."

Maddie swallowed. "Oh, then I suppose it is pretty much what you think."

"Maddie!" Ashley exploded. "What are you thinking? What are you doing?"

Her boat was floating away, the water was rising again, and Maddie decided she might as well dive in and try to swim. "Listen, Ashley, I haven't much time."

Ashley nodded. "Fine. I haven't much patience."

"Well, believe it or not, nor do I," Maddie said, surprised at the exasperation in her voice. "I am tired, Ashley. So tired of fending off proposal after proposal. Every day it's another suitor, more bouquets, more flowery verses. I cannot take it any longer."

"I understand your frustration," Ashley said quietly.

Maddie knew she did. Ashley was so beautiful that she had garnered enough suitors to fill the seats of Parliament.

"Men can be bothersome," Ashley agreed, "but eloping is not the solution. What about our pledge?"

Maddie felt guilt wash over her, but reminded herself that if the matter weren't so desperate she wouldn't be breaking their childhood pact— though it wasn't as if Josie and Catie hadn't already broken it. "Ashley, I'm sorry. You know I wouldn't break my promise unless I absolutely had to. This is an emergency."

"Emergency. Right." Ashley looked at the floor. "Everyone's had an adventure but me."

Maddie shook her head. "That's just it, Ashley. I don't want adventure. I just want to do my charitable works and be left in peace. Mr. Dover won't try to stop me or control me. He'll be my partner."

"And what about this—this Mr. Dover?" Ashley motioned to the window. "Who is he? What if his intentions are dishonorable?"

The girls turned as one to peer at Mr. Dover. He had his glasses off, polishing them, and was squinting in near blindness. He looked helpless as a mouse.

Ashley wasn't convinced. "Looks can be deceiving. How do you know he's not a murderer or a kidnapper? What if he takes advantage of you and then refuses to marry you?"

Maddie smiled. "Mr. Dover needs a wife as much as I need a husband. He has two small, sweet children that require a mother. Imagine me, a mother!" The thought filled her with warmth, and she pulled Ashley into a hug. "Good-bye, my friend. I promise to call as soon as we return."

When she pulled back, Ashley's blue-green eyes were filled with determination. Maddie had seen that look and knew it didn't bode well. She hurried to retrieve her valise and hand it out the window to Mr. Dover.

"Have you acquired a coach, Mr. Dover?" she asked.

"Yes, Lady Madeleine. We are ready to depart."

Maddie nodded and prayed all would go smoothly. She wanted an uneventful elopement. No more adventures!

Sitting on the edge of the window, she gave him her hand. "Then what are we waiting for?"

And she fell into his arms.

Chapter 2

John Phillip Charles Martingale, Marquess of Blackthorne, did not look up from his copy of the *Times* when he heard the commotion.

He was used to commotion. One might even venture to say that commotion followed him.

Jack also recognized his brother Nicholas's voice, rising above the din. And though Jack wouldn't think of hiding from anyone, friend or foe—his brother being a bit of both—he wouldn't have minded if Nicholas passed through the coffeehouse without ever seeing him.

"There you are!" Nicholas bellowed, arrowing straight for Jack's table.

Clenching his jaw and turning another page, Jack noted that his luck wasn't what it had once been. Of late, it seemed bad luck was around every corner, in every coffeehouse, at every—

Nick sat down.

At every table.

"I have been looking for you everywhere," Nick said, sounding out of breath.

Jack began reading an article on the many varied uses of corn.

"I looked in at your club, then Tattersalls, then Gentleman Jackson's."

Amazing, Jack thought. He had not realized corn husks could be used to make clothing. He wondered absently if they would make good muzzles.

"No one had seen you," Nick prattled on. "So finally I stopped by your town house. Ridgeley told me you had a habit of coming here. Good man, that Ridgeley."

Jack set the paper down, extracted a pad of paper and pencil from his coat, and began to write.

"What are you doing?" Nick asked.

"Making a note to release Ridgeley from my service."

"Release your butler!" Nick laughed. "Whatever for?"

Jack gave his brother a hard look, lifted the *Times* and turned the page. Suddenly, the paper was whisked out of his hands, an article on naval strategy superseded by Nicholas's smiling face.

The fact that his brother was smiling was not half so annoying to Jack as seeing that smile on a face that looked so much like his own. Not for the first time, he wished his brother resembled him more in personality and less in appearance.

The two men were of a similar height, which in Jack's opinion was rather more average than tall, and they shared a similar athletic build. Both had hair so dark the ladies called it blue-black, and bronze complexions from extensive time spent outdoors. Their eyes differed, Jack's being dark and Nick's a sky blue. And that summed up their divergent personalities as well.

Jack had a reputation for being dark and brooding, while Nick was all sunshine and blue skies. It wasn't that Jack was never happy. He had been . . .

Once or twice.

It was more that when he was near Nicholas, say within a hundred miles or so, he fell into a perpetual scowl.

Jack felt the scowl take hold of his facial muscles now, even as Nick continued to grin. Wrapping his hand around his coffee cup, Jack pretended it was his brother's neck.

"I'm in a bit of trouble," Nicholas said, and Jack gripped the cup tighter.

"You don't say."

"This is no time for sarcasm, Blackthorne." Nick signaled a waiter to bring him a cup of coffee. "I need your help."

"I'm shocked. Truly."

"You will be when you've heard what I've done. Well . . . what we've done."

"What *we've* done?" Jack growled. Was it him or did Nick have a target painted on his forehead? Where was one's archery set when one needed it?

"You are going to be proud this time. I, your inept younger brother, have restored our family honor."

"Was it lacking?"

Nick dismissed the question with a wave of his hand. His coffee arrived, and he took a moment to stir in sugar before tasting it. "I have managed—single-handedly, mind you—not only to rescue a damsel in distress, but to humiliate the Duke of Bleven in the process."

Jack felt his face turn red, felt his hands begin to itch and his throat close up. "Did you say the Duke of—" The tightness in his throat choked off his voice, and Nick gave him a concerned look.

"You should take care with that cup. You're holding it rather—"

"You humiliated the Duke of Bleven?" Jack managed to squeeze out. "Our enemy?"

Nicholas shifted in his chair. "He deserved it."

Jack seethed. Of all the men in England, Nick had to choose Bleven to torment. The Black Duke had been a family enemy ever since their mother had spurned him to marry their late father. Bleven would relish a chance to humble the Martingale family.

"I attended a ball last night and stumbled upon Bleven in the Earl of Wycliff's conservatory. He had some terrified housemaid backed into a corner," Nick was saying.

"This is over a woman?" Jack barked. The handle of the coffee cup snapped off in his hand and the remnants of the container splashed over his buff riding breeches.

"Bleven had her there against her will. What was I supposed to do? Stand by while she was assaulted?"

Jack closed his eyes and rubbed the bridge of his nose. "What did you do?"

Nick took a deep breath. "I might have gone a bit too far there."

"What did you do?" Jack grit out.

"I rescued the girl."

"And?"

"I might have publicly denounced Bleven."

Jack stared at his brother.

"I might have called him a rapist in front of half the *ton*."

Jack closed his eyes. "Jesus."

"And—"

"There's more?"

"Just a challenge. To a duel."

"The devil you did! Nick—"

"Shh!" Nick said, looking concerned for the first time that morning. Jack had no illusions that the feeling would last. "I don't think the duke will wait for the duel to attempt to kill me."

"Well, yes," Jack said through clenched teeth. "That's the trouble with humiliating immensely wealthy men with enough power to amass their own private army. *They come after you.*"

"Don't look so smug, brother." Nick waved an arm at him. "They're after you as well."

"And why in bloody hell are they after me?"

A lady at a nearby table gave a loud gasp and rose to leave. Jack ignored her, focusing on his brother, who, amazingly enough, looked even more concerned than he had a moment before. Perhaps Nick sensed that his death was imminent.

"I might have mentioned that you thought the duke was a filthy whoreson scoundrel. Something to that effect."

Jack reached across the table, gripped his brother's arms and hauled him close. "And what the devil would possess you to say that?"

Nicholas tried unsuccessfully to pull free. "It's the truth."

"And the king is daft as a loon, but you don't hear me spouting it all over Town."

Jack knew he was bellowing, and he knew the remaining patrons of the coffeehouse were staring at him. But he didn't care. Only one of the Martingale brothers was leaving this establishment alive.

And it wouldn't be Nicholas.

"I might have lost my temper and said too much," Nick argued. "But it was for a good cause."

Jack slumped in his chair. How could he remain angry when the honor of a poor, innocent girl was at stake?

"And," Nick said with a wink, "she was most appreciative."

"That's it." Jack wrapped his hands around his brother's neck and pulled Nicholas to his feet. "We can cease worrying about Bleven. After I kill you, I'll be imprisoned in the Tower. Not even Bleven can reach me there."

"After you—"

Jack began to squeeze, cutting off Nick's words. Choking his brother felt wonderful for three seconds.

Until Nick slugged him with a hard right hook.

Jack stumbled back, regained his balance, then went down hard when Nick pummeled into him. Jack hit his shoulder on the table and it slid into the chairs. There was a crash, and then scalding coffee smacked him in the chest.

Jack lay on the hard floor, his jaw aching, his shoulder throbbing, and his chest burning from the hot coffee. If he could have moved enough to retrieve his pocket watch, he would have taken note of how long it took his brother to cause mass chaos. He guessed that from the instant Nick entered the coffeehouse until this moment couldn't have been more than five minutes.

Not a new record for Nick, by any means, but still impressive.

Jack looked up and saw Nick coming for him. He tried to roll to the side, but a chair was in the way, and the full brunt of Nick's weight hit him like a charging bull. Jack had a moment to reflect that his brother was heavier than he looked, and then Nick's famous right hook came down again and pain exploded in his nose and eye. Jack groaned, and Nick pulled back.

"Sorry," Nick said. "Are you all right?"

But the pain had reignited Jack's fury. He shoved Nick off him and kneed him in the groin. Nick yelped, and Jack used the distraction to elbow his brother hard in the jaw.

"I said I was sorry," Nicolas moaned.

"I'm not."

Nick went down on one knee, and Jack pounced. He got in a good blow to Nick's stomach before his brother clutched his face with one hand.

"Just like old times, eh, Jack?" Nick said, sounding far too cheery for Jack's taste.

Jack grasped Nick's wrist and attempted to pull Nick's hand off his face before his brother could gouge out his eyes. "And like old times," Jack wheezed, "I'm going to win."

Nick shoved his hand hard, clipping Jack on the ear. For a moment all Jack heard was ringing, and then Nick was scrambling away and pulling Jack up beside him.

Jack shook his head to stop the ringing, succeeding only in making it worse. Somewhere through the clanging he heard his brother shout. Something about eleven . . .

Jack shook his head again. *Eleven? What the hell?*

Nick grabbed him by the shoulders, and Jack prepared for another blow, but Nick only yelled, "Eleven! Eleven's here!"

Jack glanced over his brother's shoulder and out the window. There, stepping down from his sleek black coach and four, was the Duke of Bleven, a veritable army of thugs on horseback surrounding him.

"Bleven's here," Jack murmured.

"I know! Run!"

Jack grabbed his brother's shoulder and yanked him back. "We're not going to run. We're going to face this thing."

"Face it?" Nicholas motioned toward Bleven's thugs, one of whom carried a club that resembled a medieval torture device. "If we get in that guy's way, we won't have a face left."

"Stand your ground," Jack ordered.

"You're only saying that because you want me to die," Nick moaned, but Jack noted that his brother braced his feet and stood straight.

Outside the now-empty coffeehouse, Bleven amassed his troops, placing the men so they stood in a solid wall behind him. The duke was tall and thin, handsome for an older man. His raven black hair and the silver streaks that flanked his temples even gave him a distinguished look. But Jack had known the duke for more than two decades. When he was a child, his father had pointed Bleven out and warned him to stay away from him. He had heeded the advice, never exchanging more than a cursory hello with the duke. But over the years, Jack had been close enough to look into the older man's eyes.

There was no warmth in Bleven's gaze. His eyes were predatory. The man was cold as a hawk, and when he attacked, just as deadly.

"I do want you to die," Jack said to Nicholas as Bleven and his men moved forward. The man with the club pulled the coffeehouse door open. "Problem is, I'm the only one allowed to kill you."

"I don't think our friend knows your rules."

Bleven stepped through the door, followed by his men, and Jack assumed a casual stance—as though standing in an empty coffeehouse, dripping blood on the floor from the nose his brother had pummeled, was an everyday occurrence.

He gave Bleven a stiff nod. "Your Grace."

"Ah, the Martingale brothers," Bleven said, his characteristic high-pitched voice contrasting with his otherwise formidable demeanor. "I've been looking for you."

"We're not hard to find." Jack reached down, righted a chair from the floor and sat backward, crossing his arms lazily over the chair's top rail. Nick followed suit, taking an extra moment to swipe a full coffee cup from an abandoned table.

Anyone who walked in at that moment would have thought that the two brothers owned the shop, which was precisely the impression Jack wanted. "Take a seat," he said to Bleven. He motioned to a table of abandoned cups. "Coffee?"

Bleven's men fanned out on either side of the duke. Jack counted six—all large men who looked as though they had no aversion to violence.

"Let's forgo the chitchat, Blackthorne. You know why I'm here."

Jack shrugged. "I've always thought chitchat the mark of a civilized society."

Bleven gave him a thin grin. "I'm not feeling particularly civilized at the moment."

"Haven't felt that way for the past several years, from all accounts," Jack countered.

Bleven's face darkened. "Lord Blackthorne, your presence grows tiresome. If you leave now, I'll spare you today. It's your brother I want at present."

"That makes two of us. What's he done to you?"

"He has challenged my honor."

Jack glanced at Nick as though this accusation was a complete surprise. Nick shrugged. "Impossible," he said.

Jack raised a brow as Bleven's men moved closer.

"The duke has no honor," Nick added.

"You shall pay for that," Bleven said, removing his gloves and slapping them in his hand.

Jack held up a hand. "There must be another way to settle this."

Bleven's gloves slapped his hand again. "Certainly. If you boys get down on your knees, beg forgiveness, and admit *you* are the whoreson scoundrels, I'll consider merely maiming you."

Jack glanced at Nick, but it was too late. Nick stepped forward. "Love to, Duke, but I don't apologize to rapists."

Bleven's face went crimson, and he lunged for Nick. Jack had to admit the old man was quick. Nick was quicker, though. His brother grabbed a chair and shoved it in Bleven's path.

Jack closed his eyes and wished he'd left his brother to fend for himself. Damn his parents, and damn their misplaced sense of honor. Why hadn't they taught him to be a coward?

Jack stood. "Look, Bleven, perhaps we can come to some sort of agreement. Perhaps my brother can . . . write a letter of apology."

Nick gave him a horrified look, and Bleven burst into loud cackles.

"Oh, he will apologize, Blackthorne. You both will. I've been waiting for this day." He motioned to his men. "Catch them and put them in my coach. I'd like a private meeting."

The six men, armed to the teeth, advanced, and Jack exchanged a look with Nick. Jack wrapped his fingers around the back of the chair he'd been occupying, and Nick did the same. As the first two men came forward, brandishing pistols, Jack stood still, waiting. The men, smiling at their easy victory, raised their guns.

Then, with a howl, Jack raised his chair and threw it. It hit one of the gun-carrying men in the shoulder, glanced off him and thwacked the club-toting man in the temple. Nick's chair took out the other man, then landed on the floor and skidded to a hard stop against Bleven's shin.

Bleven wailed, "Get them!"

One of the gunmen fired a wild shot, and Jack felt it whiz by his ear. He stumbled back, grabbing Nicholas in the process.

"What now?" Nick said, crouching in anticipation of the next shot.

"Now, we run!"

"Ashley, get out of the coach," Maddie said. "This is my elopement. You're not invited."

"Nevertheless, I'm coming," Ashley said, and Maddie knew that stubborn look in her cousin's eye. "You're not the only one who's allowed to have an adventure."

"But it won't be an adventure, Ashley. It will be boring, I assure you."

That was unless Ashley insisted on coming along.

Maddie glanced at Mr. Dover, seated beside her. He looked agitated and impatient. In his hand, he held a pocket watch. "We are now precisely eleven minutes behind our scheduled departure," he said.

Maddie massaged the bridge of her nose and tried to be patient.

And optimistic—an act that was becoming increasingly more difficult every time one of Mr. Dover's precious seconds ticked away. "Ashley," she pleaded. "Get out."

"No."

Maddie was about to leap across the coach and forcibly evict her friend when Dover raised his hand. "As time is of the essence, might I suggest an alternate solution?"

Ashley shook her head. "Where did you find this . . . man?"

Dover sniffed. "As I was saying—or about to say"—he gave Ashley a reproving look—"it might be more expedient to allow Miss Brittany to travel with us."

Maddie stared at him. "Come with us?"

He removed his spectacles and began polishing them. "Yes. After all, what is the harm in her coming?"

"You obviously don't know her very well," Maddie grumbled. Ashley could find trouble in a nunnery.

"Well," Dover said, looking at his watch again. "Perhaps she could be our chaperone. We didn't think to bring a chaperone."

"That's because eloping couples don't have chaperones!" Instantly, Maddie felt guilty for raising her voice. Especially as Mr. Dover had turned his reproving look on her. "I'm sorry for that outburst, Mr. Dover. I'm extremely agitated at the moment."

"I think Mr. Dover has a splendid idea," Ashley said with a smile for Maddie's fiancé. "I would make an excellent chaperone."

Maddie would have laughed if she didn't feel like crying. They really did not have time for this. Any moment her parents were going to realize she was missing and begin searching for her. It wouldn't be long before they or one of the servants discovered the note she'd left on her pillow.

"Ashley, please," Maddie begged. She never begged, but she was at her wit's end. "My father will be after us, and if we don't leave soon, we won't get away."

Ashley, who by all appearances had settled into her seat permanently, said, "Then by all means, tell the coachman to drive on."

Defeated, Maddie dropped her head in her hands. Mr. Dover, seeming to understand that a decision had been made, rapped on the roof of the coach.

He rapped three times, waited, then rapped again.

Nothing happened.

Maddie lifted her head and peered up at the hatch, where the errant coachman should have appeared.

"Where—"

There was a loud crash on top of the coach. Maddie ducked, afraid the ceiling would fall in on them. The ceiling held, but the crash was followed by a scrambling sound. She stared at Ashley, who for once in her life looked frightened.

Maddie almost groaned. The dreaded adventure was starting already.

Mr. Dover reached for the hatch, but the coach lurched and he fell back. Maddie staggered against the window with a small squeal, then almost tumbled out the door when it was thrust open and a dark-haired man with a bloody nose and a coffee-colored stain on his buff breeches climbed inside.

He barely got the door closed before the horses were whipped into frenzied motion and the coach pitched violently.

The man practically fell into the seat beside Ashley. He pushed his dark hair out of his eyes, his gaze falling on each one of them. When his dark eyes met hers, Maddie gasped, unable to breathe. There was something feral and untamed about this man. The space between them seemed to buzz with heat.

He gave her a wicked smile, and she swore she heard the hiss and crack of lightning.

She tried to close her mouth or to make it function, to say something. Her mouth moved, but no words would form.

The man settled in, stretching one booted foot out to rest beside her, and said, "So, where are we going?"

Chapter 3

The two women and the man stared at him as though he had three heads. Hell, he might. At this point, Jack figured anything was possible. He and Nick had run at least a mile, probably more, through London. They'd felt the hot breath of Bleven's men on their necks the entire way.

There'd been several minor scuffles. Jack had taken out one of the thugs with a step into a lucky doorway and an equally lucky find of a loose board. Nick had managed to lose two of their pursuers by taking a side street and doubling back. But the men always caught up to them again.

Five against two weren't bad odds. Jack had faced worse. But when the five had pistols and various other weapons, and the two had naught but bare hands, the odds changed a bit.

Jack knew he and Nick could keep running, but he worried that eventually they'd take a wrong turn and find themselves looking down the barrel of a gun. That fear was confirmed when he and Nick rounded a corner and slammed into one of

Bleven's thugs, who had managed to get ahead of them without realizing it.

The next thug might not be so unprepared.

That was when Jack had seen the carriage. The horses were harnessed and ready to depart, and while Jack watched, the coachman climbed off his box and stepped into an alley to answer nature's call. Jack couldn't believe his luck. Maybe it was turning after all.

He motioned to Nick, who understood the plan immediately—there were some benefits to getting in trouble with one's brother—and Nick indicated that he'd take the coachman's place. Jack had the more dangerous task of subduing the coach's natives.

His plan had been to throw them out and steal the coach outright, but one look at the blue-eyed, dark-haired beauty, and Jack felt the ground give out from under him.

True, it might have been that Nick chose that moment to urge the horses into motion, but whatever caused the heady, falling feeling, Jack knew he was never going to toss that exquisite creature out on the road. If anything, he was going to pull her into his arms.

He shook his head. The direction his thoughts were taking seemed to indicate the coffeehouse squabble with Nick had done more damage than he'd thought. When was the last time he'd allowed a woman—no matter how beautiful—to interfere with his plans?

When was the first time?

Never.

And he wasn't going to start allowing women to run roughshod over him now. He'd toss the man, then the blonde, then the petite brunette.

No, he'd start with the brunette.

He gave her an ominous smile and prepared to reach for her. And then the chit had the audacity— the out-and-out gall—to turn those huge blue eyes on him. How was he supposed to toss her out on the street with those sapphire eyes practically begging him to help her? He didn't know what she needed help with, but somehow, he knew she needed him.

And so, instead of tossing the chit out the carriage door, he found himself asking their destination.

Not that he was going to help the brunette. He was done with helping damsels in distress—and that included his brother. Jack slipped his head in the noose for no man.

Or woman.

Not anymore.

But that didn't mean he couldn't ask.

It was the blonde who answered him, and once Jack got a good look at her, saw who she was, he wasn't surprised.

"We're going to Gretna Green," she told him. "Without you. Get out."

Jack blinked at her forceful response, though he

shouldn't have been surprised. "Miss Brittany," he said easily. "Why am I not surprised that you are eloping to Gretna Green?"

The blonde exchanged a look with the brunette, then spat, "Obviously my reputation precedes me, sir. And you are?"

"Not impressed by you."

Jack glanced at the couple across from him. The man would be no threat. He wasn't a fighter by nature. By the way he watched the events unfolding in the carriage, Jack knew the man was an observer. He reminded Jack of his professors at Cambridge.

Dismissing the professor, Jack directed his attention back to the brunette.

"Now, you," he said, allowing his gaze to caress her pink cheeks, her ripe mouth, her slender neck, and—

Jack took a shaky breath.

—her other ample charms.

He was in more danger than he'd anticipated. "You impress me."

He extended a hand, which she didn't take.

"Jack Martingale, Marquess of Blackthorne."

The blonde took in a sharp breath—which was the usual response when he met a young lady— but the brunette showed no sign of knowing who he was.

"I do not mean to impress you, sir," the brunette said, and her voice was rich and velvety, like her long, chestnut curls. "I only mean to get to Gretna Green. Mr. Dover and I hope to marry as soon as possible."

The punch Jack felt in his gut was as real as any his brother had given him in the coffeehouse. Only it hurt like hell. It hurt as bad as that time he'd been in a dockside brawl and one of the sailors had knifed him in the ribs then twisted it just to hear him scream.

Jack hadn't given the sailor the pleasure. It had been that man who'd screamed in the end, but Jack never forgot the pain of that knife blade. He felt it now.

The brunette and the professor?

He couldn't stop himself from glancing down at those ample charms again. Perhaps it was a good thing the professor had a claim on her. Jack didn't think he could be responsible for his actions otherwise.

"Lord Blackthorne," Ashley Brittany was saying.

Jack looked back at her. She was a lovely girl. A classic beauty who had turned the heads of all his friends. He didn't know why she didn't turn his head as well. Perhaps because she was too perfect.

Perfection bored him.

"I don't know what you are doing here, but you are going to have to leave."

"I don't think so," Jack said.

"Sir, I am afraid I must concur with Miss Brittany," the professor said. "This matter does not involve you. Unless . . . " He exchanged a glance with the brunette. "Speak up now, sir. Were you hired by Lord Castleigh?"

Jack blinked. "Castleigh? Why the hell would I be working for that old frump?"

The brunette sat forward. "Perhaps because my father suspected I might run away and wanted to keep an eye on me."

"You're Lord Castleigh's daughter?"

The brunette gave him a quick nod. "I'm the frump's daughter. Lady Madeleine."

Brilliant. He finally met a woman who took his breath away, and he began by insulting her father. Not that it mattered.

She was eloping and would never be his.

Which was a good thing.

He didn't want her.

Very much.

"So let me get this straight," Jack said. "You, Lady Madeleine, only daughter of the Earl of Castleigh, are eloping with *him*?"

The professor bristled. "I'm Conlan Dover, and I happen to be the world's foremost expert on dog breeds and—"

Jack waved a hand and addressed Lady Madeleine. "And this is your . . . ?" He glanced at Ashley Brittany.

"Cousin," Miss Brittany supplied. "Well, actually, I'm her cousin's cousin."

"I see." He didn't, but no matter. "Your cousin's cousin is coming along as well because . . . ?"

"We need a chaperone," Lady Madeleine supplied.

"Of course," Jack said. Who didn't need a chaperone when they eloped? "You're right. I don't want to be in this carriage. I'll order my brother to stop immediately."

A quick look out the window confirmed that they were well away from the center of London and should be free of Bleven's thugs.

Jack rapped on the coach's roof.

"Your brother?" Miss Brittany asked, her voice sounding strained.

Jack raised a brow as the hatch opened and Nicholas poked his head inside. "Have you met Lord Nicholas Martingale?"

Maddie stared at the dark-haired man with his head through her carriage hatch, taking up the space where her coachman should have been.

"What have you done with my coachman?"

Lord Nicholas looked taken aback. "Your coachman? Never touched the man. He abandoned his post. Blackthorne and I simply filled a need."

"No you didn't," Ashley said. "We had a coachman, and therefore had no need of one. You stole our coach!"

"I resent that imputation of my character," Lord Nicholas said.

"What character?" Ashley cried. "You're a rogue."

Maddie blinked at this new information. She told herself she had to start reading the papers on

a regular basis. First, she had no idea who the notorious Lord Blackthorne was, and by Ashley's reaction to the revelation of his name, Maddie knew
he must be very wicked. And now, apparently, this
Blackthorne's brother was equally scandalous.

Lord Nicholas bristled. "You'd better be careful
with your unfounded accusations, Miss Brittany.
You, of all people, shouldn't be the first to throw
stones."

Ashley reddened, and Maddie's mouth fell
open. Ashley was never embarrassed. Had something happened between Lord Nicholas and Ashley that she was unaware of?

"It's not unfounded, Lord Nicholas," Ashley
said.

"Do you have proof?" he demanded.

"You know I do."

"Then, by all means, expose me for the scoundrel I am."

Maddie watched as the two locked gazes.
Amazingly, Ashley was the first to look away.

Lord Nicholas disappeared for a moment, presumably to check on the horses—an action for
which Maddie was profoundly grateful, as careening along London's streets without a driver
was not her notion of an ideal elopement—then
reappeared.

"So where are we going?" he asked his
brother.

"We are going no further," Lord Blackthorne
told him. "Stop the coach."

"Done." He disappeared again.

Maddie peered out the window and didn't recognize a single building. She had no idea where they were, but by the looks of their surroundings, it wasn't Mayfair. And the smell . . .

"Oh, no," she said. As much as she wanted these crazed men out and her calm, adventure-free elopement back, this wouldn't do. "We're not stopping here."

"Not my concern," Blackthorne said, without taking his eyes from the dingy gray shacks they passed.

She glared at Blackthorne. "It should be. You cannot think to abandon us here without a coachman."

He frowned at her. "As I said, that's not my concern."

"Take us back to our coachman," Maddie said, but Mr. Dover was already shaking his head.

He consulted his trusty pocket watch. "According to my calculations, we are now twenty-two minutes behind schedule. We haven't time to go all the way back, find the coachman, and then start again. That would put us approximately . . . " He looked as though he were tabulating in his head.

"Your point, sir?" Ashley said impatiently.

"Lord Castleigh might already be looking for us."

Maddie knew he was right, and poor Mr. Dover had more cause to worry than anyone else.

If her father caught them, he was well within his rights to shoot Mr. Dover for absconding with his daughter.

She didn't want to believe that her father would act so monstrously, but undoubtedly he would take a different view of the situation. He wouldn't hesitate to shoot Mr. Dover.

Maddie sighed and stared at her clenched hands. All she had wanted was to marry and then pursue her charitable causes unfettered, as she and Mr. Dover had agreed. And now it seemed she couldn't even elope without trouble. She was a failure at adventure. A miserable failure.

She glanced up. Everyone was looking to her expectantly. She couldn't afford to be pessimistic now. The coach was slowing, and her friends needed her.

Her gaze locked with Lord Blackthorne's, and she steeled herself for opposition. "I am afraid, my lord, that I have to insist you drive us to Gretna Green. At least until such time as we can acquire another coachman."

Blackthorne raised a black eyebrow. "You can insist all you want, Lady Madeleine, but I'm not going anywhere close to Gretna Green. Especially not with two unattached females in tow."

Ashley snorted. "As though either of us would marry you!"

"Oh, the feeling's mutual, Miss Brittany. But I'm not taking any chances. You know my reputation. Throw Gretna Green into the mix, and you would be compromised. And don't think I'll marry you out of some misguided sense of honor."

"Obviously, you don't know the meaning of the word," Maddie shot back.

To her surprise, Blackthorne didn't grow angry at her impudence. Instead, he leaned forward, so close that she caught the scent of coffee and soap on his skin. His dark eyes bore into hers, their intensity making her insides heat. "Remember that, sweetheart," he said, voice dark and low.

Maddie didn't know why she was reacting to him. She couldn't stop her gaze from traveling to his mouth and wondering what it would be like if he whispered other, more scandalous words in her ear. She wondered what that blue-black hair would feel like under her fingertips. She wondered . . . Jiminy, she wondered what he'd look like with his shirt off!

"Lord Blackthorne," Dover interjected. "I must ask you to refrain from taking a familiar attitude with either of these ladies. I *will* defend them."

Ashley laughed. "With what? Your pocket watch?"

"Ashley!" Maddie said reprovingly. Poor Mr. Dover. He was trying. Blackthorne would probably beat him senseless for it, but at least her fiancé had honor.

But Blackthorne didn't beat Dover senseless. Instead, he nodded in agreement.

Maddie blinked in surprise. She knew a man like Blackthorne wasn't intimidated in the least by the likes of Mr. Dover, who though taller than Blackthorne, possessed nothing of Blackthorne's obvious strength or wiles.

But Blackthorne seemed to respect Dover. Either that or he couldn't be bothered by him. "I have no intention of becoming any more familiar with the lot of you," Blackthorne said. "Good-bye, and good riddance."

With that, he opened the carriage door and stepped into the ambush.

Chapter 4

Jack felt the cold metal of the pistol at his temple before he saw the man holding it.

"Who the hell are you? And what are you doing with my daughter?"

"I didn't touch her," Jack protested. It wasn't the first time he'd said it, but this time it was definitely true.

He had stepped out of the carriage and was facing a small shop with a slab of meat painted on the sign above. He didn't dare turn his head—no need to make his attacker nervous—so he continued to stare at the slab of meat.

It wasn't a comforting picture.

"I saw you step out of this carriage, and I saw my daughter get inside. If you put just one of your grubby fingers on her—"

"I didn't even look at her. I swear," Jack said. Well, now that wasn't exactly true, but at this point Jack wished he hadn't looked at Lady Madeleine.

Wished he'd never even heard of the chit.

He didn't have much hope that Lady Made-

leine's father would believe him. Fathers of girl
children were a notoriously bad sort. He had seen
even the sanest, most reasonable men turn daft
when it came to their daughters.

The best he could hope for was that Lord
Castleigh would shoot him in the head. Then it
would be over quickly.

All over.

Unless he could figure out a way to distract
Castleigh . . .

Where the devil was Nicholas? Probably halfway back home by now. That was gratitude for
you.

"Sir," Jack said, trying to buy time, "it was an
honest mistake. I stepped into the wrong carriage.
I had no idea your daughter was inside or that
she was eloping to Gretna Green."

"Gretna Green!" the man exploded.

Jack winced as the pistol slammed into his
temple. Perhaps he shouldn't have mentioned
Gretna?

"*I'm* not involved. That's why I'm getting out
here. I don't want to marry your daughter."

"What's wrong with my daughter?"

Bloody hell, he couldn't say the right thing today. "Nothing. She's lovely."

The pistol dug deeper. If he survived this,
he was going to kill Nicholas. Bloody coward
bastard!

"She's lovely, *but* I don't want to marry her. Or
any woman!"

"Yes, he does, Daddy!" a familiar voice called
from the carriage. "That's my fiancé, and if you
shoot him, I will never forgive you."

"What?"

Pistol be damned, Jack couldn't stop himself
from turning to look at the speaker.

The blonde smiled sweetly at him from the
open window of the carriage.

Damn it all to hell! Was the woman mad? What
the hell had she gotten him into now?

"Ashley Gweneira Brittany, get out of that carriage at once!" the man who'd been holding the
pistol to Jack's head bellowed. Jack saw now that
it was not Lord Castleigh at all but Sir Gareth,
Ashley Brittany's father. "I forbid you to run off
on your own and elope."

The blonde shook her head. "I'm not on my
own, Daddy. Maddie's with me."

Lady Madeleine poked her head through the
opposite window. "Good afternoon, Sir Gareth."

"Does your father know about this?" Sir Gareth
wanted to know.

But Jack didn't hear her answer. Nicholas chose
that second to emerge from his hiding place on
top of the carriage.

Jack shook his head frantically. Trust Nicholas
to pick the moment when they were finally getting things worked out.

But Nick either didn't see him or ignored him.
With a whoop, his brother tackled Sir Gareth, flat-
tening him.

Jack jumped out of the way just in time, watching as Sir Gareth's pistol skidded along the ground, stopping with a thunk against the wall of the butcher shop. But the loss of his weapon didn't deter Sir Gareth. He came up fighting. A hard left to Nick's jaw sent Jack's brother sprawling.

With Nicholas down momentarily, Gareth looked at Jack. "You think you can take me, boy?"

Jack tried to raise his arms in a gesture of peace—he had no intention of fighting an old man—but Sir Gareth charged, knocking him down and forcing him to defend himself.

Jack tried to be gentle, restraining the older man as much as possible. Sir Gareth fought hard and was soon out of breath. Jack released him and was stumbling to his feet when Ashley Brittany came flying across the road. "What did you do to my father? How could you hurt a helpless old man?"

Helpless? Jack lifted his aching shoulder, where the helpless old man had rammed him into the ground.

Ashley ran past him, and Jack reached out to catch her, but she evaded him, attacking Nick instead. "Don't you dare hurt my father. Don't make me repay that wrong, too!" she shrieked.

Jack took a step back. Repay?

There was obviously some unsettled business between his brother and Miss Brittany. Jack was prepared to let them reconcile it on their own. Nick had already caught the blonde's wrists and was trying to calm her when Jack noticed Sir Gareth beginning to rise.

Damn. "Nick! Watch out!" he called.

Nick turned to look at Sir Gareth, and the blonde kicked him. With a sigh, Jack interceded. He pried Ashley Brittany off his brother and propelled her back toward the carriage. "You wanted to go to Gretna Green?" he panted, still trying to catch his own breath. "We're going to Gretna Green."

Jack nodded to his brother, and Nick trotted up. His movements were a bit gingerly—when the Brittany family decided to do someone violence, it usually succeeded. But with one Brittany down and the other almost secure in the carriage, Jack figured his brother would survive another day.

Over Miss Brittany's curses—she was teaching him some rather inventive phrases—Jack called, "You don't have to come along. I can handle this."

Nick shook his head. "I'm coming. It's better if we aren't seen in London for a while."

"And it might be harder for Ble—" He glanced at Miss Brittany, who was listening now. "— for our *friend*, if we split up."

"What, and let you have all the fun?" Nick winked at the blonde, and she started cursing again.

A quick glance at Sir Gareth, and Jack knew they were out of time. The old man was shuffling toward his pistol.

"Fine, come along," he said, moving toward the carriage. Nick headed for the coachman's box. "But you know what this means?" He gestured at the irate Sir Gareth.

Nick grinned. "Better you than me, Blackthorne!"

Jack scowled. His brother said it so often, it was practically a motto.

Ashley Brittany yelled a last insult at Nick's back, and Jack shoved his new fiancée inside. He climbed in after her just as Nick whipped the horses into motion.

The blonde flew across the coach to complain loudly to Lady Madeleine, and Jack looked behind them.

Sir Gareth was standing in the road, arm raised, face red, and curses ringing out after them.

Jack glanced at the two women across from him and knew exactly how Sir Gareth felt.

"Ashley, calm down. Everything will work out," Lady Madeleine said.

Jack snorted at her misplaced optimism. Nothing was going to work out. Not anymore. He was beyond help.

She ignored him and looked at Dover, now seated beside him. "Mr. Dover, I regret that this is not turning out as we had anticipated. If you have reconsidered and wish to call off our elopement, I will understand."

Jack looked at Mr. Dover, who sat with his pocket watch open on his lap. Some part of him wanted Dover to bail out. Even though he knew he would never have Lady Madeleine, he didn't want Dover to possess her either.

Dover looked up. "My lady, if you will still have me, I am most willing to undertake this journey. I gave my word, and I do not do so lightly."

Lady Madeleine nodded soberly, and Jack rolled his eyes. He felt miserable, and Dover's flowery speech wasn't helping.

"Ashley," Lady Madeleine said to her friend, "I don't know how your father found us, but it's not too late for you to go home."

"What, and let you have all the adventure?" the blonde said. Jack coughed. He was going to have to watch this one. She was the female equivalent of his brother.

"It's not an adventure," Lady Madeleine corrected. "It's practically a fiasco. You should go home now and—"

"She can't go home," Jack broke in, his misery doubling. "Not anymore."

Lady Madeleine turned her stunning blue eyes on him. "Why not?"

"Because I'm going to marry Miss Brittany in Gretna Green."

There was a chorus of dissent in the carriage, and Jack wished he could join it. More than anything, he wanted to get the hell out of the carriage and never see any of them again. Including his brother.

But they'd sped right past that fork in the road.

His course was set now, and, little as he liked it, he was stuck with it.

"I'm going to marry Miss Brittany in Gretna Green," Jack repeated over the noise. He was impressed how easily the words came out, especially when his stomach heaved at the very thought.

"No you're not!" Ashley shrieked.

Jack wanted to cover his ears. Dover, on the other hand, merely nodded. At least someone understood that this was the best and only way. Lady Madeleine obviously did not fall into that camp. She was gaping at him.

Damn, even that wide-eyed innocent look he hated on women was attractive on her.

"But—But *why*?" Lady Madeleine asked, her shock evident. "Before, you said—"

"That was before," Jack interrupted. "Before her father ambushed us and your friend there basically forced me into this elopement." He gestured to his fiancée—God, the very thought of having a fiancée made him want to empty the contents of his stomach—and she sat up indignantly.

"I did not force you to elope!"

"Then why the hell did you tell your father I was eloping with you? I might have convinced him I had nothing to do with this and gone on my way."

Ashley Brittany shook her head. "I was trying to help. I surmised that if he thought you were important to me, then he wouldn't hurt you. I don't want to marry you."

"Well, you're stuck with me now."

Lady Madeleine shushed her friend, cutting off Ashley's next remark. From the look on Ashley's face, that was probably for the best.

Lady Madeleine gave Jack a long look. "So you do have a sense of honor."

He laughed. "Honor be damned. I'm saving my own neck. Now that the chatterbox over there claimed me as her fiancé, I've all but ruined her. If I go back to London and we're not married, her father will shoot me. Hell, any peer with an eligible daughter will shoot me. I'll be labeled a defiler of young girls."

Lady Madeleine actually looked sorry for him, which almost made Jack laugh. He hadn't thought he could be any more disreputable.

Of course, if the brunette knew what he really was, she wouldn't pity him. She'd say what everyone else would: that coward Blackthorne got what he deserved.

"Oh, don't pity him, Maddie," Miss Brittany told her friend. "If you read the papers more, you'd know he's a scoundrel, and so is his brother. The two Martingale brothers are known for drink and debauchery. Why, they've corrupted my brothers completely."

Jack laughed. "Your brothers need no corrupting from me, Miss Brittany. Like you, they find enough trouble on their own."

"How dare you—"

"This isn't helping," Lady Madeleine broke in. Her voice was still calm and soft, but it held authority. "What we have here is a misunderstanding. I'm sure if we went back and explained everything to Sir Gareth, you two would not have to marry."

"But—" Mr. Dover began.

"Shh!" Lady Madeleine said, and looked from her friend to Jack hopefully.

Jack shook his head. If only Sir Gareth was the sole reason he had to get out of London. But he wasn't about to worry her with mention of Nick's little altercation with Bleven. Even if Bleven weren't involved, only marriage to his daughter would stop Sir Gareth from shooting him on first sight.

"You're noble to ruin your own plans to help me, my lady," Jack told her, "but no one would listen at this point anyway. By now Sir Gareth's gone to fetch your father, and we probably have a bevy of footmen after us. The time for talking is done. I don't want to see anyone's father again until I'm someone's son-in-law."

"I have to agree with him, my lady," Dover said. "If we go back now, we're all doomed. Your reputations are ruined—"

"I don't care about my reputation!" Lady Madeleine argued.

"That makes two of us," Jack said. "But, as I said, I'm doing this to save my neck. You might not care about my neck, but you probably care about your fiancé's. He'll fare no better than I if we go back now."

Jack watched as Lady Madeleine turned those big blue eyes on Dover, reassuring her fiancé with a look that she would never allow him to face danger.

Jack felt like killing the professor. No one had ever given a damn whether he was endangered or not, especially not anyone like Lady Madeleine. He felt another stitch of jealousy knot in his heart and looked away.

Let the couple have their moment.

It was late afternoon by the time Jack looked back. He'd been watching the country roll by and assisting with the change of horses. They were making good time. He hoped to reach Stevenage before nightfall. The carriage had turned quiet, and as he surveyed his fellow travelers, he saw that all but Dover were sleeping.

Like him, the other man was peering out the window and occasionally checking his pocket watch. Each glance at the pocket watch was followed by a slight tsk.

Across from Jack, the two girls were slumped together. The brunette had her head on the blonde's shoulder. Lady Madeleine's eyes were closed and she breathed evenly.

Jack studied her, trying to remember if he'd ever seen her in Town. He didn't attend many of the *ton*'s functions, so it was unlikely. Besides, he knew he would have remembered this exquisite creature. In fact, if they'd met under different circumstances, he might be the one sitting in Dover's place.

Dover. That required another glance at the man beside him. Jack could not figure what the polished beauty saw in the professor. He supposed the other man wasn't unattractive—not that he knew how to judge that in other men—and the other man definitely appeared intelligent. Even now he was polishing his spectacles and looking ponderous.

Lady Madeleine obviously preferred intelligence over passion. There couldn't be much passion between the professor and the earl's daughter. He couldn't begin to imagine the dull Mr. Dover kissing the luscious Lady Madeleine senseless.

Too bad, because that was so obviously what the little brunette needed. He turned his gaze back to Lady Madeleine. She worried too much. Even in her sleep he could see that. There was a small crease between her two slender eyebrows that told him she was worrying.

Jack longed to reach across the carriage and smooth the line, to make it vanish forever. But he knew once he touched her, he wouldn't be able to stop. Sure, it would start with an innocent caressing away of that line, and next thing he'd place his palm on her smooth, creamy cheek.

He could imagine the silky feeling of her skin

beneath his own flesh. She'd be warm and soft. So soft. He wouldn't be able to resist the temptation of trailing a finger or two to her lips.

Even now, in the dim carriage, he could see they were rosy and full and lush. Those were lips a man begged to kiss. Those were lips that promised so much more than they ever took. Jack imagined slipping his thumb inside that rosy mouth, and then had to shift and look away.

With a sigh, he went back to staring out the window. Riding across from Lady Madeleine all the way to Scotland was going to be miserable. He was half aroused just thinking of touching her face. He hadn't even begun to imagine exploring below her neck.

His eyes darted to the bodice of her pretty dress. The gown was purplish and white with small bows along the hem. The bodice was unadorned. No dainty bows for him to push askew there. If he just slipped one finger inside and touched—

"Sir?"

Dover spoke, and Jack pulled his eyes away from Lady Madeleine with a jerk of his head.

"What?" he barked far too sharply. Lady Madeleine moved and stretched, and Jack had to look away or embarrass himself.

"I was going to say," Dover continued, "that by my calculations, there should be a village up ahead. This would be an excellent opportunity to stop and change horses."

"Oh, good, we're stopping," Ashley Brittany

said sleepily to Lady Madeleine. "My— er, legs are so sore."

"There's no time for that," Jack said shortly, rapping on the carriage's roof to alert his brother. "Your pistol-waving father is on our heels, and we have a long way to go to Gretna Green."

The hatch opened and Nick, looking wind-whipped but relaxed and happy, peered down. "I'm going to stop and change horses again up ahead," he said.

"We had the same idea," Jack replied. "But we tarry no more than a quarter hour."

"Agreed. Between their fathers"—he gestured to the girls—"and our own friends, we had better keep moving."

"Agreed," Jack said.

Nick dropped the hatch closed and began to slow the weary horses.

Across from Jack, the two women were now awake. Lady Madeleine, damn her, had her eyes on her professor. And Ashley Brittany was watching him, her look slightly less endearing.

He gave his fiancée a tight smile. "Excited about reaching Gretna Green?" he asked sarcastically.

"Ecstatic." She curled her lip at him. "I can't wait."

"Maybe we'll get lucky and break an axle. Your father will have the opportunity to shoot me after all."

"Sir, it's not polite to raise a lady's hopes."

* * *

Maddie stepped out of the coach, despite Lord Blackthorne's strict orders for them to stay put and be ready to depart immediately. Ashley had snorted at Blackthorne's command and jumped down as soon as the marquess walked away. Maddie and Dover had waited a bit longer, and then her aching muscles protested too loudly to ignore and she hobbled down.

The first few steps were difficult, but after a moment she managed to work out some of the stiffness. It was growing late, but she took a moment to observe the little village in the afternoon sun.

The town was a pretty place, full of snug cottages on a hill and neat shops on the main street. Maddie could imagine happy families living in those pretty cottages, sweet-faced children grasping the aprons of their patient mammas, who stirred pots full of hearty dinners for handsome husbands.

She sighed. Her mother had never cooked a day in her life and had certainly never worn an apron. Her aristocratic friends and family would not find her musings romantic in the least. But she couldn't help but admire the common people and their simple lives. How many times had she wished her own life were so simple?

They had stopped at a posting house, set some way apart, but, as was usually the case, it was near a pub, and Maddie could smell the succulent aroma of fresh bread and stew.

Her stomach grumbled and she tried to remem-

ber the last time she'd eaten. She'd had a small
tart or two at Josie and Lord Westman's wedding
breakfast but had been too nervous about her
elopement to eat much more. Now she wished
she'd followed Ashley's example and taken a bite
of everything.

Ashley.

Maddie turned about, looking for her cousin,
only to find that she'd disappeared. Typical.
Knowing Ashley, she'd be gone for three-quarters
of an hour and get them all caught and dragged
back to London.

Maddie's stomach growled again, and she decided to check the pub. Perhaps Ashley was hungry and had ventured that way. But the pub was
empty. It was too early for the locals to come in for
dinner, and she was with the only group of travelers. Maddie did find a serving girl and paid for a
small chunk of bread. Afraid time was growing
short, she wrapped her spoils in her handkerchief
and headed back toward the coach.

The new set of horses was almost harnessed,
and Maddie took a moment to admire the large
bays. But as she took the first steps toward the
door of the coach, she heard the men.

It was Blackthorne and his brother, talking in
low voices near the coach box. With the big horses
in front of her, Maddie didn't think the men had
seen her.

She didn't intend to eavesdrop, but their next
words stopped her.

" . . . no reason for you to go with us to Gretna Green," Lord Blackthorne was saying. "Wales or Ireland will hide you until Bleven's temper cools."

"You want to get rid of me."

"Can you blame me?"

Lord Nicholas laughed. "No, but I have my reasons for tagging along with you."

"Is she blond?"

Maddie blinked. So Ashley and Lord Nicholas did have a past. Funny, she didn't remember Ashley ever mentioning him . . .

"Maybe I like driving a carriage," Lord Nicholas argued.

"Maybe there was something between you and Miss Brittany."

"Oh, no, you're not fobbing her off on me, Blackthorne. You're the one she told her father she was marrying, not me."

"So I'm doomed," Blackthorne said, and Maddie thought that the man actually sounded it.

"Doomed?" Lord Nicholas laughed. "There are worse fates than being married to a girl who looks like that. She's got every buck from seventeen to seventy-two after her."

"Are you one of them?" Blackthorne asked. "I'm not having some chit come between us."

There was a long pause, and Lord Nicholas finally said, "I'm through with that one. You're welcome to her. She'll make you an excellent marchioness. She's certainly haughty enough."

Maddie clenched her fists. Just like a man to talk about a woman as though she were a piece of property for them to barter or show off to friends and neighbors. Did either man consider poor Ashley, and how she would be forced to marry a man she didn't know and—from what Maddie could tell—didn't like much?

Of course not. Arrogant men. They thought every woman wanted them.

"She is beautiful," Blackthorne was saying, and Maddie leaned in closer. His voice was low and quiet, decidedly not boastful, but that didn't mean he wasn't gloating. "But she's got a bit of a temper."

Lord Nicholas laughed again. For two brothers so alike in appearance, Maddie couldn't believe the difference in behavior. She'd yet to hear Blackthorne laugh, while his brother seemed to do it all the time.

"What's a bit of a temper?" Lord Nicholas went on. "Could be fun, and I'm certain she's nothing you can't handle."

"Oh, I'm looking forward to handling her," Blackthorne said, and Maddie took a step back, unwilling to hear more.

It sounded very much like Blackthorne was anticipating his marriage to Ashley— or at least the wedding night.

Maddie had nothing but worry and reservation about her own wedding night. She hardly knew Mr. Dover. She'd met him at a meeting of the . . .

Society of Animal Studies—oh, the society had a much fancier name than that, but she couldn't remember it.

She'd gone because she was concerned about bear baiting. Actually, she hadn't even known the cruel sport existed until she took a wrong turn after delivering food to a widow. The woman lived in a decidedly questionable area of town. When Maddie had gone out a back door, instead of turning a corner and seeing her coach and footmen, she'd walked into a circle of men, a chained and bloody bear, and two vicious dogs.

She had cried for the poor bear all the way home. She'd begged her father to go back and buy the animal, but, as usual, he refused. The next day, when she'd seen an announcement for a meeting of the Animal Society, she had made arrangements to attend.

But the men there had ignored her concerns about the bear. Instead, they'd been more interested in talking about new species and poring over a book of insect drawings by a man living in India.

Only Mr. Dover had listened and seemed concerned. He alone had commiserated with her over the fate of the poor bear. Later that night, when her parents dragged her to a musicale, during which she had to endure not one, but two whispered proposals, she thought again of Mr. Dover.

As a child, she had sworn not to marry, but it was becoming increasingly clear that she was going to have to renege on that promise. Two of her cousins had already left the ranks of the Spinster's Club, and Maddie knew her turn was next. If it had to be, why shouldn't she choose someone who would be a partner with her in her charitable causes? Yes, Mr. Dover was officious and fond of lecturing. But what man wasn't?

She'd gone to several additional meetings of the Animal Society and, after talking with Mr. Dover more, made her proposition. At first, he was as surprised as any man might be, but she knew from their conversations that he was a widower with two small children. She argued that he needed a wife.

He didn't disagree, but he did point out that her family would never accept a man like him—a scholar not of the aristocracy.

And so they hatched a plan to elope to Gretna Green, and to Maddie's amazement, all they'd envisioned was coming to fruition.

Well, except for Ashley's interference.

And Lord Blackthorne and Lord Nicholas.

And Ashley's father.

And . . .

Maddie shook her head. She pulled open the carriage door and climbed up the steps, chiding herself for being so negative.

Everything was going to work out just fine. Just as it should. She would marry Mr. Dover, and Ashley would marry Lord Blackthorne, and then all her cousins would be happily married.

Catie had the smart and successful Lord Valentine. Josie had the handsome, adventurous Lord Westman. Ashley would have the dark and dangerous Lord Blackthorne.

And she herself would have . . . Mr. Dover.

Maddie felt like crying. It wasn't fair! Of all the carriages in London, why did Lord Blackthorne have to jump into hers? She had never met a man like him. She'd never even been this close to such a superb male specimen.

She knew she shouldn't be thinking of Blackthorne like that, especially on the way to her wedding with another man, but she couldn't stop herself anymore.

From the moment Blackthorne dove in the carriage and turned his black eyes on her, she hadn't been able to take a deep breath. Longing, like none she'd ever known, stole over her every time she thought of him.

She didn't know why. He'd had a bloody nose, a coffee stain on his trousers, and his hair was too long and completely disordered.

He looked like he'd been thrown in the gutter and run over by a curricle or two.

And it didn't matter.

He made her knees weak and her heart pound. He made her want to reach over and run her fingers through his hair. He made her want to straighten his hopelessly wrinkled cravat. He made her want to climb into his lap and feel those big arms around her.

She knew Mr. Dover would never make her feel that way.

And she knew something else as well.

She was going to be miserable watching Blackthorne—*her* Blackthorne—marry Ashley. She loved Ashley, but the thought of Ashley with Blackthorne made her seethe.

Maddie put her head in her hands. Now she was not only being negative, but jealous as well. She should be happy for Ashley and happy for Blackthorne. He was obviously pleased with his future wife. He obviously couldn't wait to be alone with her.

And besides, she knew that Blackthorne was all wrong for her. She hated adventure and risk, and Blackthorne seemed to court it. She refused to be controlled, and she could tell Blackthorne was one of those men who liked to be in charge. Her father was the same. He'd halted her charitable activities under the guise of keeping her safe for years. She simply hadn't been able to take it anymore.

And so she'd chosen Mr. Dover.

You've made your bed, Maddie told herself. *Now you'll have to—*

The carriage door flew open and Blackthorne forcibly pushed Ashley inside. On the other side, Dover scrambled in as the coach began to move.

Maddie heard angry shouts but had no time to decipher them as Blackthorne shot into the seat beside her, barely getting the carriage door closed before the conveyance was moving at full speed.

"Goddamn lousy luck," she heard him mutter.

"Sir!" she said in surprise, but he didn't look the least bit contrite.

"Brace yourself, sweetheart," Blackthorne said, voice grim. "We've just made some new enemies."

Chapter 5

"**E**nemies? But who—" Maddie began before
the carriage jolted and she was slammed
against the door. Ashley pulled her back up again,
and the two girls clung to each other as the vehicle
made a sharp turn on what felt like two wheels.

Behind them, angry shouts and curses were
hurled at the conveyance. The sweet, sleepy village of a moment before had awakened with an
unfriendly growl.

"What happened?" Maddie said, still clutching
Ashley tightly.

"Lord Nicholas happened," Ashley answered
with a glare for Lord Blackthorne. Not that her
fiancé noticed or cared. All his attention was focused on the town disappearing behind them.

Ashley looked back at Maddie. "The innkeeper
caught Lord Nicholas with his daughter."

Maddie gaped. "But how—when? We were
there for less than half an hour."

"Lord Nicholas works quickly."

Blackthorne must have been listening after all

because he gave Ashley an irritated look before glancing back out the window. "You have it all wrong. The girl cornered Nick. It's a simple mis-understand— Get down!"

He grabbed Maddie's shoulders and pushed her forcibly to the floor. She landed hard, and would have cried out if she hadn't been startled silent by a crash.

Blackthorne released her, and she looked up to see that the back of the carriage, between Dover and Blackthorne, had a hole in it. She turned to peer at her seat and saw that the stuffing had exploded where the bullet hit.

Bullet?

Beside the protruding stuffing, Ashley was sitting immobile, her face pale and frozen in shock. Maddie reached for her, but Dover was quicker. He took Ashley by the arms and lowered her onto the floor, covering her with his body.

Maddie had a moment to wonder if she shouldn't be the one Dover was protecting, and then another bullet crashed through the carriage, and all she could do was cower at Blackthorne's feet.

Her heart was slamming so hard against her sternum that she was afraid the bone would break. And her lungs seemed to have shrunk. She couldn't fill them with air, and she gasped and heaved like a fish tossed from the lake onto shore. She closed her eyes and prayed— or at least tried. She couldn't think of any actual words at the moment, so she hoped God could read her mind.

Another shot rang out, missing the carriage, but loud enough to make Maddie scream. And then the carriage wheel hit a hole and she was pitched forward, straight into Blackthorne's lap.

His knees closed protectively around her, and she was suddenly warm and cocooned. He smelled like coffee and tobacco and man.

"Love the idea, sweetheart," Blackthorne said. "But now's not the time."

Maddie looked up and realized her head was buried in his nether regions. A wave of mortification rushed over her. The feeling was so strong that she would have fainted—except that would have put her right back where she'd been.

She scrambled to escape her compromising position, but Blackthorne held her prisoner between his legs. He was staring out the window at their pursuers, so she couldn't be sure he was aware of what he was doing. But she had the distinct feeling that he was enjoying all of this a little too much.

"Sir! Release me!"

No response. Blackthorne completely ignored her.

"Sir!"

He gave her a distracted look, then actually scooted forward on the seat. Maddie gasped. She was now closer to the area she was trying to avoid.

"Sir!"

Blackthorne kept her locked between his knees and struggled to remove his tailcoat. He had it unbuttoned but couldn't seem to free his broad shoulders from the form-fitting material.

"Sir!" Maddie said more loudly.

"Stop whining and help me get this coat off."

"*Whining*? I'm not—"

He freed the garment, and the blue tailcoat was stuffed into her face. Then she fell backward in surprise as he released her from between his legs. Maddie struggled to find her way out from under the garment, and just when she freed her head, she looked up to see Blackthorne trying to open the carriage door.

"What are you doing?" she screamed. She sounded like a lunatic but couldn't help it and didn't want to. In light of the situation, it was perfectly appropriate for her to scream hysterically. What else was she to do when the deranged idiot before her opened the door of a moving carriage? What kind of mad fool put himself in the path of a bullet?

Blackthorne threw the door open, and Maddie had her answer.

"Hold on," he called over his shoulder. "I'm going to show my brother how to drive this thing."

"But—"

And then he was gone, scrambling out the door and holding onto the side of the carriage. The door swung wildly, its hinges creaking, and the next bullet ripped right through the window, spraying Maddie with glass.

"Are you all right, Lady Madeleine?" Mr. Dover asked. At some point he'd released Ashley and was now moving toward her.

Maddie wanted to say no. She wanted to creep under her seat and hide for the rest of her—what was sure to be short—life. Instead, she gave Dover an encouraging nod, then watched as he crawled over her, reached for the door, and pulled it closed again.

That done, he extracted his pocket watch and tsked at what he saw.

Outside, she heard shouts and the thunder of hoofs but no more gunshots. She listened for Blackthorne's voice but couldn't make it out amidst the other noises. She thought she heard a thump on the roof of the carriage, and she looked up, expecting to see Blackthorne open the hatch and smile down at her.

But then the coach lurched violently and there was a horrible wrenching sound from underneath. Outside, the shouts grew more frantic as the carriage seemed to careen uncontrollably from this side to that.

Maddie held onto the seat, the floor, Ashley—whatever she could—but she was still thrown wildly about. The carriage went left then right, swaying like a drunk sailor on his first day in port.

Her head hit something hard and a sharp ringing overtook the noise outside.

Everything in the carriage flew around them, and Maddie saw her reticule flop onto the floor and then bounce out the open window.

Slack-jawed, she watched all the money she had tumble out of sight. With a groan, she closed her eyes and clutched her throbbing head.

Finally, the carriage slowed and, with another screech, came to a shuddering stop. Maddie slowly opened her eyes, wary of the sudden quiet.

Nothing moved or breathed for the space of five heartbeats, and then Ashley rolled over and their eyes met. "I feel horrible," she moaned.

"Are you hurt?" Maddie asked, surprised at how weak and breathless her own voice sounded.

Ashley opened her mouth to reply, but outside they heard, "Come out where we can see you! Make it slow, or I'll shoot."

Silence.

The cousins stared at one another. Where were Lord Nicholas and Lord Blackthorne?

The door was flung open, and Maddie jumped, then jumped again when it promptly fell off one hinge and hung at an awkward angle. It was almost dark outside now, and the man standing in the doorway was in shadow.

"All of you out. Hands up or I'll shoot you dead."

Maddie rose quickly, to do as she'd been told, but Dover held her back and whispered, "Let me go first."

He crawled out, hands in the air.

"Where are the rest of you?" another male voice asked.

"There are only two ladies inside," Dover said. "They are no threat. Let them be."

"Get them out here now, or I'll go in and bring them out," the first man said.

Ashley and Maddie exchanged a look, and then Maddie climbed out, hands in the air. Ashley followed, but she didn't put her hands up. Instead, she stood, braced her hands on her hips, and gave the men her most condescending look.

"What is the meaning of this?" she said haughtily.

Maddie looked at her in shock. There were two men on horseback and one standing beside his mount. He was at least fifteen stone, probably heavier, and his blunderbuss looked like an extension of his beefy arm. The other two men were armed likewise. All three looked angry enough to shoot.

But Ashley didn't look the least bit afraid. She grabbed Maddie's upraised arms and pulled them down. The three men were staring at them, so Ashley spoke again.

"Sir. *You*," she said, pointing at the large man. "I asked what you think you're about. Chasing innocent women and shooting at unarmed travelers."

The man's eyes widened in shock, and he opened his mouth, then looked to his friends for assistance.

"Sir, I am speaking to you," Ashley demanded.

"So sorry, miss," the beefy man sputtered. "And miss." He nodded to Maddie, and she blinked at the newly contrite look on his face. Why, the big man actually looked sorry.

Of course, Ashley usually had that effect on men.

"That's Lady Madeleine, not *miss*," Ashley corrected him. "You are in the presence of an earl's daughter, so behave accordingly."

Ashley would have said more, but Maddie reached over and pinched her. Next, Ashley would be telling everyone they were eloping. As it stood, these men would be able to help her father and his men immensely when he passed this way looking for her. Not only did they have her physical description, but they knew she was an earl's daughter as well.

Her father was definitely going to catch them. And then he'd kill Mr. Dover and probably Blackthorne as well—though she shouldn't feel quite so anguished about that—and then her father would drag her home and she'd never be allowed to leave the house again and . . .

Oh, why had she ever decided eloping was a good idea?

"I'm sorry, my lady," the beefy man said, "but yourn coachman dishonored me daughter. I'm not leaving until he returns and makes an 'onest woman of her." He looked back at his friends, who shifted their weapons menacingly.

Maddie nodded regally. At least she hoped it

looked regal. Her hair was loose and a lock of it fell in her eyes when she moved her head. But she had to remain calm if she was going to save everyone.

"I was informed of my— er, coachman's mishap once we were en route. But I'm told this is simply a misunderstanding. We might have been able to resolve the dispute had you not begun shooting."

"An 'undred apologies, my lady," the big man said. "But it weren't no misunderstanding. Might we speak with your coachman now?"

"Certainly."

"Good. Where is 'e?"

Maddie had been afraid he was going to ask her that. She'd seen no sign of Lord Nicholas or Lord Blackthorne since she'd stepped outside. Slowly, she turned to look at the coach. The box was empty, but she couldn't see on top of the roof. Surely both brothers couldn't have hidden up there without being spotted.

But if they weren't on top of the carriage, they had to be—

The howl that came from underneath the carriage confirmed her theory and sent her stumbling back in fear. In a blur, Blackthorne rushed at the men. At least she'd thought he was rushing for them. Instead, he grabbed her, pulled her arms behind her back and dragged her toward the panting horses.

"Don't move," he shouted to the village men,

who were staring at her, and to Dover, who was coming after them. Dover ignored the order.

Maddie didn't know whether to beg her fiancé to rescue her or encourage him to escape now, before Blackthorne did something worse. Poor Mr. Dover. What had she gotten him into?

"Don't make me hurt her, Dover," Blackthorne growled as Maddie's fiancé came closer. Blackthorne twisted her arms, and she squeaked in protest.

But Dover must have thought she was hurt because he slowed. Blackthorne called, "Another step, Professor, and I kill her."

Jack watched as the professor halted. Surprisingly, the man looked ready to attack. So Lady Madeleine's fiancé had some passion in him after all.

By the look of him, the professor wasn't going to be put off for long, which meant Jack would have to act quickly.

He pulled Lady Madeleine farther back, into the shadows and behind a copse of trees. "Hurry up," he growled when she dragged her feet.

"I'm not going to help you kill me," she retorted.

Jack snorted and paused to survey their location. Satisfied that they couldn't be seen from the road, he said, "I'm not going to kill you. I don't even have a pistol."

"Mr. Dov—"

Jack slammed a hand over her mouth. The little chit was going to ruin everything. Holding his hand over her lips, he backed her up against a tree and peered into her eyes. "Bad idea, my lady."

She glared at him and mumbled something from under his fingers. He paused a moment, deciphering her muffled syllables.

"Actually, I do have a better idea."

Though at the moment he was having a hell of a time remembering it. He hadn't anticipated what it would be like to be so close to her. Her big blue eyes blinked up at him, and he noticed that her lashes were incredibly long and thick. She had that worried line between her eyebrows again, and he wanted to smooth it away.

But it was hard enough concentrating with his hand pressed innocently against her lips. His fingers grazed one soft, satiny cheek, and Jack knew he'd never touched skin so soft. He imagined her lips were equally soft. And warm. And if he moved his hand, and bent lower, he could . . .

Jack cleared his throat. "I do have a plan."

And the plan did not involve seducing Lady Madeleine. He had to rescue five people. He didn't have time to fantasize about kissing the Earl of Castleigh's daughter and another man's fiancée.

"Lady Madeleine!" Dover called from beyond their cover of trees. Her eyes widened, and Jack swore.

"Listen," he told her in a low voice, "my brother is innocent."

"Mow, mo mou mow?"

"I know because the girl tried to corner me as well."

Her eyes widened. "Me mon't melieve mat." She gestured toward the men with the pistols.

"I know they won't believe it. No father wants to hear that his daughter isn't pure and innocent. And even if he does believe it, he'll kill us for insulting his daughter."

"Mo, mat—" She broke off and pulled at his hand.

Jack gave her a warning look. "No shouting."

She nodded, and he lifted his hand. But he didn't move back. He might not be touching her face, but he had her backside against the tree trunk, which meant the rest of her was pressed intimately against him.

She was petite and womanly, curved in all the right places. And he knew in his head that he shouldn't be enjoying feeling all those sweet curves press against him, but he couldn't get his body to agree. He was obviously a scoundrel, but as long as he had Lady Madeleine close, he didn't care.

"Now what are we going to do?" Madeleine's voice, low and tinged with impatience, pulled his thoughts once again to the situation at hand. "Where's Lord Nicholas?"

"That's another problem." Jack lifted a lock of her hair and rubbed it between two fingers. Jesus, but it was like silk. Was there any part of this woman that didn't arouse him? He glanced into her eyes. "Nicholas hit his head. I left him unconscious."

"Oh, Lord." She looked past him, back toward the carriage. "Where is he now?"

"On the far side of the carriage. Hopefully, he'll wake when I put my plan into action."

"Plan?"

"Right. You and I walk out of here, then you scream and distract the innkeeper. I'll disarm the fat one—"

"Are you mad?" she hissed. "That will never work."

"You have a better idea?"

"I'm not allowing some asinine scheme like that when Mr. Dover and Ashley are in the middle of harm's way."

Jack frowned. What? Did the woman think he hadn't thought of her friends? "That's where you come in. You grab Miss Brittany and—"

"No. No, no, *no*."

She pushed him back, and Jack complied before he realized what he'd done. She started marching toward the carriage, but Jack grabbed her arm and hauled her back. "What the devil are you doing?"

She shook her arm out of his grasp and rounded on him. "I'm going to fix this."

He moved to block her path. She tried to go around him, but he checked her. "How?"

She glared at him, but he wasn't moving. Finally, she ground out, "By telling that man the truth."

"That his daughter is a trollop?"

"Yes."

"And you think *I'm* mad."

Her eyes grew dark with anger, and Jack actually considered stepping out of her way.

"Not only are you mad." She poked him in the chest, rising on tiptoe so her eyes were almost level with his. "You are the most reckless, most imprudent, most idiotic man I've ever met. Now, quit acting the fool, and get out of my way so I can take care of *your* mishap.'"

"Lady Madeleine!" Dover called again. "Are you all right? By my calculations, we are now one hour and three minutes behind schedule."

"Jiminy!" she muttered. "We have to keep moving." She turned toward the road. "Yes, I'm coming out!"

Jack scowled at her. Irritating, foolish woman. "So, you want to stroll out there and get yourself killed?"

He was washing his hands of this one. He was done saving people. Let the little chit have her way. And good riddance.

"Go right ahead." He made a show of stepping out of her way.

She raised her chin. "Good."

"Good."

With a nod, she marched past him.

"Just one more thing before you go, my lady."

And he reached out, took her in his arms, and kissed her.

Chapter 6

Maddie tried to pull away, to escape Lord Blackthorne's embrace.

Until his lips touched hers.

The man might be reckless, arrogant, and dashed in the head, but his lips were achingly addictive.

One touch, and she couldn't pull away. One touch, and she didn't want to pull away.

She had been kissed before. More than once, but not more than she could count on one hand. And before this moment, she could honestly say that she didn't care if she were ever kissed again. She'd found the activity boring at best and sloppy at worst.

Blackthorne was neither boring nor sloppy. In fact, he was slow, deliberate, and tantalizing. His lips were firm and cool, so gentle as they brushed against hers that she wasn't even sure at first that he was kissing her.

And then he kissed her again, and this time she felt his mouth move, felt the tingle of pleasure zing through the sensitive skin of her lips. It almost tickled. She wanted to reach up and rub her lips, but she knew that would not remove the ache.

Only Blackthorne could do so. And he did.

He pushed her back against the tree, cupping her head in his hand so he had complete control. Then he pulled back slightly, and their eyes met.

Maddie's lips were still tingling, and she couldn't help darting her tongue out in an attempt to quell the strange sensation.

His black eyes grew darker yet, and he took her chin between two fingers.

"I'm going to enjoy kissing you," he murmured.

She swallowed and shook her head. "I don't think you should."

One dark eyebrow lifted. "Kiss you or enjoy it?"

"Either," she whispered. She was Lady Madeleine. She shouldn't be allowing this. But already her traitorous gaze had lowered to focus on his mouth. She wanted it on hers again. She wanted more.

"Then tell me to stop," he murmured while his finger trailed from her chin to her lips, parting them slightly.

"I will," she said, feeling his finger move as she spoke. But she didn't. His body was warm against hers. He felt like liquid steel—so hard and yet so flexible.

"I'm waiting," he whispered.

"So am I," she answered. Oh, Lord. She shouldn't have said that. Lady Madeleine wouldn't have said that.

She was going to go to hell for encouraging him. But she was in a hell of anticipation right now. She needed him to kiss her again.

With infinite slowness, he obliged. He lowered his head, his gaze holding hers until the last possible second, then he touched his lips to hers. She felt like a feather had brushed her skin, only no feather had ever made her skin zing before.

She moaned slightly as the tingle infiltrated her body—traveling from her lips to her neck, her shoulders, the tips of her fingers. She felt numb. Drugged. Intoxicated.

Seemingly of its own volition, her hand came up to touch his back. As he wore only a linen shirt, she could easily feel the cords and bands of his muscles. Wrapping both hands around his waist, she pulled him closer. She felt his mouth curve in a smile against hers.

"Do you want more, Maddie?" he whispered against her mouth.

She nodded.

He caught her bottom lip, and she felt his tongue trace her mouth slowly. The shock of that erotic sensation made her body come alive. She shook with the zing of pleasure, feeling it shoot through her—from her fingers back up her arms, straight to her back, where her spine tingled and the tiny hairs on the back of her neck stood up.

"Tell me."

Maddie closed her eyes. She shouldn't allow this to go any further. She should walk away, walk back to Mr. Dover, who was waiting for her, worrying about her.

Or at least worrying about being behind schedule.

"Give me more," she whispered.

With consummate skill, he slanted his mouth over hers. Maddie felt her nipples grow erect and hard, felt her legs grow wobbily. Blackthorne deepened their kiss, taking it from playful and innocent to somewhere she'd never been. Somewhere dark and dangerous and exciting.

And then he opened her lips, and she gave in to the sweet surrender of his invasion. The way he moved, the way he explored her, and encouraged her to explore him in return, took her breath away.

Or it might have been that she was pressed so tightly against him that she wasn't sure where he ended and she began. And still she couldn't get close enough.

It wasn't until he broke away that she realized she hadn't been breathing. She was light-headed and dizzy, and she had to clutch him to keep from falling over. She closed her eyes, hoping the world would stop spinning.

When she opened them, he was still looking at her.

"You were right," he said.

She shivered at the husky timbre of his voice. It made her want to grasp his shirt and pull him back to her.

But she didn't.

"Right?" she asked, managing to keep her voice from wavering.

"We shouldn't have done that."

"I'm always right," she moaned, not in the least pleased by that fact at the moment. "I should start listening to myself."

"Lady Madeleine!" Mr. Dover called again. "These men are growing quite . . . impatient!" His voice squeaked, and Maddie knew she had better get out there.

"I have to go," she said.

"Oh, no you don't." He put his hands on either side of her head, trapping her. "I won't let you risk yourself."

Maddie scowled at his attempts to control her. She'd been right again. "Move out of my way. I don't need protection."

"The hell you don't."

She tried to hold her temper. "You're just like my father, always trying to stop me from helping."

"Maybe he stops you because he doesn't want to have to rescue you. Now stay here."

"*You* stay here." And she darted under his arm and sprinted back toward the road.

Blackthorne was close on her heels. She thought

she heard him mutter, "You'd better be right this time," but then she saw poor Mr. Dover, and she slammed to a halt.

The large man from the village was holding Mr. Dover captive, the man's big beefy arm tight about his skinny neck.

"Mr. Dover!" Maddie's hand flew to her lips.

"We won't 'urt him, me lady. Just give us the coachman and we'll let you pass."

Maddie took a deep breath and moved forward. Cutting her gaze to the carriage, she saw Lord Nicholas hidden in the shadows. He was rubbing his head, looking groggy. She prayed he would stay put.

Blackthorne was a lost cause. He was so close on her heels that he stepped on her slipper.

When she was beside the carriage, she turned to glare at him, but he only rammed into her. "Stand back," she hissed.

"Lady Madeleine, I'm not your problem." He indicated the beefy man.

She turned back to the road. "Sir, I have what appears to be unfortunate news."

The beefy man's eyebrows came together, and Mr. Dover whimpered. Maddie opened her mouth again, then closed it abruptly. She simply couldn't tell this man his daughter was a loose woman. She glanced at Blackthorne, took a deep breath, and lied. "Our coachman has apparently run off and left us."

There was a sound of protest from underneath

the conveyance, and Maddie kicked dirt back, hoping a mouthful of grime would shut Lord Nicholas up. Didn't he realize she was trying to save him?

She gave the beefy man and his companions a sad smile. In fact, she did feel sad for them. "We are as distraught as you. And I can only imagine how your daughter must feel," she said sympathetically. "Perhaps she will find another suitor?"

One of the men on horseback sniggered. "'Ardly likely! She's got a face like an 'orse—"

The beefy man turned abruptly, and the man quickly closed his mouth. Poor Mr. Dover swung this way and that as the beefy man moved.

Maddie pretended she had not heard the other man. "Is there anything we can do to make reparations? Perhaps we can give you something toward her dowry?"

As soon as the words were out of her mouth, she remembered her reticule flying out of the carriage window. She glanced at Ashley, who was unusually quiet. Hopefully, her cousin, who claimed to be ready for an adventure at a moment's notice, had thought to bring a few pounds with her.

The beefy man frowned at her offer of reparations. Obviously he was less than pleased at the prospect of returning with anything less than a groom.

Finally, he lowered the blunderbuss and released Mr. Dover. The poor scholar immediately fell to his knees and cowered.

"I suppose we can come to some sort of arrangement," the beefy man said after perusing them. Most likely he was evaluating the quality of their clothes and carriage and tallying up their worth. "Ten pounds would be some help."

Maddie blanched. "Ten pounds?" she squeaked.

"My daughter is worth it," the man said with a nod.

Maddie stared at him, blew out a puff of air, then bit her lip. She gave a tentative smile.

"Of course she is, sir. One moment."

She moved closer to Ashley, and Blackthorne followed. The three of them made a tight circle. "How much money do you have?" Maddie asked Ashley.

"A fiver. You?"

Maddie shook her head. "None. I lost my reticule—"

"Don't worry about it," Blackthorne interrupted. "I have a better plan."

Maddie whipped around to face him. "I already know your plan, and I don't agree. If we don't have enough money, perhaps we can give him something else of value. I have these earrings."

But Blackthorne wasn't watching her. He was staring at the coach as though it were new and he'd never seen it before. Then he moved away from her, saying, "Hold onto your earrings. In fact, hold onto everything!"

There was a howl from the front of the coach and the horses reared up. Maddie and Ashley jumped back, out of the horses' way for fear of being trampled. But Blackthorne—fool that he was—raced toward the animals.

Maddie had a moment to glance at the men from the village. She prayed they didn't startle easily and accidentally shoot Mr. Dover, but they were staring at the commotion in surprise. The big beefy one was moving toward his horse. The other two frowned in confusion.

Wondering at their bewilderment, Maddie looked back and blinked in disbelief. Lord Nicholas was on one of the bays, racing toward the armed men. He was howling at the top of his lungs, trying desperately to control the spooked animal.

Behind him, Blackthorne was mounting another carriage horse and turning his animal to charge as well.

"Are they armed?" Ashley asked as the men rode by in a blur of dust and horseflesh.

"I don't think so!" Maddie yelled over the noise. And then as the two groups of men converged, she shut her eyes.

The Martingale brothers were obviously going to die. They'd be shot dead in the middle of the road. She didn't want to be pessimistic, but they were clearly doomed.

She squinched her eyes closed and tensed,

waiting for the shots to ring out. The sound of the horses' hooves grew farther away, and still she waited.

When Ashley put a hand on her arm, she jumped in surprise and opened her eyes. The road was deserted. Except for poor Mr. Dover, still huddled across the way, the men had disappeared.

"What happened?"

Ashley shook her head. "Those idiots from the village took off, and Lord Blackthorne and Lord Nicholas went after them."

"But Blackthorne and Lord Nicholas aren't armed."

Ashley gave her a foreboding look. "I imagine that will become apparent soon enough."

Mr. Dover had cocked his head at the sound of the girls' voices. "Are—Are they gone?"

Ashley shook her head and muttered, "Where did you find him? I thought Sir Alphonse was a simpering fool."

Maddie ignored her and went to help Mr. Dover up. Poor man. He wasn't used to these types of adventures.

She wished she weren't either.

Jack and Nick chased the men within a few yards of the village before the men realized the brothers weren't any real threat.

One moment Jack was whooping and hollering, trying to distract the men lest they realize he hadn't fired any shots, and the next the men had

turned on them and Jack was screaming for Nick
to go back.

Nick barely got his horse to retreat before the
first shot rang out. Jack cursed and bent low. He
glanced behind him, saw his brother riding fast
and hard, and veered his mount toward the trees
off to the side of the road. Nick followed. They
were too vulnerable out in the open, and Jack
hoped they could lose the men in the woods.

He couldn't lead them back to the carriage.
That would put the women in too much danger.
Damn fool woman put herself in enough danger
as it was. Lady bloody do-gooder Madeleine.

He ducked to avoid low-hanging branches as
another shot rang out. It chipped the bark of the
tree beside him, and a spray of wood flew in his
face.

Jesus, that was close.

Nick had entered the woods to his left, and Jack
steered his horse toward his brother's. The animal was moving considerably slower as the foliage grew thicker, but that was just fine with him.
He wanted the foliage thick. Nick glanced back
and slowed enough for Jack to catch up.

"Let's find a good place to ambush them,"
Nick suggested. "Maybe somewhere near water.
We leave the horses in sight so they think we've
paused to let them drink."

"You think they'll keep following us? It's almost full dark."

Nick was silent for a moment, then said, "I

still hear them behind us. They're mad as hell by now."

Jack sighed and then brightened. Ambush it was, then.

"If we can waylay them for a bit," Nick was saying, "we'll have enough time to get back to the carriage and grab the girls. Hopefully, Miss Brittany isn't stupid enough to let the other two horses run off."

"And the carriage?" Jack asked. He had a bad feeling he already knew the answer. "The axle's broken?" He'd heard that awful pop and screech and known it wouldn't be taking them any farther.

"Clean in two," Nick answered, his voice muffled as he bent to clear a low branch. "We'll have to ride on horseback."

"That'll be interesting."

"Up ahead," Nick said. "Hear it?"

Jack listened and caught the distant gurgle of a stream. Behind him, he heard their pursuers calling out. They were getting closer.

Jack grinned. He loved a good ambush.

Maddie paced the length of the carriage for the tenth time that night, rubbing her cold arms with her equally cold hands. Now that it was dark, the temperature had dropped, and she was freezing.

She really shouldn't have worn the white and lavender muslin. All those times her cousins had made her dress in boys' clothing for their adventures, and she'd never appreciated how practical it was.

Now she was shivering in her thin dress, her dainty slippers ruined and so thin that she felt every rock and pebble in the road.

She passed Ashley and Mr. Dover, both sitting dejectedly in the carriage. She couldn't bear to look at her friend or her fiancé, much less sit with them. If they knew what she'd been doing in the woods with Lord Blackthorne, they'd hate her.

How had she turned from the girl everyone called kind and tenderhearted into a girl capable of betrayal and adultery?

Well, it wasn't adultery yet, not technically, but what did it matter? She was a horrible person, even more so because she'd enjoyed her treachery.

"Stop pacing," Ashley said. "It's too cold to be outside."

"I'm colder if I sit still," Maddie answered, beginning to pace again. With each step forward she chided herself for her stupidity in planning this ridiculous elopement. With each step back, she told herself to think positively.

Everything would work out in the end.

Not that she had any proof of that. Nothing had worked out so far. In fact, things had only become worse. At first it had merely been the inconvenience of having Ashley along. Then, as if having her friend tag along on her elopement weren't bad enough, they'd been kidnapped by Lord Blackthorne and his brother, Don Juan.

Of course, that led to more problems, and she'd barely taken a breath before they were being shot at by angry men from the village.

Now she was stranded who knew where—well, Mr. Dover probably had the location on his schedule, which was precisely why she wasn't going to ask him—and Blackthorne and his brother were gone, abandoning her and Ashley for another adventure. It would only be a matter of hours—actually twenty-seven minutes, if Mr. Dover was correct—before her father found them or the thugs from the village returned.

Then she was truly damned.

The sound of hoof beats made her jerk her head up, and she raced back toward the carriage.

"Someone's coming!"

Ashley jumped out and grabbed her by the hands. "What should we do? Who do you think it is? Should we hide?"

In the carriage, Mr. Dover moaned, and Maddie had to speak loudly to make her voice carry above his noise. "I think we should hide until we know who it is."

"I think you're right."

The girls stumbled toward the copse of trees where Maddie and Blackthorne had kissed earlier, but before they reached it, they heard a wild shout.

"We're back!"

Chapter 7

Maddie knew that voice. It caused equal and opposite reactions in her. On the one hand, she wanted to flee and hide. On the other, she wanted to run toward Lord Blackthorne.

Neither seemed preferable, so she chose to stop, turn, and face the Martingale brothers. They arrived, smug and smiling. Conquering heroes.

Ashley rolled her eyes at Maddie. "Every time I see that look, which with five brothers is fairly frequently, I want to retch."

"Perhaps they've saved us, and we can finally be on our way."

"Well, they certainly *think* they saved us," Ashley retorted. She tapped her foot and crossed her arms. "We'll see."

"No need to worry, my ladies," Lord Nicholas said when he was beside the carriage. He jumped off his horse and bowed dramatically. "We have triumphed over our tormentors. You won't see them again."

"Well, considering you're the one who began

the trouble in the first place, and we still see you,"
Ashley spat, "that's not at all comforting."

Lord Nicholas huffed and moved away, but
Maddie was watching Lord Blackthorne dis-
mount. She swore the king of scowls smiled at the
way Ashley took his brother down a peg.

But she might have been mistaken. It was rather
dark.

"As relieved as we are to see you," Maddie
said, "I'll be more relieved when the horses are
harnessed again and we're on our way. We're—
Mr. Dover, how far behind schedule are we?"

From the carriage interior, he called, "Precisely,
one hour and—"

"We'll no longer be traveling in the carriage,"
Lord Blackthorne barked, all scowls again as he
strode past Maddie. He headed for the other two
bays, who were grazing on the side of the road,
and she followed.

"What do you mean, sir?" she said, rushing to
catch up to him. "Why can't we continue in the
carriage?"

He continued walking. "The axle is broken."

Maddie felt her heart stop. Truly. It ceased beating for a good three seconds. She couldn't breathe,
couldn't think, and she almost doubled over from
the weight of Blackthorne's revelation.

Ashley rushed to her side. "Maddie, are you
well?"

She tried to nod.

"She's fine," Blackthorne said, barely glancing

at his fiancée as he led the horses by. "I'm sure you're ecstatic, Miss Brittany. Didn't you wish the axle would break so your father could catch us and shoot me?"

"Being stranded by the side of the road was hardly my wish. And I think we all know who is to blame for this." Ashley gazed pointedly at Lord Nicholas, who stood, hands on hips, studying the broken conveyance.

He held up his hands in mock surrender. "I can't help it if I'm irresistible."

"Why, you—" Ashley began.

"But what will we do without the carriage?" Maddie interrupted. She looked into Ashley's pretty face, now lit by the half-moon rising over the trees. "My father—"

"Isn't going to catch us," Lord Nicholas assured her. "We're going to ride on horseback for now. We'll make better time that way."

Maddie nodded. He was right. They would make better time on horseback—providing he didn't unwittingly seduce any women in the next village.

"But there are only four horses and five of us," Maddie pointed out. "And what about my luggage?"

"Leave it," Blackthorne said. He was moving about the horses, checking to see that they were in good condition.

"Oh, no," Maddie argued. She'd already lost her reticule and all her money. She wasn't about to give up her change of clothing and the dress she intended to wear to her wedding. "I'm not leaving it behind."

Blackthorne looked ready to argue—he always looked ready to argue—but his brother was nodding. "We'll strap your valise and any other luggage to one of the horses, Lady Madeleine. We need a pack animal anyway. Your coachman was obviously prepared. He packed blankets, food, and extra tack in the box."

"Too bad we had to leave him behind," Ashley muttered.

"Get everything we need and drop it here." Blackthorne indicated a spot directly behind the carriage. "Hurry. We have to keep moving."

Blackthorne and his brother strode toward the coachman's box, and Maddie followed. "But if we use one horse to carry supplies, that leaves only three horses to ride."

Blackthorne was handing reins and a bit to his brother. "What's your point, sweetheart?"

"Sweet—" Maddie fisted her hands and reminded herself to keep to the point, no matter how rude Lord Blackthorne became.

Sweetheart, indeed. If he knew what she'd like to say to him at that moment, he wouldn't think she was so sweet.

"There are five of us, sir, and three horses." Her tone indicated that this should be obvious.

Blackthorne looked at her, his black eyes twinkling. "We'll have to ride double. You and

Miss Brittany may ride with Nick and myself."

"Certainly not!" she said, taking a step back. The image of Lord Blackthorne kissing her in the woods an hour or so ago flashed before her eyes. She could still feel the weight of his chest against hers. She could still feel the warmth of his skin.

She would probably combust if she had to ride for hours pressed against him on the back of a horse. Even now her face heated simply thinking about it.

"I didn't say you'd be riding with me," Blackthorne said, a wicked twinkle in his eye. "Though I can see you're thinking about it."

Jiminy! He was right. Of course she wouldn't ride with him. What kind of friend was she to Ashley to even imagine doing so?

"I'll—I'll ride with Mr. Dover," she stuttered.

"Suit yourself." Blackthorne winked and turned his back on her again.

But she didn't ride with Mr. Dover in the end. Apparently, while Mr. Dover was very good with schedules and mathematics, he was not so good with horses. He climbed on one of the docile bays, accidentally kicked the horse, and when the animal shifted forward, Mr. Dover fell backward.

They got him back on his horse, and Lord Nicholas used some rope from the coachman's box to secure him.

"This is humiliating," Mr. Dover groaned.

"It won't be for long, old boy," Lord Nicholas

assured him. "We'll have to stop for the night before too long."

Stop for the night? Maddie couldn't prevent her gaze from flicking to Lord Blackthorne. She had not considered that she would have to spend a night or more in his presence.

He seemed to feel her eyes on him—or perhaps he was thinking of her as well—and he met her gaze.

Quickly, she went back to the work of securing her valise. And though she had a hundred questions, she didn't dare ask for any details. But her mind screamed its worry. Where were they going to sleep?

A village meant they risked more problems like those this afternoon.

But without the shelter of the carriage, they had to find a village.

And if they paused to sleep, would that give her father time to catch up with them?

"Stop worrying," Lord Blackthorne said, halting his bay beside her.

"I'm not worrying," she said, trying to see past him. She hoped the rope held Mr. Dover.

"Yes, you are."

She frowned up at him. Really, the impudence of this man was extraordinary. "How do you know?"

"You have that line right between your eyebrows." He reached down, and she thought he would touch her. Instead, he held his hand out to her. "Let's go."

Maddie blanched and shook her head. "I'm not riding with you." She glanced over at his brother, but Ashley was already seated behind Lord Nicholas.

How had that happened? Blackthorne was Ashley's fiancé; she should be riding with him. Then she might have ridden with Lord Nicholas. It was as improper to ride with him as with his brother, but at least the younger Martingale was affable.

But Ashley with Lord Nicholas, and she with Lord Blackthorne, was all wrong. What was Ashley doing? She'd acted as though she hated Lord Nicholas even more than Lord Blackthorne.

Maddie eyed Ashley, studying the way her friend's arms were wrapped around Lord Nicholas. As soon as she had a moment, she was going to quiz Ashley on her past with Lord Nicholas. Whatever had been between them didn't appear to be quite over.

Blackthorne snapped at her, and Maddie whipped her head back. Had the man just treated her like a dog?

"Lady Madeleine," he said impatiently, "I have neither the time nor the inclination to argue with you any further. Take my hand and climb up or walk the entire way. At this point, I don't care what you do."

Maddie ground her teeth together and glared at him. Who was he to order her about and snap at her as though she were his trained hound? Odious, uncouth man.

But he was an odious uncouth man she was stuck with, at present anyway. It wouldn't serve to anger him. She might find herself walking to Gretna Green.

So, with firm determination, she clapped her hand into his, hard, and allowed him to help her up behind him. But all the while, she was imagining when and how she would force him to apologize and beg her forgiveness.

The horse wore no saddle, and when she was behind Blackthorne, it took a moment for her to adjust. She was still finding her balance and attempting to seat herself comfortably when Blackthorne spurred the horse forward. She almost did a Mr. Dover.

Maddie was forced to clutch the marquess around the waist and hang on tightly. The act of touching him was agony and ecstasy all at once.

Increasingly, she disliked him and his rude, selfish, I-stick-my-neck-in-the-noose-for-no-one behavior. And increasingly, she found herself imagining him touching her and kissing her.

Touching him again made her forget how much she despised him, and it brought those unwanted, disloyal feelings of desire rushing back.

She could be grateful, at least, that he had donned his tailcoat when he returned from chasing the men of the village. She didn't know how she would have survived if she'd had to hold onto that muscular chest with only a thin layer of linen between them.

The group once again began the long trek to Gretna Green. Maddie and Lord Blackthorne led the procession, followed by Lord Nicholas and Ashley, the packhorse on leading strings, and, in the rear, a wobbily Mr. Dover.

Blackthorne began at a brisk pace. It might be dark, but he intended to make good time. Maddie worried that the speed might be too much for Mr. Dover's weak horsemanship skills, but when she looked back, she saw that her fiancé was still seated. Thank the Lord for small favors.

She twisted forward and stared at Blackthorne's back. She couldn't see a thing over his shoulders.

"Comfortable?" Blackthorne asked.

"No," she answered immediately, not caring that it sounded rude. He was so uncouth, she didn't think he'd even notice.

She felt rather than heard the low rumble of laughter in his chest. "You don't like me much, do you?"

She wanted to say no, that she didn't like him at all. Not in the slightest. But she couldn't be that impolite. She had standards. "I don't wish to discuss my feelings for you," she retorted. Her mother had always told her that if she had nothing pleasant to say, she should say nothing whatsoever. She was following that advice.

"But you liked kissing me, didn't you?"

Maddie inhaled sharply and stiffened. Then, aware that Blackthorne could probably feel her reaction, she tried to relax and pretend his question hadn't concerned her.

"I don't wish to discuss that earlier incident," she said coldly, and felt Blackthorne chuckle again.

"I'll bet you don't."

Maddie shot daggers into his back with her eyes. "What do you mean by that, sir? Are you implying that I want it to happen again? Because I assure you that kissing you is the furthest thing from my mind."

There was a long pause, then, "Actually," he said, voice full of amusement, "I wasn't implying that you were dreaming of kissing me again. I only meant that you probably don't want your fiancé to find out."

Maddie opened her mouth and shut it again. "Oh," she said weakly.

"So kissing me is the furthest thing from your mind, eh?"

She wanted to say, *Absolutely. I haven't given it a second thought.* But she was afraid he'd know she was lying. She'd never been very good at it, and always felt guilty later and confessed.

But she couldn't tell him the truth—that she hadn't *stopped* thinking about kissing him. And now that she was pressed against him, it was every bit as horrible as she'd anticipated. The heat of his body seeped into her. The feel of his heartbeat was steady against her fingertips, and the smell of his hair was clean and fragrant. With all of that assaulting her senses, she really couldn't stop thinking about kissing him.

The appalling fact was that she was no longer thinking about kissing him solely on the lips. The more time she spent inches from the back of his neck, the more she wondered what the flesh there would taste like. What if she touched her tongue to that spot where his black hair ended and the bronze flesh began—

"Thinking about kissing me again?" he said.

Lord, the man sounded arrogant.

"I do not wish to discuss it," Maddie said through tight lips. She forced her gaze away from his neck. The trees were very pretty at night.

"I don't want to discuss it either," Blackthorne told her. "But that doesn't mean I don't want to do it."

"Sir!" Maddie smacked him in the chest, then grabbed hold again as she lost her balance and tipped to the side.

Blackthorne chuckled again.

"You mustn't say things like that," she scolded. "I am engaged to Mr. Dover, and you—you are to marry my cousin."

"I thought she was your cousin's cousin."

"What does it matter? You are not free."

"Well, when you say it like that, I can't help but get excited."

"You're not supposed to be excited," Maddie

lectured. "You are supposed to enter into the union of marriage soberly and pensively. It's not something to be taken lightly."

"My dear Lady Madeleine, have you been attending church again?"

She sighed. "Obviously, there's no talking with you."

"Oh, you can lecture me all you want. I'm good at listening to lectures," he said. His voice sent small vibrations through her, tickling her and making her chest feel warm. "But I don't like hypocrites."

"What?" She almost slapped him again but remembered what had happened the last time she let go for a moment. "Are you calling me a hypocrite?"

"Do you call eloping to Gretna Green sober and pensive?"

"I resent that!" she said, loud enough to attract the attention of Ashley and Lord Nicholas.

"Everything all right, Maddie?" Ashley called.

"Fine," Maddie answered over her shoulder, try-ing to sound cheerful. She even smiled, though she doubted Ashley could see her face in the darkness.

She turned back to Blackthorne's hair. "I have given this marriage much thought. In fact, it's all I've thought about. You have no right to imply that I am behaving rashly."

"Have you thought about what the reaction will be when you return to Town?"

"Of course. It will be difficult at first—"

"Ah, so then you *are* returning to Town. Where will you and Mr. Dover be residing?"

Maddie opened her mouth to answer and realized she had absolutely no idea. Where did Mr. Dover live? She'd never even thought to ask.

Jiminy, she hoped it wasn't somewhere like Chelsea or Cheapside. That would be most inconvenient—

Stop it! she berated herself. *Where you live is not important.*

Blackthorne seemed to read her mind. "I'm sure Mr. Dover can't afford to reside in Berkeley Square, next to Papa Castleigh. Hell, I can't afford it."

"Where we live isn't important."

"Right."

They came to a fork in the road, and he guided the horse to the left. Maddie could see no road sign, and she hoped this was the right way to Gretna Green.

"Then let's talk of what is important," Blackthorne said. "Why are you eloping? What's the hurry to marry?"

"That, sir, is none of your affair."

"Are you—what is it you ladies say?—indisposed?"

"Sir!" This time she did smack him in the chest. She'd rather fall from the horse than allow that comment to go unpunished. "You are the most impudent person I have ever met."

"Am I? Well, you'd best get used to it. Not everything is gilded and polished below the lofty heights of Berkeley Square. Someone might actually tell you something you don't want to hear."

"Oh, and I suppose you think you have sage advice for me."

"It doesn't take a sage to see that your marrying Dover is a mistake."

"I *knew* you were going to say that."

"And?"

"And, you don't know the first thing about it."

"Don't I?"

The tone in his voice cut off Maddie's next retort. Why did he suddenly sound like he did understand? Impossible. He couldn't see into her mind or her heart.

"You think the unmarried daughter of a wealthy earl and a bachelor marquess have nothing in common? How many proposals do you receive a month—no, a week? Just the average."

"Three," she said quietly.

"Three? That's it? I would have thought at least five before you'd take such drastic measures." He gestured to Mr. Dover.

Maddie huffed. "I knew you wouldn't understand. How can you? Women don't propose to men. They don't corner them in libraries or garden benches and pledge their undying love."

"No, but their mamas do. It got so bad that I couldn't even take a piss—forgive my language— without some desperate mother sneaking up behind me to tell me how lovely her daughter was and how many sons she'd birth me."

"No!" Maddie could not believe it. She'd heard stories, but never imagined anyone would be so shameless.

"Oh, yes. The widows are worse."

Now she knew he was exaggerating his trials. "As though the attention of a widow is bothersome." She had heard far too many stories about widows who had bevies of lovers. She'd even had such women pointed out to her.

Blackthorne shrugged, his movement causing her breasts to tingle. "Did your first few marriage proposals bother you?"

Maddie bit her tongue. He had a point. But he couldn't really understand, not more than superficially, at any rate. Yes, the proposals had been bothersome and inopportune, but she was no dainty miss.

She had seen the seedier side of London. She'd comforted lonely orphans, who cried themselves to sleep. She'd sat by the bedside of a dying colonel, wounded in the peninsular wars. She'd fed the hungry, tried to clothe the homeless, cried for bears who bled for sport, and hares, dogs, and bulls who died for entertainment.

None of that proved she was not spoiled. She was, and she knew it. But the difference between her and the rest of the *ton* was that she appreciated her soft linen, her maidservant, and her full plate at dinner. In fact, it was because of the hardships she saw that she didn't expect her small luxuries. Instead, she cherished them.

And she hated that Blackthorne thought her so weak as to assume that she could not tolerate the inconvenience of three marriage proposals a week. But it wasn't the proposals that wore her down. It was the insincerity.

Above all, Maddie was an optimist. She had her dark moments and her doubts, like everyone else, but she always hoped for the best. Each time a new suitor approached her, she tried to keep an open mind. She hoped for the possibility that this man was the one she would fall in love with. This man was the one she would not be able to refuse.

She'd watched two cousins experience this type of love, so she knew that it did exist. She hoped and prayed it existed for her.

She wasn't supposed to hope for such things. She was a member of the Spinster's Club and not ever supposed to marry. But even as a child, she'd known their childhood pact exempted true love. None of her cousins would have ever begrudged her, or any of their club, true love.

But one after another her false suitors began to extinguish even the notion of true love. Worse, the more they flattered her, the uglier and more repulsive she felt.

Did no one care for her—the real her? Would anyone look at her twice if her father was not wealthy? Would anyone look past that wealth to try and know the real Lady Madeleine?

Not one.

Not even the most persistent of suitors knew

even the most fundamental truths about who she was.

They didn't care to know. Why would they? She wasn't beautiful like Ashley or so many other girls on display for the Season. She wasn't overly accomplished. She'd spent more time at Society meetings for widows than she had practicing her drawing or piano. She wasn't witty or a sparkling conversationalist. She didn't spend her time trying to think up clever bon mots.

But Maddie knew she had other qualities— good qualities—if only one of those suitors had looked deeper. She was kind; she was nurturing; she was loyal.

And when she'd finally looked to Mr. Dover, it was because she'd been in danger of losing all those good qualities. All the disingenuous proposals and declarations of love were turning her bitter and cynical. Where once it seemed her world was populated by happy couples, now she only saw philandering husbands and treacherous wives. Where once she saw the good in everyone, now she saw only artifice and corruption.

She had to find herself again, and the only way to do so was to get back to what was truly important: helping those less fortunate. Only her good works could restore her faith in the world and drive the bitterness away. She might not love Mr. Dover, but their wedding would take her off the marriage mart and allow her to focus on what mattered.

Then she could restore her faith in herself and in the essential goodness of man. She could be optimistic again and see love in the world.

But not if she allowed Lord Blackthorne into her life. He was just as his name implied, and if she opened her heart to him even an inch, he would infect her with his poison.

She'd been a fool to kiss him, a fool to make herself vulnerable. He was callous and selfish. She did not need him in her life.

A tiny voice from deep inside her whispered, *Perhaps he needs you.*

"No," she said aloud and shook her head. She couldn't save everyone. She didn't want to save Lord Blackthorne. Right now, she could hardly save herself.

"No?" Blackthorne said, jolting her out of her thoughts. "So your first few proposals did not bother you?"

"Actually, sir, I was saying no to this conversation. You and I have nothing in common, and I'm sorry to say that I am glad of it."

He did not respond, and Maddie wondered if she'd hurt his feelings. She hadn't wanted to upset him, but she needed to distance herself from him.

"Village up ahead," Lord Nicholas called from behind them. "Dover says it could be Stevenage. We should proceed with caution."

"Too late for that, Martingale," a voice said from the darkness on Maddie's right. "We 'ave you now."

Chapter 8

Jack froze, and his first thought was for Lady Madeleine. Why had he insisted she ride with him? Now she was as much a target as he.

"Come down off those 'orses, 'ands in the air," the man said.

Jack didn't recognize the voice. It could have been one of Maddie's father's men, or someone from the last village, or—and he prayed this wasn't the case—Bleven's men.

"You're wasting your time," Nick called from behind Jack. "We don't have any money or valuables. Go back and wait for a carriage."

"Ah, but Lord Nicholas. It is Nicholas, isn't it?"

Jack closed his eyes at this new voice. It was high-pitched, refined, and menacing. He'd know it anywhere.

"Now that we have you," the Duke of Bleven continued, "our wait has been well worth it. Not wasted time at all."

A man stepped out from the forest concealing the other men, his rifle pointed straight at them.

Jack had no way of knowing how many other weapons were aimed at them.

"Damn," he heard Nick swear. "Jack?" he said softly.

"We're going to climb down," Jack told Bleven. If only he could see the duke or his men, then he could gauge the odds. As it was, he had no idea what they were facing. "We have two ladies with us. They have nothing to do with what's between us. You have to let them go."

Bleven laughed. "I don't *have* to do anything, Lord Blackthorne. Now get on the ground before I shoot the lot of you."

"Don't shoot! Don't shoot!" Dover called. "I can't get down. I'm tied on my horse."

"I'll get you," Nick called.

Jack had no choice except to lower Lady Madeleine first, making her vulnerable. But he swung down beside her as quickly as he could. He pushed her behind him, so he was protecting her from the front and the horse was at her back. If anything happened to her, he would never forgive himself.

And he was quite good at not forgiving himself.

In the filtered moonlight, Jack saw Nick lower Miss Brittany, then pull her with him as he went to untie Dover.

Dover promptly slid off his horse and crumpled to the ground, whimpering something about "hopelessly behind schedule."

"How does that man know your name?" Lady Madeleine whispered in Jack's ear.

Jack clenched his jaw. He'd been afraid she was going to ask him that. "We're old friends," he said vaguely.

"Interesting friends you have."

"'Ands up!" Bleven's man called.

Jack obliged. Why the hell hadn't he thought to bring a weapon with him? Of course, when he'd left his town house this morning, he'd only intended to have a cup of coffee and read the papers. No weapon required.

Perhaps if he'd known his brother was in Town . . .

There was the hiss of flame, and then three lanterns illuminated the road, revealing at least eight men, including Bleven, moving out from the forest. Jack caught sight of his brother, hands in the air, and then one of Bleven's thugs stepped in front of Jack, blocking his view. The thug grabbed his arms and dragged him away from Lady Madeleine.

Another thug went for her, but Jack growled, "Don't touch her."

He was backhanded for his efforts, but he saw Lady Madeleine rush over to her friend. The two women stood huddled together.

"Your traveling companions have improved," Bleven said, stepping in front of Jack and Nick, who had been brought before the duke. "But your manners haven't. Show some respect, boys."

He snapped his fingers, and Bleven's men pushed Jack and Nick onto their knees. Jack didn't resist. He wanted Bleven to think he was docile and accommodating.

Bleven looked down at him. "That's better. But not good enough."

In a flash of black, his booted foot struck Nick in the jaw. With an ominous pop, Nick fell over.

"Lord Nicholas!" he heard one of the girls call, but Jack saved his strength. When the blow came for him, he was ready.

Bleven was a wealthy and powerful man. He was shrewd and cunning and ruthless. But he wasn't particularly creative. The duke moved to strike him exactly as he had Nick. Anticipating the move, Jack brought his hand up, caught Bleven's foot and pushed.

Arms careening wildly, Bleven went down. As Jack expected, the duke's thugs—mindless bullies eager to please their master—rushed to help him. There was a moment of chaos during which Jack grabbed his brother, pulled him to his feet and yelled, "Run!"

Of one mind, Jack and Nick arrowed for the girls. Jack grabbed Maddie and pushed her into action. Nick did the same for Ashley. Behind him, he heard shouts of "After them, fools!" Jack spared a glance for Dover, who was huddled in a ball on the ground, then pushed Maddie in front of him and steered her toward the trees.

They'd barely cleared the road when the first shot exploded behind them. It was wild and hit a tree far to their left, but Jack pushed Maddie down to protect her from the next shot.

"Goddamn it!" Nick swore, crouching beside Ashley, who had jumped behind a tree. "How the hell did he find us?"

"I don't know," Jack panted. "But we've got to go back."

"Back?" Ashley screamed.

"Not you," Jack told her, but he was looking at Maddie. "You two keep running. Nick and I will go back and distract him while you two escape."

"But we can't leave you," Maddie protested. She was on her knees now, and Jack wished he could push her back on the ground, cover her with his body, and keep her safe for the rest of her life. Instead, he'd have to do the next best thing.

"Don't argue," he ordered as another shot, this one hitting closer, rang out. "Run and hide. We'll find you."

"But—"

He silenced her with a quick kiss—a press of his mouth on hers—then pushed her forward. "Go!"

With steely determination, he turned again to the road and Bleven.

As soon as Jack heard the girls' footfalls receding, he called, "Okay, Bleven, you have us! Stop shooting and we'll surrender."

"No more tricks," Bleven called back. "One wrong move and I kill you where you stand."

"Agreed!" Jack called. He looked at Nick, grim-faced and white. "First chance you get, escape and find them."

"I'm not leaving you with Bleven."

Jack grabbed Nick about the throat and pushed him hard against a tree. "Goddamn it, don't argue with me. This isn't going to be like what happened with—" He stopped, swallowed hard. "First chance you get, you go find the girls. Got it?"

Nick nodded, and Jack released him.

"Let's go." The two put their hands up and marched out.

One of Bleven's men was questioning Dover near the duke's carriage, but the others immediately descended. Jack and Nick were pulled apart, and Jack's arms were bound. As soon as he was defenseless, the thugs got their revenge.

Jack didn't blame them. He'd humiliated Bleven and his men today, forced them to leave London to chase him all the way to—wherever the hell they were—and then humiliated them again.

The men weren't in a good mood.

It took about seven kicks and punches before Jack went to his knees. He looked over and noted Nick was already on the ground, curled into a protective ball. Smart man, he thought, but something about his own pride—or was it stupidity?—wouldn't allow him to go down.

His head felt as though it had split in two. He

wanted to reach up and piece it back together again, but the men held his arms so tightly that there was no feeling in them anymore. He knew they would hurt like hell once the numbness receded.

He bent to try and cushion the next blow to his ribs, and his stomach blazed up with fire. It hurt to breathe, to move, to exist. He looked up, tasting blood in his mouth, and saw Bleven sauntering over to him

Finally, thank God, the thugs stood back.

"So you thought you could outsmart me," Bleven seethed. He was out of breath, and Jack realized he must have taken a few swings at Nick. "You thought you could humiliate me and get away with it."

Jack shrugged, ignoring the pain the movement caused. "You showed us. If you're done proving what a big man you are, Nick and I have other more pressing matters to attend to."

"You arrogant whoreson," Bleven spat, his boot landing in Jack's stomach, just to make the point. "I never liked you."

Jack doubled over. His intestines felt as though they had been kicked out through his back and shoved in again, but he managed to stay on his knees. "The feeling's mutual," he wheezed.

"Shut up!" This time Bleven caught him on the right cheek, and Jack's head snapped back. The pain was like a knife thrust in his flesh, but he forced himself to stay upright.

When his balance returned, he looked up at Bleven and smiled. "Having fun?"

Bleven moved to kick him again, then seemed to think better of it. One of his thugs grabbed Jack's arms and pinned them behind his back. Bleven leaned close, so close that Jack could smell the brandy on his breath.

"Oh, I'm going to have fun. I've been waiting a long time for this." His face swam in Jack's vision, his leering smile huge and distorted. "I'm going to take you boys back to London with me, and we're going to have lots of fun. As much fun as we had all those years ago in that dark alley."

Jack tensed and shook his head. Had he heard Bleven correctly?

"Do you remember that, Jack? Do you remember how you cried and hid your face? Oh, yes. I stood in the shadows behind you, and I saw it all."

Jack strained against the man holding him, almost breaking free. "You bloody bastard. Come here where I can reach you. Fight me like a man."

Bleven only smiled thinly, then turned to one of his thugs. "Shut him up."

The thug pulled his fist back, then all went black.

Maddie grabbed Ashley's arm and pulled her behind a large tree. The two girls leaned against it, huffing and panting.

"We ... should ... keep ... going," Ashley wheezed.

"We ... can't," Maddie responded. She bent over, took a deep breath, and looked at her friend. "We can't leave them."

Ashley frowned at her. "Yes, we can. Whatever was going on back there had—" She took a second to catch her breath. "—nothing to do with us. That was the Duke of Bleven."

Maddie stared at her. "Are you sure?"

"Positive."

Maddie knew it was true. She'd seen Bleven many times, enough to recognize him even on a dark road. But she hadn't wanted to admit it had been him just now. She'd heard stories about the Black Duke. Horrible, twisted stories. Stories that she knew couldn't be true, and yet she suspected they were.

What could the Martingale boys have done to anger Bleven? How could they be such complete fools?

And why was she surprised?

"It doesn't matter, Ashley, we still have to go back."

"Why?" Ashley said. She was staring at Maddie like Maddie often stared at her. Like she was completely insane. "You heard Blackthorne. He said we should run."

"We can't leave them there," Maddie protested. "We have to return and help."

Ashley grabbed her hands. "Listen to me, Maddie, we cannot help. Not this time. I know you want to save everyone, but you're taking it too far."

Maddie yanked her hands out of Ashley's grasp. "You and all your talk of adventure. You act like you're so brave, but in the end you're no better than a coward!"

"And you're a fool! You want to rush back there and get yourself killed. Or worse."

Ashley was right, and yet she knew she couldn't do anything else. She was no hero. She was terrified. But she was even more terrified not to go back and help.

Her lips still tingled where Blackthorne had kissed her. He'd kissed her and sent her to safety, while he returned to the gates of Hades. What kind of man did that?

Maddie was afraid she knew. She was afraid she had sorely misjudged Blackthorne. But even if he was nothing more than a selfish scoundrel who probably deserved Bleven's wrath, she couldn't leave him to Bleven's nonexistent mercy.

She couldn't leave him at all. Not while there was still the chance that he would touch her, hold her, kiss her.

She glanced at Ashley, feeling guilty.

"Maddie, come on. Please," Ashley urged, tugging at her.

"No." Maddie stepped away from her. "Keep running. Go save yourself."

Ashley stared at her. "What are you going to do?"

"I'm going back."

Jack woke up when the horse he was tied to farted. It was just loud enough and smelly enough to rouse him from unconsciousness. But he didn't move, didn't show any sign of being awake and alert. Instead he stayed slumped over the horse's mane and listened.

The horse was stationary, which made it easy for Jack to identify the sounds and deduce that he was behind Bleven's carriage and surrounded by Bleven's men, who were preparing to depart.

Ahead of him, Mr. Dover whimpered and tsked and generally made feeble pleas to be set free. Jack heard a slap, and then Dover was quiet.

But he heard nothing from his brother. He eased his eyes open and tried to focus. His head was spinning, and he immediately wanted to vomit. Instead, he clenched his fists, which were bound behind his back, and waited for the nausea to pass. The spinning slowed, wobbled, teetered, and finally ceased. His vision cleared and he realized he was staring at the ground.

Darting his eyes to the right, he spotted another horse's hooves. He allowed his gaze to travel higher—aware that at any moment he might be noticed and knocked out again—and he saw a boot. Nick's boot. His brother had been dropped

over the horse beside him. Nick appeared unconscious, unless he too was playacting.

Jack stared at him, but Nick didn't stir. His
breathing was deep and irregular, and he was
slumped over his horse with his hands bound.

Damn it. Jack wanted to kick his brother, wake
him, tell him to get moving. Maddie was probably cold and scared in that wood.

Unless . . .

Jack's heart skipped. Unless Bleven had gone
after her and found her.

No.

Jack forced his racing heart to slow. She was
safe. He had to believe that. He listened to the
quiet conversation and movement around him.
Nothing indicated that Bleven had found Maddie.

And if Bleven had, fat lot of good he would be
anyway. He was tied to a horse, weak as a puppy,
and on the verge of passing out again. What could
he do to help? He couldn't protect her.

Jack shook his head. He was a man now. And
that was a long time ago. That was a different lifetime.

Or was it? How had Bleven known what had
happened all those years ago in that dirty alley?
Had he been there? Been part of it?

Rage made Jack's breath come quick. He would
get to the bottom of this. And if Bleven had any
part, he would personally rip the man into a
dozen pieces.

He forced his breathing to slow and tried to concentrate on the present.

"Hey, I think this one's waking up," one of the men near him called out.

"Doesn't matter," another man replied. "We're 'eading out."

There was a chorus of yahs and hups, and the wheels of the ducal carriage creaked into motion. Slowly, the rest of the party followed. The horse's movements jarred Jack's sore and bruised body, and he hoped Nick felt the same pain.

Anything to wake his brother.

Jack took another peek at Nick, trying to gauge if his brother was close enough to kick, but a flurry of movement above him caught his eye instead.

Something white had moved in the treetop.

Jack closed his eyes. He was seeing things. Or perhaps it was an owl.

An owl with blond hair?

He bolted upright, a warning cry on his lips, but it was too late. He turned in time to see Ashley drop from the tree and onto the back of the unsuspecting thug riding the last horse in line. Ashley and the man went down with a thud, then Maddie ran out from the undergrowth and conked the thug on the head.

Jack stared in horror. He waited for the horse to scream and bolt. He waited for the thug to grab Maddie and snap her small body in two. He waited for pandemonium to erupt and the girls to be caught.

There was no way that the girls' plan would work.

But none of that happened. The thug stayed down, Ashley grabbed the skittish horse's bridle and calmed him, and Maddie began dragging the unconscious man into the undergrowth.

"Hey!" The man behind Jack was now waving a pistol at him. "Get yourn 'ead down. There ain't nothing to see back there."

Jack didn't argue. He ducked his head back down on the horse's mane and closed his eyes. He didn't know how long it had been since he'd last prayed. Years. Too many to count. But he began to pray anyway.

"Just knock her out, God," he mumbled. "Trip her, get her lost. Whatever. Just keep her away for a little while longer."

But, as usual, God didn't listen.

With a whoop and a cry, the rider on the newly commandeered horse galloped at full speed past the duke's entourage. Maddie was on the horse's back, her chestnut hair and lavender ribbons whipping out behind her.

He was going to murder her for risking herself like this.

"What the—" the man behind Jack began, but a shot rang out, drowning his words.

Jack's horse reared and he struggled to control him. Unable to use his arms, he clamped his legs tight and made soothing sounds. When he looked again, Maddie was in the middle of the road, her pistol pointed at Bleven's carriage.

The entire train had slowed to a stop, and the horses were dancing from side to side, their nerves frayed from yet another commotion.

"What the 'ell do ye think yourn doing?" the coachman called to Maddie as Bleven threw open the carriage door and stomped out.

"What the devil is the meaning of this?"

Maddie leveled her gun at Bleven, and though Jack knew this was her best and only strategy, he winced as a half dozen other pistols were immediately trained on her.

"Maddie," he muttered. Why the hell couldn't she have run, like he'd told her to? If one of the men shot her, he would kill them all.

"Ah, Your Grace," Maddie said with a sweet smile for the duke. "Just the man I wanted to see."

Bleven put his hands on his hips. "Is that so? Have we met, miss? You look familiar."

"Lady Madeleine, daughter of the Earl of Castleigh, Your Grace. And before you ask why I'm here, let me just say that if you don't ask questions, I won't."

The duke, clearly not bothered by a petite girl with a pistol, shrugged. "Very well. Why have you stopped us? Playing at highway robber?"

"Actually, I've come because you have something of mine, or rather, *someone* of mine."

Her eyes met Jack's and then slid away. Jack followed their path, saw her gaze drift to Nick, who was now sitting and looking somewhat woozy, then to Dover.

Jack scowled. Of course. She'd come for Dover.

Maddie pointed to the professor, who was staring at her anxiously. "My fiancé."

All eyes turned to Mr. Dover, and the professor smiled weakly.

The duke laughed. "That one is your fiancé? More trouble than he's worth. Take him and be on your way."

Maddie nodded. "Ride into the woods, Mr. Dover," she ordered, but she did not lower her pistol. And Jack continued to hold his breath.

The men were silent as Dover disappeared, and then the duke said, "Is that all, Lady Madeleine?"

"One more request, Your Grace." She prodded her horse forward, closer to him. "A private request."

He looked up at her, and she leaned down to whisper in his ear. When she had his full attention, she glanced up and screamed, "Now, Ashley!"

Everyone looked around, uncertain what would come next, and then they heard a voice behind them: "Over here, boys!"

Everyone turned, and Jack's mouth dropped open. Ashley Brittany was naked and waving from the side of the road. "Come and get me!"

Bleven's men didn't need much encouragement. Three started for her before she even darted back into the trees. The others were hot on their heels, even as Bleven yelled, "No! Stop!"

But it was too late. Jack's eyes met Nick's, and the two men nodded in silent understanding. Nick spurred his horse into the woods, after Ashley, and Jack rode for Bleven.

The duke was facing Maddie again. She was pale, her eyes wide. She glanced up at Jack and cried, "Watch out! He has a pis—"

Bleven swung round, and Jack ducked. The heat of the bullet caressed his ear, and he felt the warm blood slide down his cheek. Ignoring it, he plowed his horse into Bleven. The duke jumped out of the way but went down, rolling into a ball.

Maddie didn't need any direction from him. She kicked her horse into motion, riding ahead. He spurred his own horse faster, caught up to her, and nodded toward the woods opposite those Nick and Ashley had disappeared into.

They had just cleared the treeline and disappeared behind thicker foliage when Maddie slowed her horse and turned the animal.

"What the hell are you doing now?" Jack demanded.

"Going back for Ashley," Maddie answered. "I can't leave her."

"She's fine. Nick went after her."

"But—"

"Jesus, woman. For once, save yourself. Nick's got Ashley. Let's get the hell out of here."

But Maddie was no longer staring behind her. She was looking at him. "Jack, you're hurt!"

"It's a scratch. Nothing to worry about."

But the words were barely out when his head began to ring and that spinning feeling returned. Jack frowned. It had been just a scratch. Hadn't it?

He tried to reach out, to clutch the horse's saddle and hang on, but he'd forgotten his hands were tied.

"Oh, damn," he swore as he slid off his horse and hit the ground.

Chapter 9

"Oh, jiminy!" Maddie cried, and dropped off her own horse to kneel beside Blackthorne. He was bound, and thus his body lay at an awkward angle.

She shook him, and when he didn't wake, she leaned close to listen for his breathing. Thank God. Then she got a better look at the blood covering Blackthorne's face and neck and wondered if she'd been premature in her gratitude.

Quickly, she reached under her skirts, tore off a good portion of her petticoat, and began wiping away the blood. She had to tear off another section before she could see the wound—a small nick at the top of his right ear.

She felt his head and neck and, other than a half-dozen bumps and knots, found no additional injuries. Lord, but that little nick bled enough for a full-fledged head wound.

He looked uncomfortable with his hands bound behind him, and she fumbled with the knots in the darkness. It took her three or four tries, but then the rope fell away and he lay flat on his back.

Maddie sat back on her haunches and sighed, but the sigh turned into a sob, and before she could stop herself, she was heaving and gulping and wailing.

Lord, but she was a baby. Why was she crying now that everything was over and done? It had all worked out as she'd planned. Even Ashley had changed her mind and decided to help.

Ashley's contribution had been most inventive. She had told Ashley to "cause a diversion," not strip bare, but that was Ashley for you. Ask for a cup of tea, and she'd give you a pail.

Maddie hiccupped, thought of Ashley naked in the woods with those horrible men after her, and started wailing again.

"At least I know someone will cry at my funeral," a gravelly voice said, and Maddie glanced down to see Lord Blackthorne looking up at her. "But you needn't put on quite a production."

She tried to glare at him through her tears. "I'm not crying for you, you dolt." She sniffled. "Well, I was, but now I'm crying for Ashley."

"My brother has her. She's safe." He struggled to sit, and when he'd managed it, he gave her a reassuring nod. "I promise."

Maddie wanted to believe him, but really, how could he know?

"Stop worrying," he said, reaching out to smooth her brow. "And stop crying."

Maddie hiccupped again. "I c-can't."

"You have to," Blackthorne said, drawing her into his arms. "I can't strangle a weeping woman."

"Strangle me?" Maddie knew she ought to pull away and peer at his face to gauge his expression. But now that she was in his arms, she didn't want to leave.

He was so warm and solid. He smelled like pine and freshly turned earth. So instead of moving away, she burrowed into his chest. "Why would you strangle me?" she asked, aware that her words were muffled.

"Because you're driving me mad," he answered. She liked the way his deep voice resonated in his chest and reverberated through her entire body. Even her toes felt the rumble of his bass tone. "Because you're trouble."

"No, I'm not," she said, and yawned. Her tears had dried up, and exhaustion weighed on her like a heavy blanket. No one had ever called her trouble before. She rarely merited any adjective more creative than *kind* or *sweet*.

She closed her eyes as it occurred to her that she should be glad of a new moniker. Maddie the Kind was now Maddie the Troubled.

She frowned. That didn't sound right . . .

Blackthorne's arms tightened around her. "How am I supposed to keep you safe when you won't listen to me?"

Maddie knew she was dreaming then. Why

would the Earl of Blackthorne care about keeping her safe? Why did the Earl of Blackthorne care about her at all?

"Jack?" she murmured. She shouldn't call him by his given name, but she was too tired to think about propriety. "May I ask you a question?" She felt him tense.

"What is it?"

"What did you do to the Duke of Bleven?" She tried to suppress another yawn—yawning belied the seriousness of her question—but the yawn escaped anyway.

"Go to sleep, Maddie," Jack said. "I'll tell you about Bleven tomorrow."

"But I want to know now. I—" She yawned again.

"Shh," Jack said. The last thing she remembered was the feel of his hand stroking her hair.

Jack felt her body go limp as she drifted into sleep. If she was even half as exhausted as he, she needed to rest. He only wished she could have stayed awake long enough for them to find a comfortable place to lie. They were close to a village, and there had to be farms nearby. He might have tucked her into a bed of straw.

Even better would have been taking a room at the village inn. But that would be the first place Bleven would search for them.

Bleven.

Jack closed his eyes and clenched his jaw. What the hell was he going to do about the Black Duke? Now, not only were he and Nick on Bleven's blacklist, but thanks to him, Maddie was there as well.

He might get her safely to Gretna Green, might see her married to Mr. Dover—if they could find the man again in the morning—but there was no way the professor could protect her from a man like Bleven.

Jack looked down at his sleeping charge and frowned. She couldn't return to London. Bleven would find some way to hurt her there. He could handle Bleven. He would handle him, but in the meantime, what to do about Maddie?

Jack shook his head. When the hell had he started calling her Maddie? When the hell had he started thinking so much about protecting her? It had to stop now. He'd get her to Gretna Green, save his own skin by marrying Ashley Brittany, then return to London and take on Bleven. If the Brittany clan didn't kill him first, they'd rally behind him and against Bleven.

Maddie—Lady Madeleine—had a different future. One without him.

Best if he kept that in mind. He had to ignore all insidious thoughts to the contrary, especially those that involved forgetting Ashley Brittany, stealing Lady Madeleine away from Dover, and marrying her himself.

That wasn't going to happen. It couldn't. A marriage to Miss Brittany was like a handshake. Nothing but a business arrangement. A marriage to Lady Madeleine would be an entirely different matter. He was growing far too fond of her, and that was dangerous.

If he married her, he didn't think he could stop himself from . . . well, if not falling in love with her, coming damn close. He didn't care how much he wanted her, he wasn't risking his heart. He liked it cold and hard, and he liked that Ashley Brittany wasn't any threat to it remaining that way.

The sooner he got Lady Madeleine to Gretna, got rid of her, and went his own way, the better.

But it wouldn't be tonight. He'd had enough of traveling on dark roads and traipsing through black woods. They'd start fresh in the morning. He'd find Nick and Miss Brittany and even poor Mr. Dover, prod Nick to help him steal—er, borrow—a carriage, and then ride hell for leather toward Gretna.

Jack figured if they drove the horses fast, changed them every five miles or so, and limited meal stops and sleep stops, they could reach Gretna in three days or less.

Assuming they didn't run into more trouble from Bleven or new trouble from Sir Gareth. And assuming Nick wasn't accosted by any more innkeeper's daughters.

Jack looked down at Maddie. Three more days. He shifted her sleeping form and wondered if he'd survive three more days. Everything ached, and he knew it would be worse in the morning.

His first priority was ensuring that Bleven wasn't going to stumble upon them during the night. He figured it would take Bleven several hours to round up his men and organize an effective search. That was, if the Black Duke even felt a search was worthwhile. For all the duke knew, he and Maddie were long gone.

Jack crept back toward the road, surprised to find that he and Maddie had made it deeper into the woods than he'd thought. Sliding through the brush on his belly, he surveyed the scene. The carriage was gone but several of the duke's thugs were milling about. He watched as eventually all the men returned. But without Bleven, the hirelings seemed lost. Eventually, they dispersed, riding toward the nearest town. As the last man disappeared, Jack sighed in relief and crept back to Maddie.

She was still sleeping where he'd left her, and he looked around for a softer piece of ground. He didn't see one, but spotted a tree that would provide good cover, should one of Bleven's men come this way. As gently as possible, he lifted the sleeping Maddie and moved her to the tree. Then he saw to the care of the horses.

Sometime later he lay down beside Maddie. He had intended to remain close to her, should anything happen during the night, but far enough away to maintain decency.

Unfortunately, he didn't anticipate how warm she'd be. She radiated heat, and his weak, cold body couldn't resist moving closer. And, actually, that was a good thing. They needed to share body heat to survive.

Oh, who the hell was he kidding? It was summer, and though the English nights were chilly, they were nowhere close to deadly.

He wanted to lie beside her, cradle her in his arms, and press his face into her lavender-scented hair. He'd wanted it since the first moment he saw her, and when would he have another opportunity? The professor—goddamn him—would be the man holding her after this night. He didn't think Dover even knew what he had in Lady Madeleine.

Maddie sighed in her sleep and cuddled closer to him, and Jack felt his heart lurch.

No emotion, he told himself. *Don't get attached.*

It was an old refrain. One he had adopted because he knew firsthand how much it could hurt when you lost someone you cared about. He was going to lose Maddie, and he'd be damned if he was going to care.

Jack stared at the tree limbs above him and the twinkling stars beyond that. Beside him, Maddie stirred and moaned softly. He clenched his hand to keep from reaching out to her.

Maddie awoke in a cocoon of warmth and safety. Without even opening her eyes, she knew it was almost dawn. And still without opening her eyes, she knew Jack was pressed against her backside.

She knew his scent by now, and knew the feel of his strong arms about her. She should. She'd imagined him holding her just like this—gentle but strong—a hundred times or more.

She sighed, content to stay like this forever. It felt so good to be in his arms. She felt so safe and so happy and . . .

Well, if she were being honest, she'd also admit she felt a bit stirred up. His face was near her neck, and his light breath tickled and teased the sensitive skin just behind her ear. And one of his hands—

Maddie was certain he hadn't done it on purpose, but Blackthorne's hand was cupping her breast.

The sensation wasn't unpleasant. In fact, she rather wished he would move that hand to stroke her, cup her more fully.

Jiminy! Why was she thinking about this? She blamed it on the early morning. She was still half asleep, still in that semiconscious state between waking and dreaming.

If she were awake, she'd be thinking clearly, thinking that the man holding her was going to marry Ashley.

Loyalty to Ashley should have made her jump at his touch, and she would have. If she'd been more awake.

And if she'd been awake and alert, she would also be thinking about how wrong Blackthorne was for her. Her parents always told her to marry someone like herself.

"Similar interests and similar dispositions. That's what makes a happy union," her father had always said.

Maddie didn't believe Blackthorne was much like herself at all. Did he care about orphans and widows? Would he have wept for the bleeding bear?

She didn't think so. Even worse, she had a sinking suspicion Jack was a lot like her father. Her father argued with her every time she had to travel to an unsavory area of Town to aid one of her charities.

"Why can't you stay in Mayfair?" her father would demand. "Stay where you're safe."

"Because there aren't any poor widows or orphans in Mayfair," Maddie argued back. Her neighbors were all rich and titled. Most didn't care about the poor; they only cared about the latest scandal or who was hosting which ball.

She knew her father had her best interests at heart, but she was tired of being controlled. That was why she had chosen Mr. Dover. He wouldn't try and keep her from helping others. And Mr. Dover wouldn't upset her life with bullets and Black Dukes and troublesome brothers.

Maddie opened her eyes and turned to look at the man beside her. Blackthorne didn't move or wake, but when she was facing him, his arms tightened on her again.

It was still dark, and in the shadows, she didn't feel like Maddie Fullbright.

It was an old game—pretending that what she did in the moonlight didn't matter. It had begun the first time her cousins dragged her from her safe warm bed into the dangerous streets of London on some madcap adventure. Lady Madeleine would never have run about in boy's clothing, climbed out second-story windows, or stayed up all night laughing with her cousins. And so she had pretended she was someone else.

Someone who was not the daughter of an earl, who didn't live in Berkeley Square, who didn't own silk gowns and satin slippers. Someone who wasn't weighed down with all the expectations and responsibilities of a peeress. Someone who liked risks.

Maddie felt that way now. She was just a woman in a man's arms. A woman with urges and feelings and who sometimes wanted to feel a man's arms around her or taste his mouth on hers.

Even if he was the wrong man.

Especially if he was the wrong man.

It was dark, the gray dark of day before the dawn, and Maddie could see the marquess's face. She didn't know what she'd expected. Perhaps that he'd look younger, more vulnerable, more accessible. Instead, he looked much the same as he did when he was awake.

He was frowning and serious, even in sleep. She remembered how he had smoothed her brow and told her not to worry, and she did the same for him now.

He didn't move or wake, so she allowed her hand to trace his black eyebrow, to feel the tension beneath it. She would have stopped there—if it had been morning and she'd been Lady Madeleine—but it was still dark and she was still free.

And so she cupped his cheek and trailed a finger to his jaw. It was rough with blue-black stubble, and the hair scratched her palm.

But his lips were soft. She couldn't resist touching them with her finger. They were pliant and yielding, so unlike the rest of him.

The longer she looked at those lips, the more she wanted to press her own against them, to taste him one more time.

The last time.

She stared at his eyes, listening for his even breathing. Satisfied, she leaned forward and pressed her lips gently against his.

It was a sweet kiss, light and innocent and quick. Maddie allowed her mouth to rest on Blackthorne's for only a moment, then made to pull away. But it was too late.

His hand on her back tightened and pulled her closer, and his lips came alive under hers, pressing hard against her mouth. His eyes opened.

"Nice to know I wasn't the only one with that

idea this morning. What else do you have in mind?"

Maddie tried to move away. She tried to shake her head but was pressed so tightly against him, she couldn't escape.

"Nothing," she said against his lips, and it was almost as though she kissed him again without intending to. "I—I shouldn't have kissed you."

He rose on one elbow and looked down at her. "I'm glad you did."

"Me, too," she whispered. As soon as the sun rose, she would behave as she ought. But in the few precious moments before, she wanted to behave as she desired.

Her heart was pounding now, beating so hard that she was afraid he could feel it. She waited and wondered what he'd do next. She should have known this would happen. She should have expected him to awake and respond.

And perhaps that was what she'd wanted all along. Perhaps she had tempted fire because she wanted to be burned.

He raised a brow at her. "You touched me," he said, voice low and incredibly sensuous.

All the tiny hairs on her body stood up, and she couldn't stop a shiver from running through her body. No doubt he felt it and knew what it meant.

She prayed the sun would never rise. She loved being held in his arms. She relished the feel of their bodies pressed together. She wanted to be closer. She wanted to do more, and she didn't want to think about all the reasons that she shouldn't. That she couldn't.

In the gray darkness, it was just the two of them, alone in the world. Nothing else mattered.

"I won't touch you again," she said, "not if you don't want me to." But even as she said it, she wrapped her arms around him and pulled him closer. She couldn't tear her eyes from his, and so she saw the way they darkened at her touch.

Touch me, Jack. Quick, before the sun rises.

"And what if I want you to touch me again? What if I want to touch you?"

Yes, please. Hurry.

Maddie licked her lips. "I suppose it's only fair."

"Fair?" Jack chuckled. "Oh, I'm not going to be fair." And he dipped his mouth to hers.

Chapter 10

She tasted like candied plums. Her mouth was ripe and sweet, and Jack couldn't get enough of it. He couldn't get enough of her, and she must have felt the same because she pulled him tighter against her.

He was already hard. He'd wakened when she had, felt her stirring beside him, felt her breathing change, and he'd instantly left sleep behind. His cock must have wakened even earlier. No surprise, considering that he was pressed against a warm, female backside, his hand cupping an ample breast.

Jack's first instinct had been to move closer to her, come as near to burying himself in her soft flesh as he could without divesting her of her clothing. His second instinct was to fondle the flesh cupped in his hand.

He did neither. Instead, he lay unmoving and waited for the urges to pass. He tried to think of something innocuous and boring. He attempted to focus on tax reform then the price of corn and had turned, desperately, to the war in the former colonies, when, much to his surprise, she turned toward him and touched him.

He could handle her touch, if he concentrated on George Washington, but when those sweet, candied lips latched onto his, that was the end of his self-control. George Washington be damned.

He had to have more of Maddie. He'd been wanting more of her since the first moment he saw her, his need poking him like a jutting spring in a worn chair.

Now, he slipped his tongue inside her mouth, expecting to be rebuffed, expecting resistance, but she offered none. She opened for him, invited him in.

No time to question, Jack accepted the invitation and stroked her tongue with his. She shuddered again, and he felt his own arousal double at her excited response.

His arms were already wrapped around her, and now he moved one hand to cup her breast again. Her nipple was hard in his hand, thrusting temptingly through the thin fabric. He flicked it with one finger, then ran his palm over it.

Under him, Maddie squirmed and pressed closer. His erection was suddenly surrounded by the warmth of her thighs, and it was pure torture not to toss up her skirts and plunge into what he knew would be slick, heated flesh.

But he held back, pulling away, trying to wrest

control from his body and put it back in his mind.

George Washington. Think of George Washington.

But she wouldn't allow him to retreat. She moaned low in her throat and followed him, her tongue invading his mouth with sweet urgency.

"Oh, God, Maddie," Jack growled, cupping her head between his hands and kissing her deeper. "You don't know how much I want you right now."

"I can feel how much," she whispered against his lips, and then, a moment later, must have realized what she'd said because she pulled back, a horrified look in her eyes.

"What I meant was—"

"I know exactly what you meant, sweetheart," Jack answered. The dawn, gray with a tinge of rose, was beginning to break, and the soft light played on her face. The colors dancing over her golden complexion took his breath away. She was so beautiful, so sweet, so innocent.

He shouldn't be the one lying with her, touching her.

"Touch me," she whispered.

"What?" Jack jerked back in surprise.

"Don't make me say it again," she said. "I feel how much you want me. I want you to know how much I want you, and I—I'm burning up. I need you to touch me. Hurry."

Jack closed his eyes, rested his head on her

shoulder. "Maddie, I'm not the man who should be touching you. You're innocent. You don't know what you're asking me."

He felt her smile and looked at her face. "I may be innocent, but I'm not uneducated. I know what happens between men and women."

"No." Jack shook his head, but bastard that he was, he didn't move away from her. "I can't be the one to take your innocence."

"Then don't take it," she murmured into his ear. "Give me an introductory lesson. Touch me, Jack."

And as though her words alone wouldn't have tempted a saint, her hand found his hard length and stroked it through his trousers. Her dark blue eyes met his. "Do you like this?" she asked. "Do you want me to touch you, skin against skin?"

Oh, God, yes.

"Oh, God, no." He'd never be able to deliver her to Dover as a virgin if he allowed that. He didn't know how much longer he could trust himself as it was.

He eased himself away from her and grasped her hand when she reached for him again. "Speaking of fair, it's my turn to touch you." He raised her hand until it was resting beside her head. "Give me your other hand, sweetheart."

He saw the question in her eyes, but she didn't ask it. She gave a quick glance at the lightening skies, then lifted her other hand to his. Amazing. She wanted this as much as he did. He imprisoned both of her hands under one of his and held them loosely.

For the moment she was his, entirely in his power. He saw her realize it, and her breath quickened.

Keeping his gaze locked on her dark blue eyes, he lowered his free hand to her bodice. He'd been dreaming about this, and he took his time drawing the material down over her thin chemise.

The more he revealed, the faster she breathed, until her breasts heaved against the flimsy material. Jack leaned down and placed his mouth over the exposed half-moon of flesh. She jerked, and when he didn't release her hands, she moaned.

"Hurry, Jack. More. Hurry."

Jack frowned. Most women liked it when he moved slowly. But he wasn't going to argue. Instead, he used his teeth to lower her chemise and stays, and her breasts, already straining, came free.

In the cool morning, her dark, round nipples were hard and taut. Her breasts were large, almost more than could fill his hand, and her skin was honey-colored. "God, you're beautiful," he whispered, allowing his breath to skate over her flesh.

He bent to the valley between her breasts, kissing her there, and inhaling the sweet fragrance of her skin, of her. Moving his mouth to one side, he laved the rounded flesh, inching higher and higher until she whimpered and pushed against him, all but giving him her nipple.

He took it eagerly, licking the large round nub, making it harder, tighter, sucking it, until she strained against him and cried out, "Hurry!"

Jesus! Demanding little chit. How was a man supposed to employ any skill with this kind of pressure?

But, obediently, he moved to her other breast, sucking and nibbling until she was crying out again. And then just when she would have urged him to hurry, he lowered his free hand and cupped her between her legs.

That silenced her.

In fact, she opened her eyes, which had been tightly closed, and stared at him. Her pupils were dark and large, those blue eyes dominating her face.

Without looking away, he let his hand fist around the material of her dress and tug it upward. Inch by inch the fabric revealed more of her body. He ached to look, but he kept his gaze locked on hers, watching as her eyes warmed to liquid sapphire.

Finally, he held the hem in his hands. Slowly, he released the material, leaving his hand free to cup her in truth. She'd told him she was burning up, and she hadn't lied. She was so hot, he almost jerked away at first.

Like the rest of her, the skin here was smooth and soft, the curls at the juncture of her thighs damp with her need. He stroked her outer lips, feeling her body shake and tremble as he did so.

And then, ignoring her previous orders, he moved as slowly as he could, parting those lips and slipping one finger inside.

Molten heat.

That was all he could think. She was so slick and ready for him. He pushed his finger deeper inside her, and she cried out, her eyes going so dark they were almost as black as his own.

And then he had to see her. Dragging his gaze from hers, he took a leisurely perusal of her, starting with those glorious breasts, spilling out of her bodice. The nipples were still hard and now wet from his ministrations.

His gaze traveled down her white gown with its little lavender bows. The bows were bunched up along her waist, and he could see her stocking-clad legs tangled with his.

And then his gaze fastened on her bare hips and thighs, the soft chestnut curls between her legs, and the tender pink skin where his finger moved in and out. Her hips rose to meet his movements, her body moving instinctively in that timeless rhythm.

Jack slid into her again and imagined all the ways he could give her pleasure. He felt her tighten around him and knew it would not be long now until she exploded.

"Oh, no!" Her voice was anguished, regretful. "We have to stop."

Her hands pushed against the hand holding her prisoner, and he freed her, slipping his finger out of her as she sat and began to right her clothing.

"What the hell—"

"I'm sorry," she said rapidly, not looking at him. "It's dawn. The sun is rising. We should—we should start moving."

"But—" His brain was still far behind hers, and his cock throbbed insistently. "So, just like that, we're done?"

He sat beside her, and she stood, jerking her dress down and covering those shapely legs. Her hands were shaking and she looked a bit unsteady on her feet. "Sir, we can't afford to lie about all day. We have to find Ashley and Mr. Dover."

"Sir? *Sir?*" Jack knew he sounded surly, but he felt surly. "What the hell's going on? One moment I have my hand—"

"Lord Blackthorne!"

"Fine. But why the rapid about-face? When you said to hurry, I thought you meant—"

"I think it best if we don't discuss the matter any further," she said, lifting her trembling hands to her hair. "Do you have any suggestions for locating the others without alerting Lord Bleven or my father or anyone else following us where we are?"

Jack frowned. She was fully dressed and had even pinned her hair up in some sort of order. She really was done with him. What the hell had he done wrong? One moment she'd been moaning and pressing against him. The next she was on her feet, pulling her shoes back on.

"Lord Blackthorne, I asked if you had any suggestions."

Jack raised his eyes to hers. They were clear blue, no trace of the haze of desire from a moment before. "I have a suggestion. Take that dress off and get back down here."

She shook her head. "Please be serious. In fact, be truthful. What did you do to the Duke of Bleven to anger him so?"

Reluctantly, Jack rose to his feet and began brushing off his trousers. The woman was obviously through with him. She'd dismissed him faster than a courtesan with money in her hand. "I didn't do anything to Bleven," he said. He'd left his boots on, in case they needed to run in the night, and now he leaned against the tree, pried one off and shook out the dust and pebbles.

"But if you didn't do anything to Bleven, then, why—" Her big blue eyes widened farther. "Lord Nicholas."

"Bang on the mark. My darling brother"—Jack slid his boot back on and stomped his foot back into it—"publicly insulted the duke. The duke was not pleased."

"But why would Lord Nicholas do that?" She was watching him struggle to pull off his second boot.

"He was protecting a woman's honor."

"I suppose it's justified, then."

"Nick insulted Bleven on my behalf as well. Called the duke a filthy whoreson scoundrel."

"Oh, Lord."

"It's a bit late to start praying."

She looked about, spotted the horses he'd tethered the night before and marched toward hers. "We have to go. Now. We have to find Ashley and Mr. Dover. I want no part of this feud with Bleven."

Jack shook his boot out and dropped it on the ground. "You should have thought of that last night. After that stunt you pulled, you're involved whether you want to be or not. Might I suggest, you and Dover retire to the Scottish countryside. Permanently."

"Don't be rid—" But she looked at his face and swallowed.

"I've heard the Americas are lovely this time of year."

She blew out a breath and closed her eyes. He heard her whispering something. It sounded like, "Everything will work out. Everything will work out."

Jack shook his head. Everything work out? That would be a first.

Maddie knelt beside Jack and tried to hold her breath. Jack's horse stank. She didn't know what the animal had gotten into the night before, but whatever the beast had eaten wreaked havoc with its digestion.

The two of them had made it to the nearby village, which happened to be Stevenage, and Jack and Maddie crouched behind the local pub and posting house. It was still early, and many of the villagers were not yet about, but the smells of baked bread and frying ham and sausage made her stomach rumble—despite the unappetizing aromas coming from the horse.

"Are you certain he knows to meet us here?" Maddie asked for what might have been the fifth time that morning.

"He knows," Jack growled. He didn't look at her.

Maddie didn't blame him for being mad. He must think her daft after what she'd done to him this morning. But, jiminy, she'd told the man to hurry. Besides, why should she feel sorry for him? She was the one who'd had to exert all the self-control and end their tryst. The sun had come up. She'd turned back into Lady Madeleine. Lady Madeleine did not allow men to reach up her skirts—no matter how enjoyable it might be.

And it was enjoyable. Oh, Lord, it was enjoyable. First Jack had shown her that kissing didn't have to be boring or sloppy, and then . . .

Well, the man was obviously blessed with many talents.

But now she had to think of poor Mr. Dover and Gretna Green, and escaping her father and Lord Bleven. Jack swore up and down that he and his brother had arranged to meet here, but so far she saw no sign of Lord Nicholas.

She hoped he hadn't wandered by any of the

shops and been accosted by a merchant's daughter. The man seemed to invite trouble.

Behind her, one of the horses nickered and stomped its foot, and Maddie turned just in time to see Ashley and Lord Nicholas leading their horses into the small courtyard behind the posting house.

Thank goodness, Ashley was fully clothed again, and Maddie jumped up, ran to her, and hugged her. "I was so worried about you!"

"At least someone was," Ashley said, with a glare at Lord Nicholas.

"Don't start," he retorted, moving forward to shake his brother's hand. "Little harpy. Next time she exposes herself to half a dozen drooling men, I'll let them have her."

Blackthorne pulled his brother aside and the two began to speak quietly. But before Maddie could ask Ashley what had happened to her the night before, she spotted Mr. Dover. He trudged behind Ashley and Lord Nicholas, horseless and bedraggled, but alive.

Maddie released Ashley. "Mr. Dover, you made it." She had intended to embrace him as warmly as she had her friend, but when she approached him, she couldn't seem to make herself do it. Instead, she held out her hand and allowed him to kiss her fingers.

The formality between them reminded her that her dress was wrinkled and dirty, that she wore no gloves, and that she hadn't bathed. Poor Mr.

Dover. He must rue the day he ever agreed to run off with her. Not only was their elopement a fiasco, she looked like a street urchin.

And, while he had undoubtedly spent the night shivering cold and alone, she had slept in another man's warm arms. And this morning . . .

Maddie bit her lip. Best not to think of that.

Feeling incredibly guilty, she was compelled to apologize. "Mr. Dover, let me express to you how sorry I am that this elopement has gone so terribly wrong. I am certain our bad fortune now is no omen to what the future brings."

Ashley, who was standing beside them, not bothering to even pretend she wasn't listening, snorted.

Maddie glared at her, then looked back at Mr. Dover. "I assure you that once we are married—"

"Maddie," Ashley interrupted, drawing her away. "I was so worried about you. How did you get away?"

Maddie gave Mr. Dover an apologetic look, then prepared to lecture Ashley. "After all of Bleven's men went chasing after you, it wasn't difficult. How could you put yourself in so much danger? I was terrified you'd be caught and—" She swallowed.

"Actually, I think exposing myself was the best idea I've had in a long time."

"Oh, Lord."

"You'd be surprised how easy it is to blend in when you're naked."

"Oh, good Lord."

Ashley smiled. "Lord Nicholas and I dove under a pile of leaves and Bleven's men all rode right by us. By the time they realized their error, I had my dress back on and we were long gone."

"But Mr. Dover? How did you find him?"

Ashley scowled at poor Mr. Dover. Maddie thought he looked lost and forlorn this morning. "*He* stumbled upon us," Ashley said. "At quite an inopportune moment, too. Though I suppose it's for the best. Lord Nicholas is completely incorrigible."

Maddie narrowed her eyes. "Wait a moment. What kind of inopportune moment? Were you and Lord Nicholas—"

"All right, ladies!" Lord Nicholas interrupted. "We have a plan."

"Oh, no you don't," Ashley protested. "No more of your plans. In fact, no more of you." She turned to Maddie. "I propose only the four of us continue to Gretna Green. We can leave Lord Nicholas behind to create a diversion for anyone following us."

"Finally be rid of you? Capital idea," Lord Nicholas agreed. "Except, who's going to steal the carriage?"

"Pardon?" Maddie asked. "Steal what carriage?"

"The one that's going to take us to Gretna Green," Lord Nicholas answered. "The one I'm going to steal for us."

Maddie shook her head. Lord, this was her worst nightmare come true. After all the trouble he'd caused at the inn, she could not begin to imagine how much worse the turmoil over a carriage would be. Perhaps as much turmoil as publicly insulting a duke. "You cannot steal a carriage, Lord Nicholas."

He frowned. "Why not?"

Maddie tried to catch Jack's eye. Maybe she could force him to speak to his brother, or perhaps—if she looked the other way—to knock some sense into Lord Nicholas. But Jack merely blinked at her, scowled, and crossed his arms over his chest.

Maddie licked her lips. "Lord Nicholas, you cannot steal a carriage because theft is wrong. It's a sin."

"So is murder, but I didn't get the impression last night that Bleven's conscience was troubling him."

Maddie bit her lip. Bleven did have a reputation for heartless cruelty.

"And what about your own father?" the younger Martingale brother asked, crossing his arms. "If he finds us, do you think his actions will be tempered by thoughts about sin?"

Maddie glanced at Mr. Dover. It was true. Her father would likely shoot first and ask repentance later.

Maddie sighed. "Very well, but can we not buy a carriage? Regretfully, in the fray, I lost my reticule and all my money, but surely if the rest of you pool your resources—"

"We don't have the time to go carriage shopping," Blackthorne said, cutting her off. "We're in a hurry and we have at least two parties, and probably more, searching for us. To openly present ourselves in this town, or any other, is suicide."

Maddie bit her lip. He was right. They needed to be on their way quickly and anonymously. But, still, she couldn't believe larceny was the only way. "I understand completely, and yet I cannot condone theft. We must think of another way."

"It's no use," Ashley said finally. "You can't reason with her on something like this. She has her morals and her good deeds, and no one can disabuse her of their worth."

"Is that so?" Jack said, coming forward. "Are you telling me that Lady Madeleine never slips from what is good and proper? That her morality never falters?"

Maddie felt her mouth go dry. Oh, Lord. He was not going to tell everyone about what had happened this morning, was he? Because she had not been Lady Madeleine then—only, how did she explain that to all of them? How did she explain that to Mr. Dover? "Well, you see, sir, in the wee hours of the morning, I'm not Lady Madeleine. Well, I am Lady Madeleine, but . . ."

It would never work.

Her gaze met Jack's, and he raised an eyebrow at her. His expression dared her to try and play

Miss High and Mighty now. She knew there was a reason she didn't like midnight adventures. She got into far less trouble in the daylight.

"Fine!" she said, throwing her arms in the air. "Steal a carriage. I'll even help."

"Really?" Ashley said. "Perhaps we should be the ones to steal the carriage. Wouldn't that be fun!"

"Actually," Jack said, stepping forward. "That's not a bad idea."

Chapter 11

To no one's surprise, in the end Maddie would not agree to steal a carriage. Jack wouldn't have allowed it anyway, but he liked to see her squirm. Preferably underneath him, but if he couldn't have that, then he would find some other way to affect her.

The village was large and bustling, and Nick had no problem stealing a carriage with four fresh horses. And so, an hour after their party had met behind the posting house, the five of them were once again on the road to Gretna Green.

Nick offered to drive first, and Jack let him, with the condition that he ride in the coach box as well. Nick might want to put as much distance between himself and Ashley Brittany as possible, but that didn't mean that he would spend this whole trip locked in the carriage with two women and the whiny Mr. Dover.

And he wanted a chance to speak to Nick alone. He had planned to tell his brother what the Black Duke had said in the clearing. Nick needed to know that Bleven could have been involved in what happened in that alley all those years ago. But now that he had the opportunity, Jack found that he couldn't speak. It had been his fault, not Nick's. So this knowledge would be his burden as well.

He was quiet until they had covered enough distance without pursuit so as to feel relatively safe. Then he said, "According to our professor, the next town of interest is Biggleswade. Dover estimates that we're approximately eight hours and fourteen minutes behind schedule reaching it."

"Good God!" Nick said, shaking his head. "Say it ain't true."

Jack smiled. His brother could actually be tolerable at times. And sarcasm ran in the family.

"Oh, it's true, all right, but I'm more worried about Lord Castleigh or Sir Gareth catching up to us than I am maintaining a schedule."

"You're not safe until you have a ring on Miss Brittany's finger," Nick said. "And good luck with that."

Jack snorted. "She threatening not to marry me?"

"Oh no." Nick gave him a sidelong look. "She's threatening *to* marry you."

Jack was quiet for a moment. No point trying to avoid fate. He had to marry her if he was ever to return to London and his life there. It was probably about time he married anyway. His father had passed away three years ago, and the family needed an heir. Ashley Brittany would make as good a wife as any. He knew her family, knew her brothers well, and though they were all mad as bulls with bees stinging their rumps, they were a good family. Good ancestry, good finances, good people.

Not the kind of people one wanted to anger. The men in the family could hold a grudge that outlasted world empires. And so he would marry Ashley, and everyone would have what they wanted.

Well, almost everyone.

No, Jack corrected. *Everyone*. He didn't want Lady Madeleine. He'd been through all that last night. No matter what happened, he wasn't going to marry her. It would have been a disaster anyway. She'd drive him mad with all her Good Samaritan deeds, and he'd drive her mad . . . well, he could think of a number of ways to drive her mad.

Ashley Brittany was safe. She didn't make his tailcoat feel too tight around his chest or make his blood pound in his head. Marry her, and he risked nothing.

She was pretty, spoiled, and wouldn't complicate his life with any unwanted emotions. Marrying her was simple.

Jack glanced at his brother again.

Or was it?

"What happened last night with you and Miss Brittany? You went after her, found her—still naked, I presume—and . . . ?"

"Dover discovered us, and we all got some rest."

"And that's it?"

Nick glanced at him. "She's your fiancé, Jack. You think I don't respect that?"

"You're a pretty good thief." Jack indicated the stolen carriage.

Nick laughed. "And would you have cared if I'd stolen something that was yours? Something to do with Miss Brittany?"

Jack didn't answer. *Would* he have cared? Aside from the general feeling of propriety any man had toward his wife-to-be, did he care what Ashley Brittany did? He tried to imagine her in Nick's arms, tried to imagine his brother kissing her, touching her, and felt nothing other than general annoyance.

But when he turned his thoughts to Maddie and Mr. Dover, Maddie and any man, anger exploded inside him. He was furious just thinking of Dover and Maddie inside the carriage together at the moment.

And that was why he was up here. Because he wasn't going to tolerate any bloody feelings creeping up on him. He was going to watch her marry Dover, and he was going to keep out of the way and allow it to happen. And though he didn't anticipate any more opportunities like last night had afforded the two of them, he was not going to touch her again.

No matter how much his fingers ached to feel her skin or his mouth longed to slant over her rosy lips and delve inside her sweetness, he would not do it.

He glanced at Nick and saw that his brother was watching him.

"Perhaps I should be the one to ask you what happened last night. I might be guilty of theft, but I stole for a good cause."

"Let it go," Jack said, looking at the rolling fields of crops they were passing. "You and your good causes almost got us all killed last night."

"And saved us all this morning." Nick grinned and indicated the carriage.

Jack suppressed a grin. "You're a regular Robin Hood."

"And I guess that makes you Little John."

"Do you think he's asleep?" Maddie whispered to Ashley, who was seated beside her in the carriage. They'd just stopped to change horses, and she'd been deathly afraid Mr. Dover would wake. She'd been waiting to speak to Ashley alone for most of the day, but the Martingale brothers would not let them out of the carriage for more than two minutes, and across from them, Mr. Dover had remained steadfastly awake and talkative.

While he'd droned on about schedules and lost time and distances from Huntingdon to Stamford, Maddie allowed her mind to wander and wished for privacy in order to talk with Ashley.

And now it appeared she would finally have her chance. Mr. Dover's glasses were askew on his face and his head listed to one side. He breathed in and out heavily, arms crossed over his chest, which contracted and expanded with every breath.

"Is he asleep?" Maddie whispered.

"I think so," Ashley whispered back. "Thank God. If I never hear another word about schedules and lost time, I'll be a happy woman."

"Me, too," Maddie agreed.

"Good luck. You're about to marry the man."

Maddie frowned. Her friend had a point. A lifetime with Mr. Dover was looking a bit long at the moment. A lifetime of "Dinner is now exactly three minutes late" or "Tea is precisely six seconds early."

And what would he be like with the children? Lord, she remembered that he already had two small children! In a matter of a day or so she would be a mother and a wife.

Maddie shook her head. Best not to think of it until she had to. If she had to.

She bit her lip. There was that optimism again.

"I asked Lord Blackthorne about the Duke of Bleven this morning," she whispered to Ashley.

Ashley looked away from the windows. "Don't tell me. Lord Nicholas did something to offend the duke."

Maddie nodded. "He told you?"

"No. I know the idiot man well enough to guess."

Maddie let those words sink in between them.

"And how well do you know Lord Nicholas? You never mentioned him before."

Ashley shrugged and looked back out the window. Maddie had known Ashley long enough to know her friend didn't lie. Evading a question was as close as Ashley Brittany came to perfidy.

"Ashley?" Maddie said, unwilling to let the matter go. "Was there—*is* there—something between you and Lord Nicholas?"

Ashley looked at her curiously. "I'll answer if you do."

Maddie blinked. "No, there's nothing between Lord Nicholas and I. Why would you think . . . ? Oh. I see." She swallowed. "You're not asking about Lord Nicholas."

Ashley shook her head. "And don't lie to me."

Maddie bit her lip and looked down at her fingers. "I don't think I should answer that question. I haven't been a very good friend."

"Why?" Ashley asked. "Did you kiss Blackthorne?"

Maddie peeked at Mr. Dover, noted the man was still asleep, his glasses now perched precariously on the end of his nose.

"I have."

"More than once?"

Maddie nodded, then looked at her friend. "I'm sorry. I know he's your fiancé, and I didn't want to do it, but I—I couldn't seem to make myself not do it."

"I know what you mean."

Maddie's mouth dropped open. She had expected anger, outrage, or hurt. Not understanding. "You know what I mean?"

"Lord Nicholas affects me the same way. I tell myself I'm not going to kiss him ever again, that I'm not even going to think of him, but I can't seem to help it."

"But you have to help it, Ashley, you're going to marry Lord Blackthorne."

Ashley raised a blond brow at her. "And you have to help it, Maddie, you're going to marry that expert dog breeder." She gestured to Mr. Dover, and Maddie sighed.

"It's for the best," she said with a sigh. "Lord Blackthorne and I would never suit."

"Nor Lord Nicholas and I."

Maddie blinked. "But Lord Nicholas and you would suit perfectly. You two are exactly alike."

"Madeleine Fullbright, I resent that. I am nothing like that odious lout."

"If you say so."

Ashley crossed her arms defiantly. "Fine. And if we are alike—just a tiny bit—do you think that's a good thing?"

Maddie hadn't considered the matter that way—the difficulties of marrying someone too much like oneself. Was Mr. Dover very much like her? She glanced at him, noted the way his nostrils flared with his soft snores, and decided no, they had commonalities but were not terribly alike.

They were not as different as, say, she and Lord

Blackthorne, and perhaps that meant she and Mr. Dover would make a good match.

"Ashley," she began, "do you think it's better to marry someone like you or someone opposite you? My father always says like should marry like."

"'Similar interests and similar dispositions,'" Ashley quoted. "Yes, I've heard him say that."

"Do you agree?"

Ashley shrugged. "I don't know. I think every marriage has its challenges." She gave Maddie a long look. "I think the real question is, why are you asking?"

Maddie looked down at her fingers.

"Say the word, Maddie, and I won't marry Blackthorne," Ashley whispered. "If you care for him, then I won't be the one to stand in your way."

The one to stand in your way.

And who or what would stand in her way, then? Certainly Mr. Dover, to whom she'd made a promise. Certainly her father, who was undoubtedly on his way to intercept them at this very moment. Certainly Lord Blackthorne, who seemed to look forward to a marriage between himself and Ashley.

Blackthorne might have kissed her and touched her this morning, but he hadn't proposed marriage, and she was under no illusion that he would do so. Ashley was the beautiful one. Ashley was the adventurous one. Ashley was the woman every man wanted.

And what would happen to Ashley if they were

caught before they reached Gretna Green? What would happen to herself, for that matter? Along with their cousins Catie and Josie, she and Ashley had always been the girls Society whispered about and shook its head at. They were too wild for their own good. They set a bad example.

But Maddie knew that if she did not make it to Gretna Green in time to marry, she would never go about in Society again. It was one thing to have Society whisper about you. It was quite another to have them hurl insults and blatantly cut you.

She couldn't allow that to happen to Ashley. And how could it be prevented except through Ashley marrying? Her friend had pointed her long, slender finger at Lord Blackthorne, and the man—in what was surely a rare moment—had shown honor and agreed.

"Ashley, you're not standing in my way," Maddie finally said. "I know this started out as an adventure, but it's become far more serious. You must marry Blackthorne."

Ashley blinked and studied her face. "I know. But that means you must marry Mr. Dover."

Maddie wanted to say she didn't *have* to do anything. But though she cared little for herself, she did care for her family. She had no desire to shame them.

And she did care for her charitable work. How could it continue if she were shunned from Society—the men and women who funded so much of her benevolence?

The answer was that it couldn't. Which meant she must marry Mr. Dover, and Ashley must marry Lord Blackthorne, and Lord Nicholas must, well . . . there was probably no help for Lord Nicholas.

"Maddie?" Ashley said.

She turned to see her friend looking at her with concern.

"Will you marry Mr. Dover? Because I'm not doing this if you're not."

Maddie's stomach clenched and sank. She felt ill and exhausted and trapped. She wished she could go back to her life before all the marriage proposals. She wished she could go back to the time when her biggest worry was whether a rain shower would ruin her plans to ride in Hyde Park.

And most of all, she wished she had never met Lord Blackthorne. Then she might have been happy with Mr. Dover. She might have been content in a passionless marriage, had she never known she could feel what she felt with Jack. She longed to go back and start over.

But it was too late for that now. It was too late, and she knew that no matter how hard she tried to smile and think positively, she was never going to be truly happy.

Never.

Not without Jack holding her in her arms.

Maddie took a breath and smiled sadly at Ashley. "I am going to marry Mr. Dover, and you'll marry Lord Blackthorne. Let's have a double wedding."

"Oh, yes!" Ashley exclaimed, clasping Maddie's hand in hers. "This might even be fun if you're standing by my side."

Maddie squeezed her hand. "I feel the same."

"It's decided, then. Together until the end."

Maddie swallowed. The words felt ominous. "Together until the end," she echoed.

For Maddie, the rest of the trip went by in a blur of rolling fields, moors, dales, and posting houses. The speed set by the Martingale brothers was punishing for all involved. She and Ashley were irritable and exhausted. In the jouncing carriage, sleep was impossible, and even if she did doze off, the frequent stops woke her again.

Maddie was hungry and thirsty and had to use the privy, but Lord Blackthorne and Lord Nicholas were immune to her pleas to escape the confines of the carriage. She knew they were right. Bleven or her father or the owners of their stolen carriage could be right on their heels. They had to keep going.

Mr. Dover, cheerful now that they had made up for so much lost time, echoed that sentiment frequently. "We must keep going," he told her when she complained that her bottom was pins and needles and her head ached. She'd given him a glowering look, but it hadn't shut him up until, near Scotch Corner, Ashley threatened to stuff her handkerchief down his throat if he spoke again.

The rest of that day had been blissfully quiet, and she stared out the window as they passed through Brough and Penrith. She knew they were close now. They need only reach Carlisle and then they could slip over the Scottish border. Carlisle was only eight miles from Gretna Green.

As noon came and went on the last day of their trip, Maddie's heart began to pound. She looked at Mr. Dover, staring silently out the window, pocket watch in hand, and knew that tonight she would share his marriage bed.

But she was determined not to marry or share his bed in the state she was in at present. The truth of the matter was that she stank. She and Ashley both, and no doubt Mr. Dover too, though she didn't want to get close enough to find out.

When Lord Nicholas called out that they were five miles from Carlisle, she pounded on the roof. A moment later Lord Blackthorne's face, impatient and annoyed, appeared. He too looked a bit worse for their hard travels. He had the beginnings of a black beard and his eyes were bloodshot. His skin was gray and his clothing haggard. One look at him made up Maddie's mind.

"We're stopping in Carlisle," she said. "I need a bath and so does Ashley, and if that stench is what I think it is, so do you two."

Blackthorne shook his head. "We don't—"

"Have time," Maddie and Ashley said together.

He scowled at them and made to close the hatch, but Maddie shoved her hand in the way.

"We have acquiesced to your timetable and made the most of this grueling journey without complaint."

He barked laughter at this last bit, but Maddie went on.

"And now I—we, your fiancée and I—are asking for a short time in which to prepare ourselves for the night to come. Surely, you can understand our desire to bathe before we . . . " She trailed off and made a gesture to the effect that he could fill in the rest.

But, as usual, Lord Blackthorne, didn't play by the rules. "Before we what?" he asked.

Maddie heaved a sigh. "Before you and Miss Brittany . . . before you are man and wife." She stammered the last and felt her cheeks redden. Lord, she hated him sometimes. Most times.

"Before we share the marriage bed," Ashley broke in unabashedly. "Maddie thought you might like me to wash off some of this reek before you bed me. It might be more pleasant for you to—"

"Ashley, we understand!" Maddie said loudly before her friend could go on. She looked at Lord Blackthorne, and he looked back steadily.

"Oh, let 'em clean up, Jack," she heard Lord Nicholas say. "We can afford to give them a quarter of an hour."

"A half an hour," Ashley demanded, "and

something more substantial to eat than bread and cheese."

"Demanding little chit," Lord Nicholas mumbled. At least that's what Maddie thought he said. The hatch closed again, and she and Ashley exchanged a disgruntled look.

But three-quarters of an hour later, the coach slowed and stopped at an inn in Carlisle. The door was thrown open, and Maddie stepped out on wobbly legs. She blinked in the sunlight and inhaled deeply of the fresh air. A few curious passersby glanced at her, but otherwise she was just one more traveler passing through.

Lord Blackthorne stood beside the door, still scowling at her. "Nick's gone to get you two a room," he said, then turned away from her to speak with the grooms changing the horses.

Mr. Dover stepped out of the coach, followed by Ashley, and Maddie gave her a tired smile. Ashley looked like she'd have enjoyed a long, luxurious bath as much as Maddie. As it was, they'd probably have to make do with a quick wash using a basin and ewer. Maddie didn't care. Anything to rid herself of the grime from the past few days.

"I hope he orders us warm water," Ashley said. "And a big tub."

Maddie shook her head. "Unlikely, and you know it."

"I can dream, can't I?"

"Dream away." Maddie leaned back against the coach and rolled her shoulders. Her back creaked as she worked out some of the tension, and she opened her mouth to yawn in a decidedly unladylike manner.

"Stop right there!" a voice boomed, and Maddie froze. Her eyes popped open and she scanned the street. It was crowded with carriages and people. No one stood out or appeared to be interested in them.

But she knew that voice. Knew it well.

"Oh, good God!" Ashley was saying. "Now what has that imbecile gone and done?"

Maddie opened her mouth to answer, but she was unable to speak. She looked frantically about, searching for the source of the voice.

And then she saw him. Lord Castleigh, dressed impeccably in a morning coat and breeches, stepped out of the building across from the carriage.

To Maddie's shock, her kind, even-tempered father was pointing his hunting rifle at Mr. Dover.

"Daddy!" She grabbed Ashley's arm for support.

"Thought you could run off with my daughter," her father shouted as he moved forward. As one, the people on the street seemed to notice the man with the rifle. A woman uttered a long scream, and then everyone was running, scattering for cover.

"Daddy!" Maddie cried, pushing Ashley behind her. "Put that rifle down."

"Stay out of this, Madeleine Richael Fullbright."

Oh, dear. He'd used her full name, which meant he was very angry. She had to calm him down.

Beside her, Mr. Dover threw up his arms and began to tremble. "Don't shoot!" His voice was high-pitched in the sudden silence. The busy street of a moment before was now deserted. Maddie looked about wildly for Jack and Lord Nicholas and prayed for them to stay wherever they were.

Keeping her father in sight, she inched closer to Dover. "Get behind me, Mr. Dover," she said quietly. "Move toward the carriage."

But then, just when she got Mr. Dover's attention, Ashley put herself at risk. She moved out from behind Maddie and called out, "Uncle William, you're scaring everyone." Ashley put her hands on her hips in a foolhardy gesture.

Not like Lord Nicholas indeed, Maddie thought. The two were both incredibly stupid.

"Put that rifle down right now, Uncle William."

"You hush, now, Ashley Gweneira Brittany," Maddie's father said, waving the rifle like an accusatory finger. "Your father will deal with you when he arrives."

"Wonderful," Ashley muttered. "Now we'll never get a bath."

Maddie's heart leapt into her throat as her father's rifle swung back toward Mr. Dover's heart.

"Mr. Dover!" she hissed. "Get back!"

Why now? She wanted to cry. They'd been so

close. Eight little miles to Gretna Green. Eight, after so many.

And now she'd go home again. In disgrace. "Daddy, please put the rifle down. You don't need to shoot anyone. I'll come with you."

"Maddie!" Ashley hissed. "What are you doing?"

Maddie continued to stare at her father, but she spoke out of the corner of her mouth. "As soon as Daddy's distracted, you and Blackthorne run. You can still make it to Gretna."

"No!"

"Daddy, please put the rifle down," Maddie called.

And she took a step forward and another, but before she could take a third, a hand reached out, grabbed her, and thrust her back toward the carriage.

A gunshot exploded, and Maddie was pushed down hard and covered by a familiar muscular form.

Lord Blackthorne.

"What are you doing?" she screeched, spitting dirt out of her mouth. "Get out of here." Why hadn't he stayed hidden?

"I'm not leaving without you," Blackthorne said. He pulled her up, shoved her in the carriage, then went back for Ashley, who came scrambling in on hands and knees a moment later. The two women crouched on the floor.

Inside the coach, Maddie heard another gunshot. "That wasn't my father," she told Ashley. The sound had come from behind the carriage, which meant it was aimed at her father. She crept up to the window, followed by Ashley.

"Oh, no," Ashley moaned, and Maddie followed her gaze. Lord Nicholas, pistol in hand, was sprinting for the carriage.

"Lord Nicholas!" Maddie screamed. Where had he found a gun?

And how dare Lord Nicholas shoot at her father? "Daddy?" she cried, trying to leap back out of the coach.

But Blackthorne appeared in the carriage door, blocking her exit. "Get down, you little fool."

He pushed her back, and Maddie tumbled onto the floor again. Blackthorne climbed in behind her, keeping his hand on her, forcing her to stay down. Maddie heard another gunshot, but she couldn't lift her head. She listened hard as Lord Nicholas clambered on top of the coach and whipped the fresh horses into action.

The carriage jerked violently, and Maddie fell back against the squabs then almost tumbled over. Blackthorne caught her arm and steadied her. Ashley pulled her onto the seat.

"My father?" Maddie cried, fear making her heart clench. "All those gunshots . . . " She tried to look out the window, but everything was bouncing too much and she couldn't see. "Daddy!"

"He's fine," Blackthorne said, reaching across to take her by the shoulders. "Calm down."

His voice and his touch soothed her, made the terror flee, but not the fear.

"I don't know how the hell he found us, but Lord Castleigh is undoubtedly right on our heels now. Even if we make it to Gretna before him, it'll be a close thing to marry before he stops us." He glanced at Ashley.

"But he's unhurt?" Maddie asked, the fear beginning to claw at her again. "How could Lord Nicholas shoot at him! How dare—"

"Isn't there anyone else you're worried about?" Jack asked, and his dark tone felt like an icicle sliding down her spine.

She looked about the carriage, saw Ashley's shocked expression and Jack's grim one.

"Oh, Lord! Oh, no! Mr. Dover!"

"I'm sorry," Blackthorne said quietly, releasing her and averting his gaze.

"Is he—is he—" But she couldn't say it. If Mr. Dover were dead, she would never forgive herself. His death would be on her conscience, and she knew she would burn in hell forever for ending the poor man's life. All he had wanted was a mother for his children, and she'd given him shootouts and carriage chases, angry dukes and irate earls.

The hatch above them slammed open and Lord Nicholas peered down. "Hold on!" he called. "They're coming up behind us."

Chapter 12

Jack didn't have time to worry about Maddie. He would have liked to pull her into his arms, stroke her back and stop her trembling. The look of pure shock and then guilt that passed over her face when she realized that Dover was not with them was heart-wrenching, even for a man like he, who everyone said had no heart.

At that moment he would have done anything to give her the prissy little professor back, if it would just erase the anguish from her features.

But her father was unhurt—at least the earl had appeared hale enough when Jack had last looked back. The white-haired man was plum-faced, shouting, and still waving that hunting rifle.

Jack turned from Maddie and tried to see out the window. "Bloody hell," he cursed. There was a coach right behind them and gaining ground. He popped the hatch open again and shouted to his brother, "Faster, man. They're right behind us."

"I'm doing the best I can," was Nick's strained reply.

"Damn it." Jack slammed the hatch shut. He was going to have to go up there. He didn't think he would do a better job than Nick at escaping the irate earl, but he couldn't sit here with his hands clasped, twiddling his thumbs uselessly either.

If he'd made one promise in his life, it was never again to do nothing.

With another curse, Jack moved toward the door and reached for the handle.

Maddie grabbed his arm. "What are you doing?"

"Going up there." He shook her hand off and reached for the door again.

"No! You'll never make it. Or you'll be shot."

He gave her a quick grin. "Your concern is touching, sweetheart. But I'll be back."

He swung the door open, grasped the coach's frame, and pulled himself out and up. Jesus, he'd obviously spent too much time sitting at his club and drinking port because it was damn hard hauling himself on top of the carriage. He huffed and puffed and sweated, but he finally made it, then reached down and slammed the carriage door shut.

Holding on tightly, he glanced behind him. Just rounding a corner was a nondescript town coach.

Normally, he would have assumed it was Castleigh, but there were so many people after them that he was making no conjectures. He narrowed his eyes to observe the green and gold livery on the coachman, then popped the hatch and peered into the carriage.

Two pairs of anxious eyes blinked up at him. He found the bright sapphire ones. "What color is your father's livery?"

Maddie stared at him as though he'd gone daft. "I— What?"

"Lord Castleigh's livery is green and gold," Ashley supplied for her.

Jack nodded and dropped the hatch closed. Well, at least he knew it wasn't Bleven again. Holding onto the sides of the carriage, he managed to push himself forward until he could climb beside his brother on the box.

Thanks to the quick work of the grooms at the posting house, Jack and Nick had been able to ensure the change of horses before Maddie stepped out of the carriage and the shooting began. But this new team was rather spirited. Nick had his hands full trying to control them.

"How close?" Nick asked through clenched teeth.

"Less than a quarter of a mile," Jack answered. "And gaining."

"Still seven miles to Gretna Green. We may be able to outrun them."

Jack doubted it. They were in an old carriage with second-rate horses. He and Nick were exhausted. The earl was in his shiny town coach and had probably paid for the best horses in Carlisle. And who knew how long he'd been sitting there waiting for their arrival? His coachman and foot-men were probably rested and ready to fight.

"How the hell did he find us?" Jack said to no one in particular. "And why the devil weren't we more careful? We should have known."

"Too late for all that now." Nick reached under the box and handed Jack a pistol. "There's one shot left. Make it count."

"Right," Jack said, turning to observe the earl's progress.

Still steadily gaining.

Well, the good news was that his brother had acquired a pistol.

The bad was that Jack wasn't a very good shot. He decided to wait until the earl closed the gap between them rather than risk shooting out of range. While he gauged the narrowing distance, he tried to wedge himself into the box so his aim would be steady.

They were on flat land now, and the earl's men pushed their horses faster. Jack could see their faces, see their determined expressions. He decided his best hope was to wound the lead horse. That would force Castleigh to cut the animal free and harness the other horses before continuing on.

By then, Jack thought, he would be married.

His stomach gave a heave that had nothing whatsoever to do with the bumpy road, but he swallowed the anxiety and returned to the task at hand.

He raised the pistol over the top of the carriage, squinted, tensed his finger on the trigger—

And the hatch popped open.

Jack jerked and his one shot went wild. "What the hell!"

"How close are we?" Maddie called from below.

He peered down and saw her hand still outstretched from opening the hatch. Damn fool chit had ruined his one shot.

Without a word, Jack slammed the hatch closed again. He turned back to Nick. "Got another plan?" he asked.

Nick gave him a disgusted look and tensed his jaw in concentration. Jack glanced back at the earl's coach, which was now neither gaining nor falling behind. No need to worry that the earl would try to run them off the road or shoot at them. With Maddie inside, he was certain that the earl would not allow his men to take any chances.

Once they arrived at Gretna, however, Jack had a feeling that all bets were off.

"My advice?" Nick said over the roar of the horses' hooves. "Pray."

They covered the last few miles to Gretna Green with the earl's coach close on their heels. But with the city in sight, Nick pushed his horses faster, taking risks by running off the road and going over uneven ground.

Jack considered it a miracle that the axle didn't snap or one of the horses falter and break a leg, but the end result was that they arrived in Gretna Green without the earl in sight.

Jack, keenly conscious that Castleigh was right behind them, didn't even wait for the coach to come to a stop in front of the blacksmith's shop before jumping down and flinging the door open.

"We're here," he barked. "Let's go."

Ashley scrambled out and rushed to the blacksmith's door, with Jack right behind her. It wasn't until he was inside and the rotund priest was rising unsteadily before them that Jack realized Maddie hadn't followed.

Nick was standing in the door, and Jack swung around to face him. "Where's Lady Madeleine?"

Nick shrugged.

"She's still in the carriage," Ashley told him in a rush. "Without Mr. Dover here, she has no reason to come inside."

"Damn."

The priest cleared his throat. "Ye'll be wanting ta marry, then." The man's Scottish accent was thick, his words marred further as he lifted a jug of brandy and took a swig. A good portion of it dribbled back down his chin.

Jack let out a long sigh. Leave it to him to find the drunk priest. Not that the man was actually a priest. Scottish law didn't require one to officiate at a marriage. From the look of the man and the plethora of brandy jugs in the shop, this anvil priest was probably a smuggler.

"We're in a hurry," Jack said.

"Och, a hurry." The man's tongue rolled over the r's and got stuck. "No' heard that before." And then he burst into laughter.

Jack scowled. He needed to get this over and done. Now, before he reminded himself that Dover might be dead, and Maddie was free. Damn it.

He looked at Ashley and took a deep breath. He was going to marry Ashley Brittany. She was safe. She posed no risk to his heart.

And yet, he couldn't leave Maddie in the carriage alone. He couldn't even leave her unmarried. He didn't want to imagine what would happen to her when she returned to London, still unwed after a failed elopement and several nights spent in the company of men who were not her relatives.

Hell. He looked to the priest, who was asking if they had two witnesses, and then at Ashley.

"Lord Blackthorne," she said, "should I ask Maddie if she will serve as our second witness?"

Jack shook his head. "She'll have to be more than that."

He knew what had to be done. He clenched his fists and told himself he was doing what was best for all of them, especially himself. But then, he'd always been a selfish bastard, hadn't he?

Jack turned on his brother.

Nick looked behind him, searching for Jack's intended victim, then realized Jack was looking at him. He raised his hands in surrender. "Whatever it is, I didn't do it."

"I need you, Nick," Jack said quickly. "We need you."

Nick narrowed his eyes. "I don't mind being a witness."

"No." Jack took a step forward. "You must marry Lady Madeleine."

"Oh, no." Nick backed up, shaking his head. "This is your wedding, not mine."

"He's right, Nicholas," Ashley said, coming between them. "If she returns to London unwed, her reputation will be ruined. Her life will be ruined. She has to be married."

"But that's not my fault," Nick argued. "I didn't touch her. I barely know the chit."

"What does it matter whose fault it is?" Ashley demanded. "Thank God I'm not marrying you. You're the most selfish man in England. Scotland, too," she added after looking about her.

"Don't start." Nick pointed a finger at her, then looked at Jack. "Where's the bloody professor?"

"Back in Carlisle. Probably dead."

"No thanks to you." Ashley began to rail again, and Jack pushed her aside.

"Let me handle this."

Jack advanced on his brother until Nick had nowhere to go but out the door. As soon as they were away from Ashley and the priest, he hauled Nick up by the shirt collar and pushed him against the building's wall.

"Listen, Nick. I've done a lot for you over the

years. I've stuck my neck out for you more times than I care to admit, and you can do one small bloody thing for me."

"Small? This isn't like not telling Father when I drank a bottle of his best wine," Nick argued. "This is marriage. Forever."

Jack tightened his grip. "You're always talking about good causes. Here's a good cause."

Nick shook his head. "But—"

"Yes or no, Nick. We both know how much you owe me."

"Oh, goddamn it." Nick sighed and scowled. "Fine. Bloody *fine*."

Maddie hunched in the carriage, her arms wrapped around her knees, tears streaming down her cheeks. Inside the blacksmith's shop, Ashley and Lord Blackthorne were being married. Meanwhile, she was out here alone. She was a widow before she'd even said her vows.

Poor Mr. Dover. He'd only wanted a mother for his children.

He'd only wanted to arrive in Gretna Green on time.

In the end, they'd been too late. And now he lay dead in Carlisle—well, perhaps not dead, but wounded. And she'd just left him there, left him for strangers to—

The carriage door was wrenched open and Blackthorne reached in, grasped her arms, and pulled her out. "What are you doing?" Something in the stony expression of his face made her struggle to get away. "I prefer to wait in here."

"Well, you can't get married in the coach." He pushed her forward, and before she could ask what he meant, she heard the clatter of hooves nearing.

"Bloody hell! It's your father."

Her feet seemed to move of their own accord then, and she all but ran inside the blacksmith's shop. She skidded to a stop and stared at the drunk anvil priest.

Ashley reached out and gripped her hand, Lord Nicholas came up beside her, and Maddie, in her horror, realized what Blackthorne had been saying. She was to marry Lord Nicholas.

"And do ye come here of your own free accord?" the priest asked.

"No!" Maddie shouted. She was not going to marry Lord Nicholas. She was not going to marry anyone.

"Maddie, don't be a fool," Ashley hissed at her. "Your father is almost here. Do you want him to find you unwed?"

That was a rather terrifying thought. Her father was not a violent man, but he'd already shot one fiancé. Could she allow the same fate to befall Lord Nicholas? "No, but—"

"She's here of her own free will," Ashley said. "Aren't you, Maddie?" Ashley poked her in the back, and Maddie nodded.

The priest frowned at a piece of paper Maddie

assumed was the marriage certificate. "So it's ta be a dooble ceremony?"

"Right," Jack said from beside Ashley. "Now, get on with it."

The priest began asking for their names, but Maddie didn't listen. She couldn't stop staring at Jack. She was about to become wife to his brother, but she couldn't spare a glance for her intended. All she could think was that she was going to lose Jack forever.

"No, it's Ashley, not Ainsley," Ashley was telling the priest, "and I'm marrying him, not him." She pointed to Jack and then Nick, and the priest nodded and wrote something down.

Oh, Lord. Maddie swallowed her fear and horror. The priest was so drunk he could barely stand. The man began trying to sort the couples out again, and Jack growled, "Hurry up, man. Hurry up."

Maddie turned toward the door as the priest began the ceremony, a simple one. "Do ye take this woman ta be yer lawful wedded wife?"

"I will," Lord Nicholas said.

Maddie heard the clatter of hooves outside cease and knew her father had arrived. There was an ominous silence. She clenched Ashley's hand.

Ashley squeezed her hand back. "He's too late," she whispered, then turned as her name was called. "I will," her friend answered, and Maddie felt Ashley's pale hand shake.

The silence outside was broken as her father's

voice rose, issuing orders to his footmen. Maddie could hear stomping and yelling.

"Do ye take this woman ta be yer lawful wedded wife?"

The shouting came closer, and Maddie could hear her father's voice raised in anger.

"Madeleine, do ye take this man ta be yer lawful wedded husband?"

Wait a moment . . .

Maddie spun round, her mind now focused on the ceremony. Could it be her turn? But hadn't Jack just—

"Lady Madeleine, answer," Jack demanded.

"But—"

"Hurry up," Lord Nicholas barked. Everyone was staring alternately at her and then the door. Maddie noted that someone had had the foresight to bar it, but now there was an ominous pounding on the thick wood.

"Hurry up!" Ashley said, and Maddie threw her hands in the air.

"I will." Her head ached and she felt dizzy.

The priest swayed—either that or she was worse off than she thought—and then said, "Weel, then, Ainsley and—"

"Ashley," they all corrected.

The priest blinked. "Verra weel, lass. Ashley and Nicholas, Madeleine and John, in the name o' the Father, Son, and Holy Ghost, I declare ye man and wife." He lifted a blacksmith's hammer—one of two items in the shop that had anything to do with metal forging—and banged it on the anvil. He looked at Maddie and Jack. "Oh and . . . er, man and wife." The hammer struck again.

Maddie took in one breath then another, and still the light-headedness persisted. The pounding on the door grew louder, and she closed her eyes to drown it out. But nothing could stifle the pounding of her heart. She did not dare to believe it, and yet—

"Wait." Nicholas held up a hand. "I'm married to her?" He pointed to Ashley. "Or her?" He pointed to Maddie.

The priest frowned and consulted the certificate. "Er . . . ye are married ta the fair one, lad. Yes. And the dark-haired lass is married ta him." The priest pointed to Jack.

Maddie glanced at Jack, who was staring at her, his face unreadable. He didn't look away and his expression didn't soften.

Her heart felt like it might burst from hammering so hard.

"But that's not right," Ashley said over the banging on the door and the pounding of Maddie's heart. "You've married the wrong brides and grooms!"

The priest frowned. "Wha' now?" He took another swig from his brandy jug and shrugged. "Ooh, weel, it's a trifling mistake."

"Trifling?" Nick hollered. "You've married the wrong couples. I'm stuck with *her*."

Maddie glanced at Jack, who had still said nothing. Did he realize *he* was stuck with her now? Or perhaps the truth was that she was stuck with him.

Lord Blackthorne was her husband.

The room seemed to swim again, and she had to clutch Ashley to stay on her feet.

The priest waved all concern away. "Ah weel, juist sort yerselves oot."

And then he lifted his jug high, tilted his head back, and toppled over.

Chapter 13

Maddie looked like she might follow the priest's example, and Jack reached out and grasped her shoulder to steady her. She jumped at his touch, and he quickly withdrew his hand.

My wife, he thought, staring at her. *My wife.* What the hell had he gone and done now?

"Open up this door before I kick it in!" Lord Castleigh's voice was punctuated by three short thumps that sounded very much like kicks already.

His father-in-law.

"Let's go," Jack said, herding everyone toward the adjacent room. "Out the back."

Nick grabbed Jack. "Wait. I'm not leaving until this is fixed." He pointed to the crumpled marriage certificate in his hand. "I didn't agree to marry *her.*" He pointed to Ashley.

"And I agreed to marry you?" Ashley said, stepping between the brothers. She poked Nick in the chest with one finger. "If I had the choice between marrying you and eating a three-course meal of horse feces, I'd grab a napkin and fork."

"Is that so?" Nick looked down at her. "Well, if I had the choice between—"

"Do something!" Maddie hissed at Jack. "My father will be inside at any moment."

Jack turned to look at his wife. She was staring up at him, expecting him to save her—save all of them. What a disappointment he was going to be.

" . . . I'd drop my breeches," Nick was saying, "and ask for the hot coals."

"Enough," Jack said firmly, stepping between the lovebirds. "Castleigh is coming in, and I for one don't want to be on the other side of his pistol."

"But we can't leave," Ashley protested. "We need the priest to do the ceremony again and marry us to the right people."

"You go try and rouse him," Jack said, pushing past her and fumbling in the darkness for the back door. "I'm getting out of here."

He found the latch, then pulled the door open and jumped back as Castleigh's startled footmen leapt to attention.

"Oh, hell," Nick said, and then he was beside Jack. The two brothers dispatched the footmen in a matter of moments, and then both couples were standing in the moonlit courtyard.

"I think we should split up," Jack said. "If

Sir Gareth is close behind Castleigh, we'll make it harder for them to catch us if we aren't all together."

"But I don't want to go with him," Ashley complained.

"Jack," Nick said, taking his brother by the shoulder, "we have to fix this. I'm going to go check on the priest. Maybe he's come around."

When Ashley followed Nick back into the blacksmith's shop, Jack turned to look at his new bride. "You want to go try and rouse the priest?"

She shook her head. "No. Do you?"

Jack looked at her for a long moment. He couldn't have orchestrated this muddle in a hundred years, and yet, while it was happening, he hadn't stopped it. He'd known this would ruin him, and yet he'd stood silently, allowing the priest to marry him to the wrong woman. And he had a feeling Maddie had seen what was happening and allowed it to go on as well.

He took her hand. "I say, let the priest sleep it off. Come on."

He pulled her into a run, leaving the blacksmith shop, her irate father, and Nick and Ashley behind.

Maddie couldn't fathom where Jack could be taking her. They'd left the small town of Gretna, with its cozy inns and houses, and were once again trudging over a dark road. Actually, it was barely a road. She doubted a carriage could have even traversed the small, muddy trail. She supposed that was why Jack had chosen it.

He was moving quickly, his hand clamped firmly around hers, forcing her to keep up.

Or perhaps he just wanted to be certain she stayed by his side. He hadn't broken contact with her since they'd left the blacksmith shop.

Maddie shook her head. The exhaustion was playing tricks on her mind. Jack did not want to keep touching her. He did it out of necessity or because he had forgotten he still held her—not because he wanted to.

He had wanted Ashley.

And she had wanted Mr. Dover.

Oh, Mr. Dover—

She focused on breathing deeply and moving her leaden legs, refusing to think of her lost fiancé. She would never stave off the tears if she thought of him. Or of poor Ashley, left with the wayward Lord Nicholas. Ashley must hate her for running off. And Maddie didn't blame her. She was a horrible friend.

And the worst part was that whenever she looked at Lord Blackthorne, she didn't care. She was glad he was hers and not Ashley's.

That was, until she remembered that he was all wrong for her.

Maddie's legs finally buckled and she tugged on Jack's hand. "I have . . . to stop," she panted. "I'm too . . . tired."

"We can't stop here," he told her, looking impatiently from her to the road. "We need to put more distance between us and your father."

Maddie shook her head. "I don't care. I don't care if he catches us. I'm going to collapse if we don't stop."

Jack stepped before her, cupped her face in his hands, and Maddie couldn't keep her eyes from closing and from enjoying the feel of his warm flesh against her chilled face. "Maddie, if we just go a bit farther, we'll arrive at a town. We can stay at an inn. You can have a bath and a meal. You don't want our wedding night to take place along the road, do you?"

Her eyes popped open. Wedding night? But he couldn't possibly be thinking of—

Oh, Lord. He probably was. He was a man. And she was his wife now.

He was right that she would have preferred a cozy inn to a patch of brush beside the road, but she was simply too tired. She could barely stand.

"I can't, Jack," she told him. "I want to go on, but I simply can't."

He took her hands. "I have another idea. Can you walk, or do I need to carry you?"

Maddie preferred to collapse right where she was, but she agreed to walk. She couldn't make Jack carry her, after all. The difficult part was getting her legs to cooperate, but with supreme effort she lifted one foot and then the other.

Her eyes were on the ground as she concentrated on making her feet continue to move. Consequently, she plowed into Jack when he stopped. She stumbled, but he caught her around the waist. Despite the fact that her body was numb and weary, she felt her skin tingle where he touched her.

"Careful," he said, and she wanted to heed the warning.

The problem was, she didn't know whether she should watch her step or her new husband. Both might prove dangerous.

"Stay here," he ordered. "I'll be back in a moment."

Maddie realized she'd been staring at his mouth. Now that he was gone, she looked around. They were on the outskirts of one of the many farms in the area, and Jack was heading for the small farmhouse. When he reached the door, he turned back and gave her a small wave, and then the door opened and light spilled out.

Maddie turned away so as not to be seen clearly. She was embarrassed at how wretched she must look. She could have certainly used a bath at an inn, but as it stood now, she would probably have fallen asleep and drowned in the water.

She didn't know what Jack said to the owners of the farm or even how long he spent talking with them. Somehow, she found herself in a clean, warm stable, resting on a bed of straw. She was able to open her eyes long enough to see Jack looking down at her with a worried expression, and she wanted to reach out and tell him that she was fine. Tired, but fine. But the words were too heavy for her mouth, and her eyes slid shut again.

She awoke the next morning when something snorted in her face. The thing snuffled and wheezed, and she opened her eyes and stared straight into the snout of a rather large pig. She jerked back, and the startled pig trotted out the stable door.

The stable where she'd been sleeping was quiet, and Maddie realized she was alone. The straw beside her was flat and matted, so she knew Jack must have slept there. Through the windows and doors, she could see that the morning was fairly advanced. The sun was out and the steel-blue skies of Scotland spread out above her.

She stood, though her muscles protested, and finally hobbled to the open stable door. She saw no one about, despite the evidence that someone had been there. The troughs were full and chicken feed had been spread. Seeing an old cloth covering a pail next to the door, she lifted it and saw bread and cheese.

She smiled and reached hungrily for a slab of the thick, country bread. She was so hungry, she might have devoured the entire contents of the pail. But she knew Jack would need sustenance as well, so with a slice of bread in hand, she began to search for her new husband.

Ten minutes later Maddie wondered if she'd

been abandoned. She'd walked around the stable and gone up to the farmhouse, but saw no sign of him or anyone else. She was about to make her way back to the road when she saw a pair of ducks lift into the sky. Maddie frowned at the tight group of trees, realizing there must be a body of water behind them. Trudging in that direction, she found a battered path and followed it to a large, clear pond.

It was now late morning, and she stood on its banks and smiled. The grass near the edge had been worn away, and she could imagine many picnics on the soft soil where she stood. Across the pond, she saw a few ducks. A mother and her golden ducklings made a long line of ripples in the water. To her left were more trees, one with a rope hanging off it, and she imagined children swinging on it in the summer. Still smiling, Maddie turned to her right, and her breath caught in her throat.

To her right was a naked man.

More specifically, her naked husband. He hadn't heard her approach, and his back was to her. He stood thigh deep in the water, arms raised, brushing his wet, black hair off his forehead.

Maddie almost stumbled when she spotted him. She'd had no idea the male body could be so beautiful. His legs were long and muscled, the thighs chiseled like a sculpture. His bottom was round and firm, the cheeks a shade lighter than his bronzed body. His waist tapered in at the hips, making the breadth of his back and shoulders stand out in contrast.

His back was hard and muscled, the water from his wet hair sluicing over the ripples and planes. As he lowered his arms, muscles moved, and her heart sped up. She could imagine that hard flesh under her fingers, could imagine those muscled arms coming around her. The thought made her mouth dry.

And then a cloud moved away from the sun, light filtered through the trees, and Maddie saw what the overcast day had been concealing. What she had assumed were shadows were actually bruises on Jack's legs and back. Some were old, turning green and yellow, and some fairly new and still black and blue. But all looked as though they hurt.

She must have made a sound, must have inhaled or issued a small cry, because Jack turned and saw her looking at him. The concern in his face mirrored what she felt, and he started for her.

"Maddie, what's wrong. Did your father—"

She shook her head quickly, unable to speak now that he had turned and she had the full fontal view of him. Lord, he was as magnificent from this angle as from behind.

He was also as bruised—no, even more so. His stomach, so lean and hard, was marred by black and blue smudges that extended over his ribs. His upper chest was relatively free of the painful marks, but as he approached through the shallow water, she could see scratches and scrapes almost everywhere.

Well, not everywhere. The poor man might be hurt, but she couldn't help gazing down at that one appendage so interesting and terrifying to virgins.

Yes, his manhood was there, and it appeared unhurt—not that she was any great judge, as this was the first of its kind she'd seen.

She quickly looked away, and Jack splashed up to her. "What's wrong?"

She reached out, grazing his shoulder with two of her fingers. "You're hurt. Jack, I didn't realize you were so bruised and—oh, your eye." Her fingers strayed to his face and the puffy, red skin next to one eye. She could see that he'd shaved this morning, and she could now make out old and new bruises on his jaw. She traced her finger down his smooth jaw and touched one fading mark.

"I'm fine." He caught her hand and held it.

When his fingers twined with hers, she realized that she was standing before a naked man and took a step back.

Jack followed.

"Perhaps you should dress," she said, looking behind her. "The owners may come upon us at any moment and—"

She trailed off as she looked back and he shook his head. "They've gone into town this morning," he said. "In fact, I asked them to let me know if they hear anything about your father or my brother."

Maddie blinked. "You told them who I was?"

Jack shrugged, obviously as unconcerned about this as his nakedness. He made no attempt to cover himself. "I don't think we're the first eloping couple to knock on their door. They seemed sympathetic, especially after I gave them a few pounds."

"You paid them?"

"The last of my blunt, too. I'll have to rely on my name and credit from now on." Jack winked at her. "Come here." He tugged on her arm, and she stumbled into him. It was an awkward tangle of limbs for a moment as Maddie tried to move away without touching him and Jack tried to pull her closer. Finally, he took her shoulders and held her still. "Calm down. You've got straw in your hair."

"Oh." Maddie giggled. Her stomach felt like it was in knots, and she couldn't stop trembling. "Straw." She felt like a silly schoolgirl before an examination.

Except her tutors had usually been women.

Clothed women.

Jack reached out, slowly, and Maddie felt his hand caress her hair. He pulled a piece of straw from the mess and then reached for her again.

"More?" she asked, her voice high-pitched and nervous.

"Mmm-hmm." His hand cupped the back of her head, fingers entangling in her long curls. "More."

He bent to kiss her, his mouth cool and moist from his earlier swim. He was still dripping wet, dampening her own clothing, but as soon as she felt his body press up against hers, she forgot about keeping her clothing dry.

She was hungry for him, hungry to feel that skin she had so admired against her own skin, and hungry for the taste of his mouth. She had gone too long without his lips on hers.

And when she finally got her first taste of him, it was like coming home. It felt so right and so wicked and so . . . shallow. She wanted more. She wanted to kiss him deeper, more thoroughly, until she could not get enough.

She responded to his kiss by devouring him with abandon. She would have been embarrassed at her enthusiasm if she'd been able to think of anything other than the sleek skin of his chest beneath the pads of her fingers and the strength of his arms as they pulled her closer.

They stumbled, Jack pulling her forward so that her shoes were soon wet and mired in the sand of the pond. But she didn't care. His hands had slipped the shoulders of her gown down, and his lips were teasing her ear, her neck, the spot at the base of neck and shoulder.

Maddie shivered when his hands cupped her

breasts, kneading them and pulling her gown down to reveal her to his gaze and the cool morning air.

"Wait," he said.

She had closed her eyes, and now opened them and stared at him. Wasn't she supposed to tell *him* to wait?

He ran his fingers through his wet hair again, and Maddie had to restrain herself from wrapping her arms around him and stepping back into the circle of his naked arms.

"Slow down," he said. "In a moment I'll have you on your back, waterlogged, your skirt up around your neck."

The idea didn't sound unappealing, as long as he kept rubbing his warm skin over her and touching her with those talented fingers and that persuasive mouth.

But then he stepped back and she saw that what she had assumed was his hip pressing against her abdomen was actually quite another part of him entirely. Hard, swollen, and thick, the sight of his manhood sent a tremor of fear shooting through her.

"Perhaps you are right," she said, moving back farther. "We should take this slow."

Jack took her elbow, halting her retreat. "Not that slow," he said, mischief in his eyes. "I want time to undress you. See you. Savor you."

"Undress me?" Maddie said, trying to step away again. "But—" She gestured helplessly to the open space around them.

Jack gestured to his own naked form. "It's only fair."

Maddie didn't have an argument for that, and yet, she felt she needed to argue. It was one thing to kiss Jack and become swept away in the moment, quite another to allow him to make love to her outside, in broad daylight. In the sunshine, she couldn't even pretend she wasn't Lady Madeleine. And though Lady Madeleine would certainly do her duty by her husband, that did not mean she would do so with wanton disregard for propriety.

"I know that look." Jack reached out and stroked her forehead. "Stop worrying. In fact, don't think at all. Just feel."

He caressed her cheek, touched her chin, and then moved his hand to run his fingers along the sensitive skin of her collarbone. Maddie shivered as he drew her in and kissed her lightly, his hands reaching back to unfasten her gown.

"Jack," she murmured. "I don't know about this."

"Shh," he said, bending to kiss her neck as he slipped the gown farther down. "You can't bathe fully clothed." His breath was warm on her ear, and his hands had worked her gown down over her hips and were lingering there. "You do want a bath, don't you?"

She dearly wanted a bath. She couldn't wait to rinse off all the grime from their journey.

But a bath with Jack watching?

He removed her stays, then reached for her chemise, and Maddie's hands caught his. "I should keep this on."

He glanced at her, then continued to undress her. "Have you ever swum naked in a pond?" he asked.

Maddie swallowed and shook her head. She could feel the cool breeze on her calves and then on her knees as her chemise rode higher and higher.

"You're going to love it," he whispered, and she knew he was right.

He tugged her farther into the water, pulling her chemise over her head and tossing it onto the bank behind them. And then, just as the cold water started to make her shiver, he closed his warm, naked body around her.

Chapter 14

Maddie shivered from the contrast between the heat of Jack's body and the cool water of the pond.

She was naked.

She was naked and pressed against her equally naked husband.

In full daylight, no less! She couldn't even blow out a candle and seek privacy in darkness. No, he could see every inch of her. And he would, as soon as he released her.

Unless he didn't release her . . .

Maddie wrapped her arms around Jack and buried her neck in his chest. He smelled like sunshine and blue skies and shaving lotion. She noted once again that his face was clean and smooth. He must have borrowed a razor from the farmer.

She'd almost grown used to seeing him with that black beard, and he looked younger without it.

Jack began to pull away, but Maddie wouldn't allow it. She stayed pressed against him, hiding her too-ample breasts and hips from his eyes.

When he tried to step back again, she went with him, and he almost lost his balance. "I had no idea you liked me this much," he drawled when she still wouldn't release him.

"I don't like you this much," she retorted, and kept her arms firmly clenched around him.

"Then let go," he said.

"What? And parade myself in front of everyone? I don't think so."

His laughter rumbled through her. "Parade yourself? And who's everyone? It's only you and me."

"That's not the point."

"Fine." Jack grasped her chin and forced her to look him in the eye. "We'll walk into deeper water."

Staring into his eyes made her think of kissing him again, and that made her shiver again, but she managed to nod and follow him farther out. Her body was becoming accustomed to the water temperature, and when she finally released him and ducked under, the water felt perfect.

She dipped her head back, wetting her hair and face, then came up smiling at Jack, who was standing in water to his neck. She could barely touch the pond's floor on tiptoes.

"Better?" Jack asked.

Maddie smiled and nodded.

"And what do you think of swimming without clothes?"

"It's deliciously wicked," she answered. "I feel like the most sinful libertine."

Maddie felt her face heat, and she ducked under again. When she came up, he was still looking at her, his swept-back hair making the hard planes of his jaw and cheekbones stand out. His black lashes were wet and spiky, and his dark eyes were filled with mischief and something that looked very much like desire.

"So I've married a wanton libertine. My luck improves day by day."

Maddie, treading water now, shook her head. "But that's the problem, Jack. I'm not a libertine. I'm Lady Madeleine. I shouldn't be doing this." She gestured to the pond and her lonely clothes, balled up on the shore.

"Who says?" He moved closer to her, and Maddie treaded water faster.

"I—I imagine everyone would say so. This isn't proper."

"Not proper for Lady Madeleine." He came closer still, and Maddie thought she felt his leg brush hers under the water. She looked down but saw only her own rapidly peddling legs. "But what you have failed to consider, my lady"—Jack reached out to her, his hand skimming the surface of the water—"is that you are no longer Lady Madeleine. Now you're Lady Blackthorne. My wife."

Maddie raised her eyebrows. She hadn't thought of that. She was Lady Blackthorne. She was a marchioness. "And who is Lady Blackthorne?" she asked. "I don't know anything about her."

"She's whoever you want her to be," Jack said, his voice low and husky. "She's part Lady Madeleine and part someone else entirely."

"Who?"

He held his hand out again. "Come here and I'll show you."

Her heart was beating fast now as she put her hand in Jack's and allowed him to pull her body into his. Even under the water she could feel the heat of him. His skin was warm and sleek and hard, and she rubbed wantonly against him. Without the constraints of gravity, he held her in his arms easily, and his hands were everywhere—cupping her behind, her breasts, her hips.

And she was just as liberal with her touches. She rubbed a hand against the light smattering of hair on his smooth chest, traced a finger down his hard abdomen, and brushed against the evidence of his desire for her.

"Put your legs around me," he whispered into her ear, and her whole body quivered. "Put your legs around my waist."

"Is that the kind of thing Lady Blackthorne would do?"

"God, I hope so," he answered.

She moved forward, wrapping her legs around him, pressing against those sleek muscles and feeling his hands support her back and buttocks. Every inch of her was molded to every inch of him, and, between them, pressed his hard member.

"I want you, Maddie," he whispered. "I want to slip inside you and make you my wife."

"I want that, too," she whispered.

"How much?" he asked, stroking her nipple until it peaked with need. "Enough to allow me to make you ready? Enough to do something truly wanton?"

Maddie felt the blood pound in her ears. She was excited, aroused—too far gone to make a sound decision. But maybe that had always been her problem. Maybe she needed someone to make her let go.

"What do you want me to do, Jack?"

"Float on your back, and let me give you pleasure."

Maddie didn't know what she'd expected him to say, but that was not it. And wasn't that what made being with Jack so exciting? He never said what one expected.

She released him and lay on her back, until she was floating comfortably. His hand was under her, supporting her. He looked down at her, and she kissed him, feeling all her need for him well up in that single exchange of mouth on mouth. "Let me pleasure you," he said when they parted. "Let me have my way."

She nodded her acquiescence, though she couldn't have refused him anything by then. She wanted him so much, needed him to keep touching her, kissing her.

He kept his hand under her back to support

her as he dove underneath the water, surfacing between her legs. Maddie jerked when she saw his head pop up between her knees. "What are you—"

"Shh," he said, reaching one hand forward to stroke her inner thigh. She shivered and flailed her arms a bit, but he kept her afloat.

"Open your legs for me," he whispered, his breath tickling the spot just above her knee. "I want to kiss you . . . here." He touched her inner thigh a few inches above her knee. "And here." He touched her higher, and Maddie inhaled sharply. "And here." He touched her womanhood, and she jerked and moaned at the pleasant shock that went through her.

"I thought you'd like that. Now open for me."

God help her, she obeyed him. *You're not Lady Madeleine*, she told herself as he rained kisses on the inside of her leg all the way to her core. "You're Lady Blackthorne," she whispered as his tongue retraced the trail of kisses. And then his mouth was on that most sensitive part of her, and his fingers were spreading her gently, so that his tongue might taste more of her.

Maddie clenched her hands to keep from crying out. Oh, Lord. She rather liked being Lady Blackthorne.

She allowed herself to float freely as his tongue laved her, creating quick, sharp jolts of pleasure that made her jerk, followed by long, languorous strokes of bliss that buzzed through her body. He knew what he was doing, and the tension inside her grew with each touch. His tongue tapped and danced and swirled over her sensitive nub until she couldn't stop herself from crying out.

"More!" she cried, too desperate to be ashamed of her gluttony. "Don't stop."

It seemed every muscle in her body clenched as the pleasure rose. She rose with it, feeling it twirl through her, take her captive, and bind her with its power. The pleasure became so acute it was almost pain, and her whole body shook with it.

And still she wanted more. "Harder!" she cried hoarsely.

And when he obliged her, she convulsed and gave in, crying out.

He caught her and pulled her close to him, holding her tightly as her mind spun. She caught her breath finally, then looked up at him and smiled sheepishly.

"I'm sorry I yelled so loudly." She closed her eyes, embarrassed. "I don't know what came over me."

"I hope it comes over you again," he said, kissing the tip of her nose. "In fact, I'd like to make that happen now."

She was hugging her legs about him again, and he began to kiss her and stroke her body.

"I want you, Maddie. Even more now than before."

"I want you, too," she said between kisses. And, unbelievably enough, it was true. Her body was responding to his touch, becoming tense and expectant once again.

He kissed her cheek, her nose, the column of her neck. "You are so beautiful."

"I'm not."

He met her gaze with those dark smoky eyes. "You are. I wanted you the first time I saw you. I can't believe you're my wife."

Maddie felt her heart lurch, felt something very much like love pour into it, and then she quickly shook her head. These were words of seduction, not love. This was a man who wanted to charm her. She couldn't allow herself to believe his words. If she believed them, she would fall in love with him.

And no matter what else happened in this marriage, she would not fall in love with a man who was so wrong for her. A man she knew would grow to hate her when she refused to allow him to control her.

He cupped her cheeks and looked down at her again. "You're mine," he said, kissing her possessively.

Her breath was stripped away. Lord, she believed he really did find her beautiful. He wanted her as much as she wanted him.

She had assumed all along that he wanted Ashley, and yet, he'd never said as much. Other than a boastful comment to his brother, he'd shown no interest in Ashley whatsoever, hadn't even looked back when he'd grabbed her hand and pulled her away from the blacksmith's shop in Gretna.

Maddie broke the kiss and looked into her husband's eyes. "You never wanted to marry Ashley, did you? You aren't sad at all that the wedding was mixed up."

He blinked at her, looking confused. "Sad? Hell, I'm relieved. When I realized the priest was doing everything wrong, I couldn't believe my luck."

"You couldn't—you realized and didn't stop him?"

Jack bent so that his face was a hairbreadth from hers. "Why? When I knew it meant I would have you?"

Maddie swallowed hard and tried not to melt at his words. Jack wanted her. Jack desired her.

And she wanted him as well. She desired him. She had begun to care for him.

She was in deep trouble.

Jack slid his hands around to cup Maddie's sweet bottom. Her skin was smooth and slick from the water, and her flesh intoxicatingly warm. He was so hard for her, he could barely think straight.

She was looking at him with those blue eyes, her lids lowered invitingly. He pulled her tight against his erection, and she gasped in a breath and tilted her head back. Her long brown hair glistened wet in the sun, and the tops of her breasts emerged from the water. He kissed the soft skin of her neck, while his hands kept her body pressed against him.

Without being told what to do, she moved provocatively against him, and he knew he had to be inside her soon or lose all sense of control.

"Maddie," he growled in her ear. "Do you feel me?"

"Yes," she moaned, and rubbed her hard nipples against his chest. Her legs closed tight around his waist as he repositioned her. His cock grazed that hot, wet place he'd been dreaming about.

She opened her eyes then and looked at him. Desire clouded the usual startling blueness. "Stop teasing me," she said, voice low and husky.

He grinned. "Demanding, aren't you, Lady Blackthorne?"

He rubbed against her intimately, inserting just the tip of his cock inside her, letting her have a taste of what was to come. She shivered in his arms. "Please, Jack. Now."

His hands tightened as he moved deeper within her. He controlled the pace, lowering her onto his shaft with tortuous slowness. The heat of her was amazing. She was so warm and so tight, it took conscious effort not to explode. He wanted to be fully inside her before he gave in to the pleasure.

He eased himself in farther, and her legs tightened around him.

"Am I hurting you?" he whispered against her neck.

"A bit. It hurts, but it also feels . . . oh, Jack."

His fingers had found her engorged nub, and he caressed it lightly until she was squirming against him. Her nails bit into his shoulder as she pressed to get closer, closer. But he held her back, wanting to spare her as much pain as possible.

He slid his finger over her again, and he felt her tense around his hard cock. "Jack," she cried, and this time when she bucked against him, he allowed it to happen. He plunged into her, burying his shaft deep inside. He heard a gruff shout mingled with her heaving cries and realized he had made the sound.

He couldn't help it. She felt so good. Grasping her buttocks again, he embedded himself deeply. She moaned, and he had enough presence of mind left to ask, "Am I hurting you? Did I hurt you?"

"Yes, but don't stop. It's a good hurt . . . oh, Jack."

He withdrew and plunged in again, the sharp contrast between the cool water and her explosive heat bringing him to climax all too soon. He thrust deeper, and her warmth enveloped him, tightened around him, and with a shout he let go.

He poured himself into her, his orgasm so strong that he couldn't stop a growl from escaping his lips. He lowered his mouth to her neck, biting her gently, leaving a small red mark.

She was his now.

She was still naked when Jack carried her back to the stable. He left their damp clothes tossed over a wooden fence to dry. They both needed new garments, and he'd have to go into Gretna Green to secure the necessary funds and supplies to see them back home.

He settled her on one of the blankets spread out over the straw where they'd slept the night before. She stretched, her glorious body tempting him once again. But he knew it was too soon for her, so instead of taking her into his arms again, as he would have liked, he said, "Tired?"

Eyes half closed, she murmured, "Mmm-hmm. Come lie with me." Her voice was low and sultry, and the sound made his chest tighten. She opened her arms to him, and it was an invitation he couldn't resist.

Just lie beside her, Jack, he told himself. But as soon as his leg touched hers, she rolled over and embraced him. Her limbs tangled with his, and he felt himself growing hard again.

Corn, he thought. I'll think about corn. Or potatoes.

She snuggled her cheek on the curve of his shoulder, wrapped one arm around his chest and looked up at him.

"Jack?"

Stew and potatoes. Potatoes with corn . . .

He glanced down at her, at those big sapphire

eyes peering up at him. "Go to sleep," he said.

She blinked. "But it's the middle of the afternoon."

Damn. Good point. "We're leaving tomorrow. You need your rest."

"Fine." She snuggled into him again, her long lashes brushing against his neck when she blinked. He could smell her, that sweet feminine scent taking him unawares. Making his hands itch to touch her. He licked his lips, and he could still taste her.

Potato pudding. Cornmeal . . .

"Jack?" she murmured, and then yawned. *Thank God.*

"Sleep," he repeated.

"I will. Jack?"

Bloody hell. "What?"

"That was wonderful. In the pond, I mean."

He felt an arrogant smile break on his face. "I know."

She looked up at him again, and he tried to frown at her but couldn't quite manage it. "Is that all you wanted to say?"

He thought a moment. "Yes."

With a scowl, she shook her head and turned from him. But he grabbed her and pulled her back. "I liked it, too," he said.

She smiled and closed her eyes. "Thank you."

When her breathing deepened, Jack put his arms behind his head, stared at the ceiling, and slowly exhaled. Maybe this marriage wouldn't be so disastrous after all. He'd married her, made love to her, and he hadn't fallen in love with her yet. Maybe she hadn't been as dangerous to him as he'd thought. Maybe he truly was immune to the softer emotions.

He planned to keep it that way.

He'd told her they would leave for home tomorrow. He'd be glad to have her under his roof and in his bed. But he didn't relish the return to London and his inevitable dealings with Bleven.

If Nick was smart, he'd stay out of Bleven's path for a while, just until Jack paid the Black Duke a visit. If there was any truth to what Bleven had said in the clearing, he would make sure Bleven suffered the consequences.

But the confrontation would take careful planning. Bleven was not a man to underestimate, and he would not rush their meeting. In the meantime, he couldn't let his guard down. Maddie had to be protected at all costs. If his new wife tripped into Bleven's path . . .

Jack took a deep breath.

No, he'd protect his new wife, even if it meant locking her in his house and keeping her under guard. No one was going to touch her. And all this do-gooder business of hers had to stop. Good Samaritans were nothing more than prey for the lowlifes of the world. He had seen it before, a do-gooder cut down by the very scum she was trying to help. He wouldn't let that happen to Maddie.

He glanced at her, watched her chest rise and fall steadily. She might not like his interference at first, but that was too bad.

It was for her own good.

Chapter 15

Maddie paced outside the livery, waiting for Jack. In the distance she could hear the roar of a crowd and what sounded like dogs barking, but the little town was otherwise quiet.

She took three steps forward, watched the wrinkled lavender bows on her gown teeter drunkenly, then turned and took three steps back. She desperately needed a new gown. The lavender and white dress had dried overnight, but it was hopelessly crumpled and more dingy gray than creamy white.

She peered across the street and saw the dressmaker's shop. She knew Jack wanted her to wait outside the livery, in front of the window, where he could see her, but she itched to take a look in the shop.

She wasn't worried about her father. The sweet couple who'd allowed Jack and her to stay in their stable had told her that the Earl of Castleigh left for London after he roused the priest and saw the marriage certificate. Even the Earl of Castleigh could not doubt his daughter's marriage.

Maddie hoped her father wasn't too worried . . . or too angry. She'd call on him as soon as she and Jack arrived in Town.

She did worry about Ashley and Lord Nicholas, however. They seemed to have disappeared from Gretna Green. Jack had told her that his brother could look after himself, but Maddie made him promise to inquire after Ashley and her new husband.

The crowd in the distance grew louder, and Maddie frowned.Why did she keep hearing dogs?

She squinted through the dingy window of the livery again and saw Jack deep in conversation with the owner. Jack wanted loan of a carriage and coachman to drive them back to London and was probably haggling over the price. He'd been in there a quarter of an hour, so obviously the owner was not as impressed at having a marquess in his store as Jack had anticipated.

She didn't doubt Jack would get what he wanted, but in the meantime, why shouldn't she walk down to the shop? Or see what the crowd was cheering about? The longer she listened, the uneasier she grew. Her belly felt tight and knotted.

Jack turned and looked at her, and she gave him a reassuring wave. With a nod, he went back to haggling.

Certain her new husband would be in the shop for another quarter hour at least, Maddie slipped away. She had to cross one street to reach the dress shop. It wasn't far at all, and she'd be gone only a moment.

Jack wouldn't mind, she thought, and started across the street, walking slowly to observe the crowd at the far end. Maybe she should slip down and look . . .

No. She was going straight to the dress shop and back to Jack. That was all. She was not going to investigate all that barking and growling.

She tried to move forward, then paused. Perhaps the dress shop could wait five minutes. She would just take a quick peek at whatever the crowd had encircled.

Maddie turned and headed toward the cheering people. As she neared, her heart pounded and the blood thumped in her head like a hammer. Before she could think about it or stop herself, she pushed through the circle of men before her, ignoring the large sweaty bodies. No one paid her the least attention. All eyes were focused on the spectacle before them.

"No," Maddie breathed, reeling back in horror.

Surrounded by the crowd, which was held back by ropes, she saw a large stake. Chained to the stake by his neck was a beautiful black bear with the saddest eyes she'd ever seen. Two large bulldogs growled and lunged at the bear, who swiped at them with his enormous claws.

The bear was bleeding from a wound to its shoulder and left flank, and Maddie could see by the way he moved, that the poor animal was in pain. The dogs lunged again, and one clamped onto the bear's tender snout. The bear howled in anguish before knocking the dog off, leaving angry red scratches on the dog's side.

"Stop it!" Maddie screamed. She hadn't meant to call out, but she couldn't seem to stop herself. "Stop this at once."

But no one appeared to hear her. In fact, the man beside her pushed her aside so he could get a better view.

"Did you hear me?" Maddie yelled. "Stop this—"

"Oh, shut up, willna?" another man told her. "I canna enjoy the sport with all yer screaming."

"But this is cruel," she countered. "We cannot allow this to continue."

"Look, lass," another man said, turning to face her with an angry jerk. "I doona want to hear yer chatter again. Go home, Sassenach."

"But—"

A hard hand clamped on her shoulder and jerked her back. "We were just leaving," Jack said.

Maddie spun round to face him as he took her hand and dragged her away from the savage scene. "But Jack," she protested, "did you look—"

There was a howl of pain, and she turned in time to see one of the dogs thrown to the ground. It was hurt badly, and she would have rushed to its aid if Jack hadn't continued to pull her away.

"Jack," she said, digging her heels in once they reached the main street. "We have to go back. We have to help that bear."

She wasn't prepared for the anger in his eyes when he rounded on her, and she took a step back. "Forget about the goddamn bear," he growled. "I told you not to move. I told you to wait right outside the shop."

He was yelling at her, sounding just like her father, and Maddie straightened her back and attempted to speak civilly. "I did wait, but I didn't see the harm in walking to that dress shop and peeking inside."

"But you didn't go to the dress shop, did you?" He grabbed her wrist and tugged her toward a carriage that was now waiting outside the livery. She realized this must be the carriage he'd secured for them. "You could have been hurt," he said.

"I know."

At her apparent easy acquiescence, he turned and looked back at her.

"But that bear is hurt, Jack. Those poor dogs, too. How could I let that happen without trying to stop it? How can you let it go on?"

"Maddie . . ." He leaned down so she could see his eyes. "I'm having a hard enough time trying to keep you safe. What the hell am I supposed to do about a bear?"

She put her hands on her hips. "Well, if you

won't do something, I will. I'm not leaving that bear, Jack. If I have to stay in Gretna Green permanently—"

"We're returning to London. Now." He grabbed her arm and tried to push her toward the carriage. Maddie slapped him away, and a woman passing on the street gave them a curious look. "Stop it," he ground out between clenched teeth. "You're causing a scene."

"*You're* causing a scene," she retorted.

"Get in the carriage."

"No." She shook her head and crossed her arms over her chest. "And if you try and make me, I'll scream my head off."

"Goddamn, bloody—"

"Profanity won't help you," she said calmly. "Now, you can either help me or abandon me, but I'm not leaving without that bear."

She saw the muscle in Jack's jaw tense, saw his fists curl into hard balls. Then he grabbed her shoulders roughly. "Stand right here." He backed her up until her spine was pressed against the livery. "Do not move. Not your feet, your arms, not even your eyes. I swear by all that's holy, if you move one inch, I'll kill you, and that goddamn bear, too."

He stalked away from her and climbed in the carriage. As she watched the carriage pull away, Maddie bit her lip.

One day of marriage, and he'd already left her.

She knew she should have married Dover. At least he would have tried to help her with the bear. Mr. Dover would have—

She swallowed a sob. Poor Mr. Dover. He wouldn't ever be helping any bears after this. And it was all her fault. How was she ever going to atone for that sin?

She'd only begun to imagine all the punishments she deserved when the carriage with Jack returned, this time pulling a cage on wheels behind it. Maddie stared at the cage, then broke into a huge smile.

The bear was inside. Jack had the bear!

The carriage door opened and Jack stuck his head out. "Get in before the owner changes his mind."

Maddie scampered forward and jumped in. Jack rapped on the coach's roof and they were off.

Her husband started to say something, to chastise her, she was sure, but Maddie didn't let him say a word.

She climbed in his lap and kissed his frowning lips until, finally, he kissed her back.

"Jack, we have to stop in Carlisle," Maddie said.

Snuggled on his lap, her face buried in his neck, she couldn't see his scowl, but he made sure she knew about it. "No, we don't," he said. "We're getting as close to London as we can before dark."

He'd barely whisked the woman out of Gretna

Green in one piece. He was not letting her free in Carlisle. Who knew what mischief she would find there?

Not to mention that he didn't know if Bleven was still looking for them. Jack assumed the duke had returned to London after his defeat a few days ago, but he couldn't be certain. He didn't want to run into Bleven on the road in the middle of the night. He wanted to confront the Black Duke in London, when the time was right, and the advantage was his, not Bleven's.

So they weren't stopping in Carlisle. They'd travel as far as they could, and then he'd tuck Maddie away at an inn, where he could keep her safe for the night.

And where he could make love to her until dawn. He'd had her in the water and on the soft straw of the stable—she'd been too delicious to resist last night—but he'd never had her in a bed.

"I don't want to stop, either," Maddie said, interrupting his pleasant thoughts, "but Mr. Dover . . . "

She looked up at him, those big blue eyes full of unshed tears.

Oh, Jesus Christ! How was he supposed to fight against tears?

"I want to know what happened to him, Jack. And if he's—if he's d-d—" She swallowed loudly. "—gone, I have to pay my respects." She buried her head against his shoulder. "This is all my fault. I might as well have been the one who pulled the trigger."

At least that's what Jack thought she said. It was hard to understand her words under all the blubbering.

"You weren't responsible," he said, trying to sound reasonable. "Dover knew the risks."

"You don't understand, Jack. He didn't want to marry me. I persuaded him." She looked up at him again. "I can be very persuasive. Poor Mr. Dover. He never had a chance."

Jack thought Dover was probably swayed more by Maddie's good looks and ample charms than her rhetoric, but kept his opinion to himself. If she wanted to canonize Dover, he knew that arguing with her would only make him look bad.

"And he has two little children. Poor babies. How are they going to survive without him?"

"We don't even know if Dover is dead," Jack argued. "For all we know, your father missed."

Maddie grabbed his coat and hauled herself up. "Do you think so? Really?"

The hope in her eyes undid him—more even than the tears.

Bloody hell.

"Fine. We'll stop, and I'll make inquiries about the professor. But you are to stay in the carriage. Understand? No bears—" He glanced at the bear's cage behind the carriage and rolled his eyes. "— no dogs, no bunny rabbits."

Maddie nodded violently. "Stay in the carriage. I promise."

Jack gave the coachman instructions to stop in Carlisle, outside the posting house. It wouldn't be a total loss. While he made inquiries, they could change horses.

Ten minutes later they reached Carlisle, and he left Maddie in the carriage, with the bear in his cage behind. She was full of more promises not to leave or even think about leaving.

Skeptical, Jack turned back several times as he walked away, to make sure she hadn't moved. His first stop was a nearby tavern. It was the best place for local gossip. And he desperately needed a drink.

He ordered a gin, swallowed it in one gulp, and asked for another. A few minutes later he had the information he needed. He returned to the carriage, pleased to see that everything was as he'd left it. A few curious townspeople were milling about, trying to get a good look at the bear, but the coachman and the outriders were keeping them away.

Jack nodded to the coachman and then inclined his head toward the coach. The coachman gave him a reassuring wave. All was as he'd left it.

Jack allowed the muscles of his shoulders to relax. Maybe this marriage wouldn't be as difficult as he'd feared. His wife could follow his directions. She wasn't as unmanageable or stubborn as she'd seemed.

He opened the door of the coach, a smile on

his lips. "Guess what? Your professor— What the hell?"

"Jack! Don't yell. You'll upset him."

And right on cue, the small snot-nosed child in her lap began to bawl.

Jack stared, blinked, then stepped back and shut the carriage door. Outside the carriage, the kid's cries were muffled, and Jack closed his eyes.

He hadn't had that much gin, had he?

No.

Impossible.

Even when he'd spent the night drinking, coming home completely floored, he had never imagined seeing children.

Jack took a deep breath, opened the carriage door again, and winced. The kid was still wailing loud enough to wake the dead. Jack opened his mouth to say something, but his jaw was clenched too tightly.

"Now, Jack," Maddie said, holding her hand out. "Don't become distraught. I didn't leave the carriage."

Jack heaved in a deep breath and blew it out again. He stared at the urchin on her lap and willed the kid to shut up.

"And I didn't find any bears, dogs, or rabbits. That's what you said. You didn't mention children."

He was aware that his breath was coming in short, fast heaves. He probably looked like a man who'd just run three miles. But it was either that or punch a hole in the carriage.

"Jack, are you all right?" Maddie asked tentatively.

The child in her lap had finally stopped crying and now was hugging her, thumb stuck in its mouth, staring at Jack with more interest than fear. Jack didn't have much experience with children—they all looked the same to him—but he guessed the kid was somewhere between three and ten.

And it was probably a boy.

Or a girl.

He didn't know if it could talk, but it looked like it could walk. It was dirty, its clothes tattered, and its face crusted with snot.

Jack pointed to the kid. "Where did that come from?"

"That?" Maddie followed his finger and frowned. "Timmy?"

Oh, devil take him. It had a name. "We're not keeping it. I've already agreed to keep the bear."

"Well, a bear is hardly the same as a child."

"We're not keeping it!" Jack bellowed, and Timmy started crying again.

Maddie ran a hand over the child's dirty curls and glared at Jack. "If you keep yelling like that, I'm going to have to ask you to leave. I won't tolerate yelling in my carriage."

"*Your* carriage? This is my bloody carriage."

He'd almost yelled again, but managed to tamp his voice down at the last moment.

"Are you going to evict a defenseless woman and child? Is that the kind of man you are?"

"Oh, bloody hell." He wanted to hit his head on the carriage.

"Don't talk like that in front of Timmy."

Jack grasped the sides of the carriage, took one deep breath, then another. "Maddie, I'm asking you as calmly as possible. Where did this—Timmy— come from?"

"Is that all you wanted to know?"

He narrowed his eyes menacingly.

"I was going to tell you," she said. "If you hadn't started yelling."

"Maddie—"

"Very well. I was sitting here waiting for you to return with word of—oh, Jack, did you find out about Mr. Dover?"

Jack held up a finger. "Timmy first."

She frowned. "As I said, I was waiting for you to return when I happened to look out the back window. I wanted to see how the bear fared, and I suggested to the coachman that he might bring the poor creature some water. Did he? Blackjack looks thirsty."

"Blackjack?"

Maddie nodded. "The bear."

Dear God, she'd named it. They were never going to get rid of the beast now.

"You looked out the back window . . . " Jack prompted.

"Right, and when I did, I saw Timmy standing all by himself, looking at Blackjack." She looked down at Timmy and smiled. The boy smiled back, and Jack saw that the child was missing his front teeth. "And I called Timmy over and—"

"Wait." Jack held up a hand. "You weren't supposed to call strangers over. You were supposed to wait in the carriage."

"I didn't leave the carriage, and you never said I couldn't speak to small children. Really, Jack."

"Go on," he said through clenched teeth.

"Timmy told me he was lost. He doesn't remember where he lives, and I was just asking where he last saw his mama when you returned and began yelling."

"We're not keeping him," Jack said, pointing at the boy.

Maddie rolled her eyes. "He has a mother, Jack. We just need to find her."

"And I suppose that's my job."

Maddie shrugged. "I'll be happy to do it. Just move out of my way—"

Jack held his arms out. "Do not leave the carriage. I'll be right back."

He closed the carriage door on his wife and little Timmy, and turned to see the coachman looking at him with raised brows. "Ready, my lord?"

Jack blew out a breath. "Not yet."

"Yes, my lord. But we're losing daylight, and you said—"

Jack walked away. More and more, he was hoping Bleven would find them. A quick bullet to the brain and Maddie, Timmy, and Blackjack—why the hell had she named the beast Blackjack?— would no longer be his problem.

And he'd thought Nicholas was trouble.

An hour later Timmy and his mother enjoyed a lengthy reunion. There were tears and embraces and profuse expressions of gratitude.

Jack sat in the carriage and scowled while Maddie hugged Timmy and his mother at least a dozen times. He'd tried to urge her to hurry the reunion along, but she ignored him. Finally, he pulled her into his lap, waved good-bye, and closed the carriage door.

"Jack!" Maddie said, the worry line he'd like to banish appearing between her brows. "That was rude."

"You think it would have been better if I'd done this in front of little Timmy?" And he bent and took her mouth with his. When he pulled back, she was breathless. "More? Or are you still worried about Timmy?"

She pulled his head down. "I'm sure Timmy's fine. Kiss me again."

He did, then traced his lips along her jawline to the soft spot on her neck, just below her ear.

"You drive me mad," she whispered.

He knew the feeling. She was driving him mad,

and not just with her wriggling body. He'd known she was a do-gooder, but he hadn't anticipated it would go this far. Bears, lost children, he was afraid to ask what was next.

Suddenly, she jumped back. "Jack, I forgot about Dover. You found out about him?"

He nodded and opened his mouth to tell her, but she was shaking her head.

"I cannot believe I forgot about him. I'm a horrible person."

"He's not dead, Maddie."

"He's lucky not to have married me, God rest his soul. He's— Wait, he's not dead?"

Jack shook his head and tried not to smile. He'd never met anyone who cared so much about everything and everyone. One minute a bear. The next a lost boy. "Dover is fine. Several people told me that your father only grazed the professor's shoulder. He was up and walking around before we'd even left Carlisle."

"But where is he now?" Maddie asked. "Is he still in Carlisle? Should we offer to take him back to Town?"

Jack didn't know where the hell Dover was, and he didn't really want to find out. He certainly wasn't having Maddie's former fiancé sharing his carriage—not when he wanted Maddie all to himself.

"Maddie," Jack said, drawing her back to him and kissing her again. "Dover is fine. He can take care of himself."

"But, Jack—"

"Forget him." He nuzzled her neck and pushed her gown off her shoulders. He kissed the soft skin there.

"I can't," she whispered.

Jack slipped his hand in her gown and kneaded her breast, taking the hard nipple between thumb and forefinger. She arched against him, and Jack murmured, "Forget him."

Pressing her body closer, she moaned. "Maybe just for a little while."

Chapter 16

It turned out to be quite a long while, as Maddie didn't think about Dover again for several hours. Making love in a coach had been fun, exhilarating, and, she was certain, most improper—even for a married woman. But Jack had ignored her admittedly weak protests. And, as usual, she had to acknowledge that when Jack wanted something, he usually got it.

That worried her somewhat. Her husband was even bossier now than he'd been before. She decided it was probably because they were newly married and that it was understandable that a new husband would feel protective of his new bride.

They stopped for the night in a small town with a pretty name that immediately flew out of Maddie's head. She was so hungry and so tired and so ready for a bath that nothing else mattered.

Well, except for Blackjack. She waited to be certain that the bear was settled comfortably and had been given food and water. One of the outriders was engaged to keep watch over the bear all night, and only after Maddie had spoken to the youth herself did she feel confident enough to go up to her room.

And Jack.

Earlier, he'd followed her so closely that he'd all but stepped on her toes, until she'd finally convinced him to go upstairs and take a bath. He had, but he'd engaged the other outrider to shadow her. Now, Maddie waved the boy away and paused outside her bedroom. Hearing the unmistakable sound of water sloshing against a tub, she took a deep breath.

She hadn't forgotten how wonderful Jack looked that first morning of their marriage. Even now, just thinking about all that bronze skin and those hard muscles made her stomach tighten and the spot between her legs feel damp.

Her hand trembled as she opened the door and stepped into the room. It was dim, lit only by a pair of candles, but she saw Jack immediately. To her disappointment, he was not naked. His hair was wet and his back bare, but he'd pulled on his trousers and was standing at the open window, looking out.

"I'm almost afraid to turn around," he said when she closed the door behind her. "First it was a bear, then a child. Don't tell me you've found a lion this time."

"That's not funny, Jack." But she couldn't stop

a small smile. When people met her, they were always surprised at how those in need seemed to gravitate toward her. It was as though she was a beacon for the sick and injured, the poor and helpless.

He turned then and took her in. "You're tired," he said. "And it's my fault you haven't had much rest."

She blushed. "I didn't mind."

He crossed to her, took her hand and drew her to him. "But I do." He put his hand on her cheek. "Another day and these circles will be as dark as your beautiful sapphire eyes."

Maddie felt her heart seize. He knew the color of her eyes. It was too dark in the room for him to see them clearly, which meant he knew without even looking. She felt the sting of tears and swallowed hard to keep them from falling.

Jack led her toward the empty tub on the floor near the crackling fire in the hearth. "I had them take away the used water and bring fresh." He lifted one of several buckets on the floor and poured the steaming water into the tub.

"Jack, you don't have to do that."

"Oh, it's not for your benefit." He emptied another bucket into the tub and winked at her. "Whatever it takes to get you naked faster. Start undressing."

A rush of heat coursed through her, and Maddie felt suddenly self-conscious. She knew she was his wife, and Jack had seen her without clothing before. He'd seen her quite intimately and in full daylight, but somehow the two of them alone in this room with its flickering candles, warm fire, and waiting bed made her new position all the more obvious.

She was his *wife*. She was Lady Blackthorne, who made love in ponds and carriages and took delight in the sight of her husband's unclothed body. She belonged to Jack, and he to her. Her emotions surged when she thought about the momentous thing they had done in marrying each other. And yet, she shied away from giving her emotions free rein. She knew she could so easily fall in love with Jack. He was everything she desired in a man. And everything she wanted to avoid.

She had the sinking feeling that outside of the bedroom, little about their marriage would be blissful.

"I'm waiting," he said, pouring the last of the warm water into the hip tub. "Or maybe you'd like my assistance."

Maddie quivered with pleasure at the thought of his hands on her body.

"I'll take that as a yes."

And before she could say anything—think of a way to express all the emotions she was experiencing at that moment—Jack was beside her, his large warm hands flicking the buttons on the back of her gown open. His breath was on her bare neck, his fingers inching her gown over her shoulders, and Maddie couldn't stop herself from leaning back against him.

His bare chest felt delicious against her exposed skin. He smelled like soap and faintly of mint.

Then Jack bent on one knee and turned Maddie to face him. He took her slipper in one hand, and she held onto his shoulder while he removed it and then its partner. Throughout the task, he never stopped touching her. A finger here, his arms there, his mouth . . .

And then his hands were on her legs, inching her shift upward, revealing more and more of her body to him as he undressed her. She closed her eyes as the shift cleared her head, and didn't open them again until she felt his arms come around her.

"So beautiful," he whispered, his hands tracing the line of her spine and then branching out to caress her hips. He guided her to the tub and held her hand as she stepped in. When she sank into the warm water, she let out a slow sigh of contentment.

"Feel good?" Jack asked from behind her. His hands came around her neck, and he began to knead away at her sore and tired muscles.

Maddie could only moan an incoherent response as his magic hands slid over her wet skin, teasing away the aches and pains and slipping her closer and closer to sleepy contentment.

But Jack wasn't about to allow her to sleep. Not yet. His hands dipped in the water, and when she leaned forward, his fingers, slippery from the soap, glossed over her.

Now she knew why he smelled of mint. The soap's fragrance refreshed her—or perhaps it was the feel of his slick hands sliding around to cup her breasts.

"Oh, Jack," she murmured as his hands dove down to her belly and lower still.

"You want me to touch you?" he whispered in her ear.

"Please."

The lower his hands strayed, the more she ached for him. He rose, moved to the front of the tub, and she saw the evidence of his need for her. He was full and hard, his trousers straining from the force of his desire.

Wantonly, she opened her legs for him when he knelt before her, but Jack shook his head. "Not yet."

He took her foot, lifted it out of the small tub and rubbed it clean. Then his hands slid up her leg, moving in slow, deliberate strokes, closer to where she ached for him. But just as she began to shake with anticipation, his hands slid back down again and he repeated the torture with her other leg.

This time, she knew, he would touch her, and she shook with need as his hands skated over her flesh, coming nearer and nearer to her core. She closed her eyes tightly, feeling as though she might explode with even the merest touch, but just when she rose to meet him, his hands skipped away again.

She opened her eyes and glared at him.

"Something wrong?" he asked, mischief in his twinkling eyes.

She bit her lip. "No."

"I want to wash your hair," he said, coming around behind her again. Maddie noticed that he'd left one pail of water beside the hearth, and she was glad for his clear thinking. She was so distracted tonight. She would have poured all the water in and left nothing with which to rinse off.

Jack began to pull the pins from her hair, and Maddie reached back to stop him. "You don't need to do that. I can wash it."

"Oh, but I want to," he growled in her ear. "I love your hair."

"You do?" No one had ever told her that before. No one had ever made her feel as beautiful and desirable as Jack did.

A moment later her hair was heavy with suds, and the smell of mint surrounded her. Jack's fingers were indeed enchanted as he massaged her scalp, coaxing away the last of her tension and worry.

She was half asleep when his hands finally ceased their ministrations, and she didn't even feel embarrassed at her nudity when he pulled her to her feet in the tub. She was the shameless Lady Blackthorne after all.

"Ready?"

She nodded, not certain what he had in mind, but knowing whatever it was, she wanted it. Warm water trickled over her head and slid down her body. She leaned her head back so the suds from her hair wouldn't fall in her eyes, and she heard Jack's quick intake of breath.

She smiled. Good. At least she wasn't the only one affected.

The water cascaded over her, soft as her lover's touch, and when the soap had been washed away, Jack wrapped her in warm linen and led her close to the fire.

She wrapped her arms around him, reaching on tiptoes to kiss him. "That was wonderful."

"Oh, wonderful hasn't even begun." He reached between them, stripping her of the linen and feasting on the sight of her. Maddie opened her arms to him, and he came to her, kissing her until she could no longer think of anything but him.

His hands roved over her, and she was equally liberal in her caresses of him. She ran her fingers over his chest, memorizing its angles and planes, loving the way he tensed at some of her touches and how his skin seemed to heat when she touched him in other ways.

She couldn't get enough of him, and now that his bruises were fading, she felt free to explore him. He allowed it, and when her hands dipped to the waistband of his trousers, his dark gaze met hers.

She unfastened his trousers, pushed them over his hips, and when he stepped put of them, she took his hard manhood in her hand. It pulsed in her grip, its velvety smoothness such a contrast to its unforgiving hardness.

She caressed the length of it lightly, trying to gauge by Jack's reaction how much she pleased him. "You're driving me mad," he said when she squeezed him gently at the base of the shaft. "I need to be inside you."

His hands slipped between her legs, and though she was slick with need for him, she couldn't stop a small cry of pain at his touch.

"Damn it." He pulled back and took her by the shoulders.

"I'm sorry," Maddie began. "I didn't mean—"

"Shh. It's my fault. Of course you're sore. I should have realized. We'll stop."

"But, Jack, I don't want to stop."

One brow rose in a cocky gesture she was beginning to know well.

"What do you have in mind, sweetheart?"

Maddie shook her head. "I don't know. I—I just want you."

He walked to a chair in the corner, grasped it and

pulled it toward her. She watched his lithe body move in the firelight and wanted him even more.

"Sit here," Jack told her. Maddie frowned. What new game was this? But she'd learned that in matters of the flesh, he knew her better than she knew herself. She did as he said.

"Open your legs," Jack told her.

Maddie stared at him and didn't move. But he took her hand, kissed it, and pressed it to her womanhood. "If I can't touch you, you'll have to do it."

Oh, but this was too wanton. She couldn't touch herself. Not in front of him. "Jack—"

"Open your legs, Maddie. Or should I call you Lady Blackthorne?" The way he was looking at her fired her blood again and hot desire rushed through her. All his touches, all his kisses—she wanted him, wanted pleasure.

And though she still felt shy, she also knew that there was no one besides her husband that she would rather share this intimate moment with. Only Jack. Now and always Jack.

Her hand moved lightly against her flesh, and Jack nodded, his dark eyes even darker than usual. "Do what feels good to you."

Maddie nodded, wanting to do what would please him, what would keep the desire hot and dark in his eyes. Lady Blackthorne was a seductress. She lifted her hands and cupped her breasts, feeling their weight, watching the nipples grow stiff and hard as her pleasure rose. She pinched one nipple, and Jack's breath grew heavy. His manhood was rigid and ready as she slid her hands down her abdomen.

Her hands met at the juncture of her thighs and slowly, so slowly, she opened her legs. Jack's gaze burned into her, making her feel warm and restless. She shifted, parted her outer lips, the way Jack had, and tapped one delicate finger against the sensitive nub that brought her so much pleasure when he touched it.

Jack let out a slow, agonized breath as Maddie began to tease the bud into aching sensitivity. Her eyes still on him, she brought her finger to her mouth, touched her tongue to the finger, and dipped it back between her legs.

"Oh, God, Maddie," Jack groaned. He touched himself, then brought his hand away, as though wanting to prolong the agony, as though not wanting to miss a moment of her ecstasy.

The moist finger against her tender bud caused a shock of sensation between her legs, the pleasure rippling into her belly and coiling into a tight spring.

She threw her head back and rode the heightened sensation, no longer caring that Jack watched her. She was a slave to the pleasure that built and built but would not peak. She dipped her finger in her mouth again, but before she could touch herself, Jack was between her legs. "I have to taste you," he said, voice hoarse. And he thrust her legs farther apart and put his mouth on her.

His slick, skilled tongue was her undoing. One

touch and she writhed beneath him. Her body shook with small spasms of pleasure. So much pleasure, and yet she knew there was more. He grasped her hips, holding her still as he plundered her gently. Maddie was aware that she was gasping, that her hands were fisted in his hair, and that the coil in her belly was so tight she thought she would die if she didn't find release.

And then the coil unraveled—not slowly, but in one quick jolt everything came undone. She jerked and cried out with pleasure, bringing her legs closed at the intensity. And still Jack continued to touch her, making her scream with the power of her climax.

Finally, he released her, rising up before her, pushing his hard manhood into her hand. Her hands were slick, and she moved them up and down his shaft, her fingers trembling and unsteady, but he was ready for her. With a cry, he threw his head back and climaxed, his seed spilling onto her chest, where it felt warm and heavy against her breast.

She herself felt warm and heavy. She closed her eyes, only vaguely aware of Jack cleaning her with the linen and soap, brushing her hair back from her face, and lifting her into his arms.

She dreamed of a growling black bear who, when she ran her hand along the soft fur of his head and scratched behind his ears, closed its eyes and purred.

* * *

On the fourth day of the trip back to London, when the coachman announced they were nearing Islington, Jack shook Maddie awake. Somewhere along the way he'd acquired a new gown for her—white with small yellow flowers—and now she straightened it and rubbed her eyes.

"We're home?" she said, her voice groggy. Beside him, she was warm and adorably disheveled, the yellow bow she'd tied in her hair falling lopsided over one cheek.

"Almost, sweetheart. Next stop is my town house."

And his bed.

They'd traveled hard these last few days, and he hadn't wanted to tire Maddie further by keeping her up late at night with his attentions. He hadn't touched her, and as a result wanted her more than ever. And he still hadn't made love to her in a bed.

He'd change that tonight.

"Do you think Blackjack knows we're almost home?" she asked.

Damn. He'd forgotten about the bear. What the hell was he going to do with a bear in the middle of London? If his country house weren't currently under renovation, he would have taken Maddie and the bear there. The estate had twelve bedrooms and as many beds. He would have liked to explore his wife's passionate nature in each of them. But as it was, they were forced to return to London—and Bleven.

Jack clenched his fists. He would finally have answers. And revenge.

"I think the bear is the least of our worries," he told Maddie, who was straightening her hair bow.

"Do you think Lord Nicholas and Ashley have returned yet?" she asked, peeking out the window, practically bouncing with excitement now.

"We'll know soon enough."

Jack gave the coachman the last bit of directions to his town house on Brook Street and pulled Maddie away from the window to snuggle her beside him.

She immediately reached up and kissed his cheek. "I can't wait to see your house and meet all your servants. Ridgeley, in particular, sounds wonderful."

"Ridgeley had better toe the line. He's the one responsible for this mess. If he hadn't told Nick where I was, I'd never have had that run-in with Bleven."

"Then you might never have met me," Maddie said. "And I'd be married to Dover right now, and Blackjack would probably be dead."

The bear again. Jack scowled. What the hell was he going to do with a three hundred pound bear?

The coach slowed, and Maddie took his hand. She always seemed to know when something was bothering him. "Everything will work out for the best," she said.

He raised a skeptical brow. "You keep telling yourself that, sweetheart." He shook his head. Little optimist. Damn, if he didn't actually like that about her.

A liveried footman opened the carriage door, and the late afternoon light spilled inside. Jack descended first, reaching back to help Maddie climb down.

Ridgeley had come out to meet them, the old man's blue eyes widening a fraction when he saw Maddie. It was a subtle gesture, one Jack wouldn't have noticed if he hadn't known the butler for twenty years.

Jack led Maddie up the steps to his town house, nodding to Ridgeley as he opened the door. "Welcome home, Lord Blackthorne. Lady Blackthorne," the old butler said without even a pause.

"Ridgeley," Jack said, nodding back, meanwhile noting that most of the rest of his staff was quickly assembling in the entryway. Not as polished as Ridgeley, they stared at Maddie with open curiosity.

She smiled at the stiff-necked butler. "Good afternoon, Ridgeley. I see you've heard the news of our recent marriage." Jack saw the worry line appear between her brows. "I'm afraid we must be the latest *on dit*."

"The Martingale family has always been popular in Society," his butler replied.

She raised a brow at Jack. "So I hear."

"I suppose introductions are in order," Jack drawled, feeling the weight of his title pressing down on him. Amazing how little he'd felt like a marquess the last few days and how heavy the responsibility, now that he had it back.

But his main priority was keeping his new wife safe. He wanted a quiet, uneventful return. When they were settled in, he would determine the best way to approach Bleven. Until then, he intended to keep her hidden away. And as he'd be hiding with her, it might prove an enjoyable undertaking.

He began the introductions with his housekeeper, Mrs. Gardener, and moved down the line. A true earl's daughter, Maddie smiled and greeted each servant, putting the staff at ease and quickly winning their approval. Hell, no wonder he'd liked her so much from the start. She could charm an ornery bear.

Unfortunately, she had.

Jack was introducing the second downstairs maid—why the hell did he need all these servants again?—when the pounding began on the door.

He swung round.

Damn. So much for his unobtrusive return.

Ridgeley opened the door, spoke quietly with the guest, and then addressed Jack. "Lord Castleigh to see you, my lord. Are you at home?"

Jack scowled. He should have known Castleigh would post men to watch for his return.

"Daddy?" Maddie said, grabbing Jack's arm. "Oh, jiminy. I hope he didn't bring his pistol."

"Pistol?" the housekeeper said in alarm.

"I bloody well know he's at home," a voice, presumably Castleigh's, boomed from the other side of the door. "I saw the bear out front."

"Bear?" one of the maids said, her voice rising.

A footman, close to the window, pointed outside. "That's right. They've brought a huge black bear with them. It's got fangs and claws big enough to eat the lot of us."

Jack opened his mouth, but Maddie had already stepped in. "Oh, no, that's just Blackjack. He's a nice bear. He'd never eat you. He's going to live here with us."

"Live with a bear!"

A few of Jack's servants were backing up, and hysteria showed on their faces.

"Calm down—" Jack began.

"My lord, are you home?" Ridgeley repeated, voice even and expression bland.

"Oh, bloody hell, just let me in." Castleigh pushed past Ridgeley, who looked down his nose at the intruding earl.

"I present the Earl of Castleigh."

"It's the man with the pistol!" someone screeched, and a few of the servants ducked behind the statues and plants in the vestibule.

"And he's got the bear," someone behind a Roman bust called out.

"He doesn't have a pistol!" Maddie assured

them, but Jack saw her glance at her father suspiciously. "And the bear is outside."

Jack was tempted to peer out the window just
to be certain. At this point he wasn't ruling anything out.

Maddie gave her father an imploring look.
"Daddy, tell them the bear isn't going to hurt
them," she said, approaching him. "They won't
listen to us."

The servants quieted and all eyes turned to
Lord Castleigh. Or at least Jack assumed they did.
He couldn't see his servants from their hiding
places behind the statues.

Castleigh smiled. "Oh, I'm sure the bear won't
eat you."

Maddie sighed. "See?"

"No more than the wolf she brought home one
winter in the country," Castleigh continued. "It
only took off half our footman's arm."

Jack closed his eyes.

"Daddy!" Maddie glared at her father. "You
know it was only a finger or two." She spun back
to look at her new staff. "Really, we told him to
stop tormenting the poor wolf. It was the man's
own fault that he was bitten."

Gasps and squeals erupted around Jack, and
the servants rushed away, leaving the statues
teetering. Ridgeley, Maddie, and Castleigh stood
in the vestibule.

Jack put a hand to his head and tried to soothe
the pounding behind his eyes.

"Welcome to the family, Blackthorne," Castleigh boomed.

"Tea, my lord?" Ridgeley asked.

Jack shook his head. "Bring me a brandy. The bottle."

Chapter 17

"If you're going to shoot me," Jack said, taking a seat behind the large oak desk in his library, "can you wait until I finish the brandy?"

Ridgeley had brought two glasses and a pot of tea, and Jack poured brandy for himself and his new father-in-law, while Maddie glared at the men and poured herself tea.

"He's not going to shoot you, Jack," she said, setting the teapot down. "Are you, Daddy?"

Castleigh sipped his brandy and smiled again. Jack didn't like that smile. It looked more like a smirk. "Oh, no. I don't have to shoot your new husband, Madeleine." He set the glass on the desk. "You'll kill him all by yourself."

"Daddy. Stop it."

Castleigh spread his arms. "Not that he needs you to do him in, dear. I hear he has problems of his own. The Black Duke?" Castleigh shook his head. "Not an enemy I'd have courted."

Not an enemy Jack particularly wanted either. But he would deal with Bleven when the time came.

Jack propped his feet on his desk and motioned Maddie closer to him. She came, and he put an arm around her waist. Castleigh's eyes narrowed. The man might act smug, but Jack knew he wouldn't be here if he weren't concerned for his daughter. Castleigh might even hate him—and Jack really couldn't blame him for that—but he wanted the best for Maddie.

Jack pulled her flush against him. "Why are you here, Castleigh? It's obviously not to wish us felicitations on our happy union."

"Is it a happy union, then?" the earl asked, turning his glass. "I call it a hasty union. I was told she'd run off with that bumbling dog breeder. Had I known, sir, that you were next in line, I would have shot you as well."

"Daddy!" Maddie glared at him from across Jack's desk. "You cannot mean that. In fact, I think you owe me an apology for shooting my fiancé. Poor Mr. Dover."

"He's poor Mr. Dover no more. When you took off for Gretna, I left one of my men behind in Carlisle. Your poor Mr. Dover accepted a tidy sum to stay out of your life, Madeleine."

Maddie gasped. "You paid him off!"

Jack actually found himself smiling. Had he known Dover was susceptible to bribery, he would have done the same thing.

"That's despicable, Daddy." She frowned. "I suppose I don't need to write him that letter of apology now."

Castleigh rolled his eyes. "The dog breeder is no longer my concern." He looked at Jack. "Blackthorne, despite my best efforts to prevent an elopement, you've managed to succeed. Therefore, I believe I owe you a dowry."

Jack tensed and shook his head. "I don't want your money, sir. I didn't marry Maddie for her dowry."

"Oh, Jack." Maddie squeezed his hand.

"Touching," Castleigh said, "but let's see how you feel when you discover how expensive my daughter can be."

"I can afford her."

"Thus far."

"Thus far?" Jack asked.

"That's right, my boy." Castleigh gave Jack his empty glass and motioned for him to refill it. "You don't need the money yet. But who's going to pay for whatever injuries that bear causes your staff? I imagine the surgeon's fees will add up."

"Blackjack won't hurt anyone," Maddie protested. "Jack will build him a secure enclosure. He won't escape."

Castleigh kept his eyes locked on Jack. "That's what she said about the wolf. Cost me a tidy sum when that footman got bit. I'm still paying his salary, though the man hasn't worked for me in over five years. Difficult to work with half your arm missing."

Jack was about to take a large gulp of his brandy, but Maddie grabbed his arm. "Don't believe him,

Jack. Danvers is doing well, all things considered. He could even come back to work . . . if he didn't jump and cower in the corner every time someone makes a sudden movement."

Jack stared at her and tried not to picture the pitiful Danvers, with his mangled arm and tattered nerves.

"But if you don't want the dowry to cover bear injuries," Castleigh was saying, "then you'll want it to help with the dues."

"Dues?" Jack asked.

"Oh, they add up." Castleigh leaned back in his chair. "How many societies do you support, my dear? Fifteen? Twenty?"

Maddie was busy stirring her tea.

"Maddie?" Jack prodded.

"Maybe a few more," she murmured, staring into her teacup and avoiding his eyes.

"How many more?" Jack asked. "Twenty-five?"

She pursed her lips.

"Maddie," he growled.

"Only thirty-seven."

"Bloody hell."

"But someone has to support them, Jack," Maddie said, pulling away to face him. "Someone has to help the widows and the orphans and the homeless."

"And the gamblers and the drinkers," her father continued.

"They're trying to reform, Daddy!"

Jack put his head in his hands. He'd known do-gooders in his life. Hell, his own mother had been a do-gooder. But Maddie was the queen of Good Samaritans.

"And your societies have missed you," Castleigh was saying. "Your mother and I have had a constant stream of callers."

Maddie brightened. "How is Mother?"

"Tired," her father told her. He produced an enormous stack of calling cards from his greatcoat and began laying them on the oak desk. "She's had so many visitors calling for you. The ladies from the Widow's Benevolent Society, the Orphan's Munificent Society, the Foundling House, the Society for War Veterans, the Society for—" He paused to read the card. "—Widows of War Veterans."

Jack watched the small white cards cover his desk and glanced at Maddie. "Exactly how involved are you in these endeavors?"

"Very involved," she said with a decisive nod. "I make it a point to visit each charity twice a month."

Jack looked back at the mounting pile of cards. Foundling houses and war widows didn't live in the best areas of Town. Who knew what could happen to Maddie if she insisted upon visiting those places? She could be robbed or assaulted . . . or worse.

And with Bleven still a threat, he didn't want Maddie out of his sight.

Jack's hand skimmed over his desk, sending the cards flying. "Enough," he told Castleigh. He stood and faced Maddie. "This is ridiculous."

Castleigh leaned back and crossed his arms over his chest, his look turning smug. "Nice beginning, Blackthorne, though 'ridiculous' wouldn't have been my first choice."

Maddie ignored her father and bent to gather some of the fluttering cards. "I know it seems like a bit much," she admitted, "but once you get to know all the orphans and the widows, you'll change your mind."

"No, I won't." Jack pulled the cards out of her hands. "You can't save everyone, Maddie. At the very least, you must give up your visits."

"Exactly," Castleigh chimed in. "Said so many times."

"But they all need me, Jack. If I don't help, who will?"

Jack opened his mouth to respond, but was stalled by the pleading look in Maddie's eyes.

Castleigh was nodding. "That one always gets me, too."

Jack rounded on his father-in-law. "Do you mind?"

"Not a'tall." Castleigh settled deeper into his chair.

"Look, Maddie . . . " Jack reached out and took her hand, pulling her close. "I need you now. More than all of these societies."

"And I'll be here for you, Jack, but you can't

ask me to give up my life's work. This is my calling. This is what I was born to do."

Jack shook his head. "I admire your generosity, sweetheart, but I can't allow you to visit all of these organizations. If you want to give money, fine, but I won't have you running about London, risking your safety to help some snot-nosed orphan who'll probably pick your pocket, given half a chance."

Maddie inhaled sharply and snapped her hand away from him. Castleigh shook his head. "Should have cautioned you against that one."

Jack could tell the man was enjoying the argument. Maddie, however, was not. She was shooting daggers with her eyes. Her hands were on her hips, fists balled.

"You don't know the first thing about my work, Jack. And if you don't want to know, that's fine, but don't tell me what to do. You don't have the right."

"The hell I don't. I'm your husband. I swore to protect you, and I'm bloody well going to do it." From Bleven, from cutthroats . . . from herself, if need be.

"By locking me up and taking everything I care about away from me?" She shook her head vehemently. "I knew I shouldn't have married you. You're worse than he is." She pointed to her father.

"I only wanted to do what was best for you, Madeleine," her father said.

"And I just want to keep you safe," Jack added, trying to keep his voice reasonable.

But Maddie was well past reasonable. "*You're* trying to protect me? Jack, the day I met you, I was chased, shot at, and held at gunpoint by three thugs. I don't think you're one to protect me." She rounded on her father. "And, Daddy, I'm tired of you always thinking you know what's best for me. I'm a grown woman." With her skirts swishing, she marched toward the door. "*I* know what's best for me, and it's neither of you."

The door slammed behind her, and Jack slumped in his chair. Across from him, Castleigh offered to refill his glass. Jack accepted the brandy, downed it, and held the snifter out for more. Outside, he heard a suspiciously bearlike noise, followed by a maid's bloodcurdling scream, then Maddie's soothing voice.

"If you're going to shoot me," Jack told his new father-in-law, "now would be a good time."

Maddie couldn't believe how many of Jack's servants were afraid of sweet, little Blackjack. Not that Blackjack was all that little. He was about two feet taller than she was when he stood on hind legs and probably weighed more than three of her put together.

But he was much tamer than she first thought. He didn't even growl. When he was afraid, he made a blowing sound. And with all the screaming going on, who wouldn't be scared? She'd intended to house him in Jack's mews until an enclosure was built, but the groom argued that a bear would frighten the horses. Being new to the household, she was in no position to argue, so she decided to keep Blackjack in a guest room—safely behind lock and key, of course.

Once she had Blackjack settled and fed, Maddie asked the housekeeper to show her to her quarters. She had thought Jack would be the one to show her to her room, but he was still ensconced in his library with her father. And she was happy for both of them to stay there.

Lord, anyone would think she was an infant, the way those two tried to protect her. Did they truly think she didn't know the dangers associated with her work? That was why she'd never argued with her father when he insisted that she take a footman with her at all times. Not only that, she'd encouraged her father to hire the biggest, burliest footmen she could find.

Most were retired pirates and smugglers she met through her work, but she hadn't told her father that.

Maddie opened the door and surveyed her room. It had obviously been cleaned recently and hastily readied for her, but other than that, she could see that no special preparations had been made.

She glanced at the bed with its pretty yellow counterpane, then wandered over to the dressing table. Laid out on the tulipwood surface were a silver brush, comb, and mirror. The antique set was tarnished with age, though it had been well cared for and kept free of dust.

Maddie touched the set and wondered who they had belonged to. Jack's mother? It was difficult to imagine Jack as a child with parents. He was so serious, so capable. Had he ever been a rosy-cheeked boy who climbed trees and played pranks?

She yawned and wandered back to the bed. Her muscles exhausted, she ached to crawl under the counterpane. Once there, she found the bed soft and the sheets silky. She took a deep breath and her eyes drifted closed.

"Bloody hell!"

Maddie awoke with a start and blinked in confusion at the dark, unfamiliar surroundings. She was warm and comfortable, but now Jack was hauling her out of her little nest and tugging her into his arms.

"Jack, what's wrong?" she murmured, rubbing sleep from her eyes.

"What's wrong?" he barked, dragging her toward the door linking their two rooms. "I leave you alone for a couple of hours and you endanger my entire household."

Maddie dug her heels in before he could pull her into his room. "What are you talking about?"

Jack lifted the candle from the dresser. "There's a bear in my house. A maid tried to clean the guest room where you hid him and was scared to death. She just resigned her post."

Maddie winced. "I tried to put him in the

mews, but the groom said he made the horses nervous."

"We're getting rid of him in the morning," Jack announced, walking through the door to his room.

"What?" Maddie stomped after him, fury making her heart pound. "What has Blackjack done? He can't help it that the maid was scared."

"I'm not going to wait around for him to hurt my staff or you, Maddie. I've made up my mind. He's gone."

Jack tore off his tailcoat and dropped it on the burgundy Aubusson rug. The room was done in dark mahogany wood, offset by deep burgundy and navy. In the center there was a mammoth bed, much bigger than the one in her room. The headboard was ornately carved and highly polished, as was all the furniture.

It was a beautiful room, but Maddie wasn't impressed. Not with this room or with Jack. Why did he have to be so difficult? Why did he have to be so controlling? By jiminy, she was not going to put up with it.

Anger surged through her. The back of her neck was hot, and she felt her face flush. In a rage, she slammed the adjoining door as hard as she could, making the room shake.

"What the—" Jack spun to face her.

"So, you've made up your mind, have you, Jack?" She stalked toward him, hands on hips.

His eyes narrowed. "That's right."

"The bear is gone." She stomped closer, was almost on top of him.

He didn't back down, but she saw a muscle in his jaw tense. "That's right."

"I've made up my mind, too," she said, voice vibrating with fury. "If Blackjack leaves, so do I."

Chapter 18

Maddie turned on her heel, prepared to march back to her room and slam the door, sealing her grand exit, but Jack was too quick. He caught her around the waist and hauled her up against his broad chest. "You're not leaving," he growled in her ear.

"Don't tell me what to do."

She struggled against him, but his grip was like a steel clamp, and the longer she was pressed against him, the less she wanted to escape. The scent of pine and leather and Jack enveloped her as completely as his strong arms. She looked down and saw his powerful bronze hand spread out on her belly. His touch was warm, the heat radiating from his hand all the way to her toes.

"Then say you won't leave."

"Say Blackjack can stay."

"Damn it, Maddie. It's not safe to have a dangerous bear so close."

"We'll build him an enclosure."

"Not good enough. I want him gone."

"Let me go." She shoved at him again, but he pulled her tighter.

"I can't, sweetheart," he whispered, and she was surprised at the need and the vulnerability she heard in his voice. Or had she simply imagined it? His steel grip hadn't lessened. "I can't let you go. I won't."

"And I won't be a prisoner, kept under lock and key and your ridiculous mandates."

"You'd like my mandates." His lips tickled her ear, his wicked innuendo making her shiver.

"I might."

His hand slid lower, sending small swirls of pleasure into her belly and between her thighs. She was wet for him, and yet she refused to give in.

She turned her head so she could look into his dark eyes. "But I'm not another one of your servants, Jack. I won't be ordered about. I want to be your partner, your equal—in all things. I have my own mandates."

Jack raised a brow, a sinful gleam in his eyes. "Oh, really? Such as?"

She turned in his arms. "Such as, Blackjack stays."

Jack scowled and began to pull away, but she ran a finger down his throat, touching him lightly, opening the placket of his shirt. Jack stood immobile as she parted the material, revealing the bonze skin of his chest. On tiptoes, she kissed the stubble under his chin, then his throat, where she felt his pulse throb steadily.

His hands came back around her, pressing her flush against him. Maddie smiled and kissed him again, trailing her lips down his flesh and then tracing her earlier path with her tongue.

"I like how you taste, Jack."

"I love how you taste. Take this dress off."

Maddie pulled back and held up a chiding finger. "Oh, no. Tonight I'm the one with the mandates."

He spread his hands. "Very well. What are your orders?"

She ran her hands over his shirt, dipping them into his waistband and pulling the white tails free. "Take off your shirt," she whispered.

Unusually obedient, Jack lifted the tails and began to pull the material over his head. As his bronze flesh was revealed, Maddie bent to kiss him, touching lips and tongue to his hard abdomen, then to the smattering of hair on his chest, and ending once again at the pounding pulse point at his throat. She noticed his blood was throbbing even harder now.

"Do you want me, Jack?" she whispered, punctuating her soft words with a quick nip at his flesh.

"God, yes." His hands were on her hips, and he pulled her against his hard erection. Maddie trailed her hand along his shoulders, down his chest, pressed against the muscles of his abdomen. His flesh quivered, and then she dipped into his trousers.

She could feel his velvet tip, and it moved at her first touch. Jack groaned, and Maddie, as aroused as he was now, flicked open his trousers, sliding them over his slim hips. He was bare underneath the material, and his manhood sprung free. Sliding her hands around to squeeze his buttocks, she cradled him close to her woman's heat.

"I need you, Maddie."

"Show me."

His hands were immediately on her, ruching her skirt up, searching for the source of that heat she knew he craved. As soon as he touched her, her knees buckled and he was the strong one again. He went down with her, kneeling on the plush rug before her, kissing her, touching her oh so intimately in the ways he knew she liked best.

She felt as though it had been years since he'd last been inside her. Her body had missed his touch, the ecstasy he could give, and before she knew what was happening, she was clutching his shoulders and crying out as pleasure shook her.

When she opened her eyes again, Jack was rising. "The bed," he said, breathing labored. "I want you on the bed."

Maddie reached up and touched his erection, circled it with her hand. Jack sank down beside her again. "And I want you here," she told him. "Lie down."

"Maddie—"

"Do it, Jack." He obliged her, and she crawled on top of him, her legs straddling him, her knees cushioned by the luxurious rug. "I have a proposal for you."

Jack's eyes were dark with desire. "A proposal?"

"Mmm-hmm." She loosened the bodice of her gown, tugged it down, then went to work on her stays and chemise. Jack's eyes were riveted. "You want Blackjack gone. I want him to stay."

"Not the bear again."

Maddie finally freed her breasts from the stays, and she tugged the chemise down. Jack's hand automatically reached up to finger her nipple. "I propose—mmm, that feels good. I propose a game."

"I don't have the patience for games," Jack said, gripping her hips so his erection brushed against her core.

"Then you'll surely lose. The object of the game is to have the most patience. Whoever finds fulfillment first, loses."

Jack was watching her now, his expression arrogant. "You'll lose."

"And if I do, then I grant you one wish. Whatever you desire. And if I win—"

"You won't."

"If I win, you grant me one wish."

"Whatever you want, sweetheart," he groaned, moving against her. Maddie readjusted, allowing the tip of his erection to enter her. But she rose up so that when he tried to plunge deeper, he couldn't.

"Do you promise, Jack? Whatever I want?"

"Yes, yes. God, you're hot. Maddie . . . "

She lowered herself a fraction of an inch, taking more of him inside. Now her mind was swirling, the feel of him inside her undeniably erotic. The urge to take all of him, to lower herself and ride him, was almost overwhelming.

"Prepare to lose, Jack," she managed before he thrust inside her and all coherent thought fled.

"Bloody, goddamn bear," Jack said some time later. He was sprawled on the soft carpet, a sated Maddie draped over him.

Unfortunately, she hadn't been sated soon enough. He'd lost her bloody proposal.

"Profanity won't help you," she murmured, her breath light and warm on his shoulder. "It was a fair fight."

"Fair? How was it fair? You were one climax ahead of me before we even began."

She rose on one elbow and smiled at him. Her blue eyes were dark with the pleasure he'd given her, her mouth swollen from his kisses. "And yet, you were confident you would win."

"I should have." He touched her rosy lips.

"You lost, Jack. My wish is that we keep Blackjack. Are you going to go back on your word? I thought you were a gentleman."

He laughed at that. "Hardly, sweetheart. But I do honor my bets. We keep the bear, but he's moving outside. And I'm keeping you nearby. You're sleeping in here, with me."

And, devil take him, one of these days he was going to have her in a bed. He glanced up at his bed, the clawed feet of which were near his head. He'd been so close.

Maddie yawned. "Sleep sounds good."

Jack agreed, and he rose, pulling her to her feet. Naked, she leaned against the bedpost while he pulled back the lavish sheets and coverlet.

"I hope that bed is as comfortable as it looks," she said. "I have a busy day tomorrow."

Jack's hand, wrapped around the soft sheets, clenched. "Doing what?"

She waved a hand and yawned again. "Visiting my charities. You heard my father. I've been terribly remiss in my duties."

"I told you that's done. Give money, host an event, but I won't have you risking yourself, running all about Town." Running right into one of Bleven's traps.

Maddie paused mid-yawn and glared at him. "And I thought I told you not to give me orders. I'm not one of your servants."

Jesus Christ. Jack felt like banging his skull on the headboard. The woman was going to drive him into Bedlam. She was going on again about orders and equality, and he knew it could continue all night.

So he did the only thing he could think of. He pushed her against the bedpost and kissed her.

She was less than receptive, so he kissed her again, then nuzzled her neck. Her arms came around him, pulling him closer. He bent to kiss her throat, his hands coming up to cup her breasts. "Sweetheart, I have another proposal for you."

Her breathing quickened, and Jack had a feeling she wouldn't be able to refuse.

Maddie frowned as she watched Jack's valet help him into his coat. "I don't see how I'm going to choose just one charity, Lord Blackthorne," she complained. "It's not possible."

Jack brushed at the sleeve of the coat and nodded to the valet, dismissing the man. "It's only for a few months. And you agreed to the proposal."

She pursed her lips. "You tricked me."

Jack laughed. "You're damn right I did. Ready for breakfast?"

The door closed behind the valet, and Maddie leaned back on the bed. "How can I think about food when I have so many other, much more important items on my mind?"

Jack shrugged. "Don't think. Just eat." He moved toward the door. "And you need have only one thing on your mind. Me."

Maddie sighed and fell back on the soft mattress. Why had she agreed to Jack's stupid proposal? How could she possibly choose between the Widow's Benevolent Society and the Orphan's Munificent Society? Widows and orphans alike needed her.

And what about the war veterans and the animal societies? Who would help if she didn't?

"Madeleine, I'm not going to change my mind. You actively participate in only one society for the time being."

She looked up to see Jack towering triumphantly over her. All her life she'd fought her father for the right to pursue her charitable interests, and then in a moment of blind lust she'd lost all she'd worked so hard for. Or perhaps she'd lost it long before—the first moment Jack jumped into her carriage.

"You really have no heart, do you?" she said, raising herself on her elbows. "How can you be so callous? How can you stand there, looking so smug, as though winning a wager with me is more important than helping children?"

"Because my first priority is protecting you. You want to help children? Fine, we'll give all the societies in the country a donation." He took her roughly by the shoulders. "But I won't risk you."

"And I won't be locked up like a pretty bird, all show and no value. That's not a life."

Jack's dark eyes turned stormy, his eyebrows coming together in a black slash. "It's better than the alternative. You think you're invincible, that nothing can touch you." He was shaking now, shaking her shoulders and shaking with fury. "But you're not invincible. You're not safe. And I'll be damned if I lose you the same way I lost—"

With a growl, he released her, pushing her back and turning away. Maddie sat stunned for a long moment and then bounded off the bed, darting under Jack's arm and blocking the door before he could open it. "Wait, Jack. Finish your sentence. Who did you lose?"

"No one." He tried to push her aside, but she wedged her shoulder against the door tightly and reached out to place her hand on his chest.

"Tell me."

She saw his jaw clench, and for a moment she was certain he would sweep past her, shutting her out once again. Forever.

And then his eyes softened and his features relaxed. The pain she saw in his face sliced through her, and she put her arms around him. "Oh, Jack," she whispered.

"You say I have no heart." His voice was raspy, but the deep bass rumbled through her. "Do you know how many times I've heard that whispered about me?"

She hugged him tighter. "I didn't mean it. Of course you have a heart."

He pulled back, a sneer on his lips. "You think so? You don't know me. No one ever told you that I watched my mother die and did nothing to save her, did they?"

Maddie swallowed hard but refused to pull away from him. That was what he wanted—to distance himself from her and his feelings. And yet, she knew if she were ever to understand him, ever to claim a piece of his heart, she had to break down this last defense. "Jack, I don't believe you. I do know you. You would never stand by when someone needed your help. Please, tell me what happened."

He stepped back, shook his head and ran a hand through his hair. The style the valet had spent so much time taming was instantly in disarray, sections of dark hair falling over Jack's forehead. But it was his expression that pained her the most. Had she ever seen a man with so much pain in his eyes? He looked shattered.

Maddie watched as he tried to compose his features and finally turned away from her, crossing to the window and parting the heavy burgundy draperies. The sun was bright in he sky, and the light touched Jack's dark hair, making the blue-black waves gleam.

"My mother was a lot like you," he told her. "She had all these charities and societies and benevolent works. She was always going to help this orphan or that widow." He turned and looked at Maddie, and the pain was still there. But now it was something hard and tight in the lines of his face. "Sometimes she took my brother and me along with her. She was away so much, I seldom saw her, so the opportunity to spend time with her—even in a hospital surrounded by sick people or a filthy flat housing ten people—was a treat."

Maddie could imagine Jack, a small dark-haired boy who missed his mother. Did he lie awake late at night, waiting for her to tuck him into bed? When he scraped his knee or banged his toe, did he wish she were there beside him to kiss it better?

Maddie bit her lip. When she looked at Jack now, she could see the loneliness and disappointment in his eyes. She moved closer and put her hand on his shoulder, but he turned away to stare out the window. "I didn't know, Jack."

"There's a lot you don't know," he said, voice cold. "You don't know what people are capable of. You don't know what they can do."

"What happened?" she asked quietly.

Jack blew out a puff of air. "My little brother was always in trouble. Even back then." He smiled faintly, probably remembering some mischief from the past. "I was two years older, so it was my duty to watch him, to keep him safe. One day my mother went to visit a widow. The woman lived in some seedy part of the city, near the river. I'll never forget the stench of that place. It smelled like rotting fish and decay."

Maddie knew that smell well. She'd come to associate it with poverty and sickness.

"Nick and I were told to wait in the drawing room—if you could call it that—and it was fine for a while, but then Nick started to get restless. I was tired and sick of dealing with him. I was stupid—only ten—and I didn't think. He wanted to go outside, and I couldn't blame him. Anything for fresh air. So I pretended not to see when he sneaked out the door. I figured he'd be back in a few minutes. The next thing I know my mother was shaking me awake and asking where Nick was."

Maddie wanted to hold him again, but she didn't dare. She was afraid he'd stop speaking or push her away.

One thing about her husband was becoming abundantly clear: He was always taking care of others. No wonder, as it appeared he knew little else.

"So we went to look for Nick, and we couldn't find him. We looked up and down every street, in every filthy nook and cranny. The more we looked, the more distraught my mother became. We split up, and goddamn it, I should have never left her alone."

"Jack, you were just a boy."

"No," he said, rounding on her. "I was supposed to protect her. Both of them. I failed. Oh, I found Nick, all right. He was playing dice with a bunch of boys and taking them for everything they had. He was always a good gambler. But when we went back to find my mother, she was gone. By sheer luck—if you want to call it that—we turned into a blind alley and saw her. Three men had her. Big men, and they—"

Maddie closed her eyes, nausea rising within her. Suddenly, Jack's arms were around her. He was shaking, but his voice was even.

"This isn't a story you should hear, sweetheart," he whispered into her hair. "This isn't something I want you to know, to think about."

Maddie pulled back, gazed into his eyes. "Tell me the end. Tell me what happened."

Jack's eyes went hard again, hard and far away. "I was too afraid to intervene. I was afraid they'd hurt me. I was paralyzed with fear. Nick and I hid, and we saw it all. I sat there and watched my mother raped and beaten and murdered, and I didn't do anything to stop it. Because I was too much of a bloody coward."

"No, Jack."

"I keep telling you that I stick my neck in the noose for no one. Now maybe you'll believe me."

"You were a child, a boy. Your mother would have wanted you to hide, to keep Nick safe."

"My mother would have wanted me to do something. To save her. I stood there and cried like a baby, and that was the last time I cried. I didn't weep when I told my father what had happened or at the funeral or even at the grave site. People say I have no heart." He closed his eyes, swallowed. "They're right."

His voice broke on the last word, and Maddie had to hold back tears. She took his hand, tried to hold it, but it was cold and unyielding. "They're not right, Jack. If you didn't have a heart you wouldn't have helped me, you wouldn't have risked your life so many times."

He straightened, once again in control of his emotions. "I did what I had to in order to save myself. Either that or I rushed in without thinking. Monstrous trait."

"No. You rush in because you care. You married me because you care. I won't believe you don't care about me, Jack. I know you do."

"You're my wife, and I made a commitment. Keeping you safe does benefit me, sweetheart. One day I'll need an heir." His voice was calculating, his smile cold.

Maddie shook her head. She knew he wasn't the selfish coward he tried to make everyone think he was. But he hadn't yet forgiven himself, and until he did, he would never see the brave, heroic man he'd become.

"I won't allow anything happen to you, Maddie," Jack was saying. "I'm not going to stand by while you're attacked, beaten—"

"Jack, that's not going to happen. I'll take precautions."

"You'll choose one charity and do work for them only if I am with you. The rest of the time you'll stay here, where I know you're safe. Discussion over. I have a meeting with my man of affairs in an hour, and I'm going to eat breakfast."

He crossed the room, and Maddie was right behind him. "Jack, I understand your concerns." He opened the door and walked briskly down the hallway, and she had to run to keep up with him. "But you can't lock me up."

He reached the stairs and began to descend. "I'm not locking you up. I'm keeping you safe."

"A cage is a cage," she said under her breath, so the maid polishing the marble at the base of the stairwell wouldn't hear. "Do you think that's what your mother would have wanted? To be locked away, prevented from doing what meant most to her in the world?"

Jack glared at Maddie and made a sharp turn at the bottom of the steps, heading toward the breakfast room.

"Don't you think your mother would have rather died doing something worthwhile?" Maddie said, following him, her voice rising despite herself. "If you can't see that her sacrifice meant something, then not only her life but her death was in vain."

Jack paused at the door to the breakfast room, his hand gripping the handle fiercely. "You don't know the first thing about my mother, and it's not your business, so stay out of it."

He opened the door, entered, and was immediately greeted by Ridgeley. "Good morning, my lord. Coffee? The *Times*?"

Maddie would have fled back to their room, but Ridgeley saw her.

"My lady." He pulled out a chair beside Jack's. "Your chair."

She tried to think of a way out, an excuse to run away. Instead, without looking at Jack, she took the proffered seat.

"My lord," Ridgeley was saying, "your man of affairs has arrived early, and I have taken the liberty of showing him into the library."

"Damn," Jack swore, beginning to rise from his seat.

"But before you bury your head in matters of business, my lord, I must inquire what time you would like the carriage this evening. The Prince Regent's ball begins at nine."

Maddie raised her eyebrows. "The Prince Regent's ball?"

It wasn't her first choice for an amusement, but the way things were looking, it might be her only chance to escape the confines of the town house. And perhaps the ball would give her an opportunity to show Jack that his overprotective nature was unnecessary. If he saw she wasn't in any danger and could take care of herself, he might relax.

"Yes, my lady," Ridgeley told her. "His lordship accepted the invitation some weeks ago, and I fear that, except in the case of life-threatening illness, it is too late to send regrets."

Jack glanced at her, his jaw tight.

"Is there a life-threatening illness?" Ridgeley asked. "Or shall I order the carriage for, say, half past nine?"

Maddie met Jack's gaze. "No illness, Ridgeley," she said. "By all means, order the carriage. I, for one, cannot wait to dance the night away."

Chapter 19

"I don't dance," Jack informed her after they'd climbed into the carriage.

"Really?" she said, raising a brow. "That's tedious."

"I'm tedious," Jack retorted, and indeed he felt as much today. He'd spent most of the afternoon locked away with his man of affairs, going over everything the man could find out about Bleven. Jack didn't yet have the evidence to prove that Bleven was involved in his mother's murder, but from what his man had discovered, Bleven possessed opportunity and motive. The Black Duke was in Town at the time of the murder, and he made no secret how much he hated the woman who'd spurned him for another.

The work dredged up painful memories, and Jack had to force himself to continue with it.

He would have much rather spent a frivolous afternoon in bed with his wife. He could have ignored Bleven for one day, dismissed his man of affairs, and enjoyed Maddie fully. But he had the sinking suspicion that was the kind of thing a man in love did.

And he was not in love.

He liked his wife. Very much. But he wasn't in love with her, and the fact that he could resist her all but proved he wasn't going to be. Thank God he didn't have to worry about that anymore.

But he had other worries. Namely, that pink ball gown she was wearing. Jack frowned. Maddie had corrected him several times—told him the dress was not pink but rose and burgundy. He squinted at her in the carriage. The thing still looked pink to him.

The idea of what his wife would wear to the prince's ball had never even crossed his mind, nor the necessity of her sending for her clothes and other personal items from Castleigh's town house. Why would she need anything? She wasn't going anywhere—except to bed with him, and the less clothing there, the better.

But now Jack found himself preoccupied with thoughts of the rest of Maddie's clothing. Were all of her ball gowns cut like this one? Did all of her dresses nip in and accentuate the sweet curve of her waist? Did they all hug her breasts like a pair of gloves? And what about ribbons? This gown had several, and he itched to tug at them and reveal the creamy flesh beneath.

And why the hell couldn't he stop thinking about flounces and ruffles? He'd never considered women's clothing much before— except to determine the fastest way to remove it.

But he would wager his best hunter that there wouldn't be a man tonight who wasn't thinking about removing Maddie's gown.

The color brought out her smooth complexion and made her sapphire eyes seem even bluer than usual. Not that anyone but he would be looking at her eyes.

Jack narrowed his gaze at his wife's bodice. There was entirely too much of Maddie's ample bosom on display. He opened his mouth to ask where the hell her shawl was, then thought better of it. They'd already quarreled over the neckline three times that evening.

But when he'd told Maddie that the gown wasn't proper, she'd exhibited her usual stubbornness and lack of concern for safety. She acted as if all he wanted was to control her. But as with her charitable works, his interest in the dress arose because he wanted to protect her from unwanted advances.

Of course, she hadn't seen it that way. She'd told him that he was being ridiculous. She claimed to have worn the dress several times before without causing a riot and assured him that the neckline was decent, far more modest than what most ladies wore.

And she was probably right.

But he was still scowling.

"Stop frowning," Maddie said from across the carriage.

"Then take off that gown," he retorted.

She raised a brow. "What, here? Now?" She fluttered her lashes in a display of mock innocence.

Jack couldn't stop a small smile, but it faded immediately when, once again, all the possible dangers his wife might face tonight flitted through his mind. If it had been anyone other than the Prince Regent hosting this ball, he would never have agreed to make an appearance. But with everyone talking about the Blackthorne elopement, the prince would be sure to take offense if he and his new bride didn't grace Carlton House. Jack did not like Prinny, and he didn't need any more powerful enemies.

And he didn't need an evening with the simpering sycophants who surrounded the fat regent.

Jack scowled again. He and Maddie were sure to be the event's main attraction.

By the time they reached Carlton House, Jack was on edge and determined not to let her out of his sight. He wasn't going to allow her to fall prey to Bleven. As they exited the carriage and started up the stairs, he grasped her hand and muttered, "Stay close to me."

Maddie nodded absently, but upon entering, inclined her head to acknowledge several other guests. The damned woman seemed to know everyone. He had to haul her back to his side several times when she would have run off to have just a quick word with Lady This or Lord That. Finally, the interminable wait to be announced ended, and they entered the Crimson Drawing Room.

The room had been renovated in the last few years and was now swathed in crimson satin damask. From the curtains to the upholstery, everything except the light blue velvet carpet dripped red satin.

Suddenly feeling the need for a drink, Jack released Maddie for a moment to snatch a glass of champagne from a passing footman. He lifted one for her as well, and when both of his hands were occupied, she reached over and gave his arm a perfunctory pat. "I'll be back in a moment."

"Oh, no you won't."

But she was already scampering away. "Don't worry!" she called over her shoulder, chestnut ringlets bouncing down her back.

"Bloody hell." Jack downed one glass of champagne and looked for a place to set the other. He couldn't find a spot, so he downed that one, too. He could just see the top of Maddie's head as she reached the far corner of the room and embraced two women—one a tall brunette and one a thin redhead with a crop of curls.

He grabbed a footman, dropped the empty glasses on his tray, and stalked after Maddie. Obviously they needed to have another discussion about how she was not to leave his side. Or rather, he would have to lecture her again.

If he could reach her.

But the path that had cleared for Maddie swallowed him whole. Men and women surrounded him, stepping in his way and trying to engage him in inane conversation. Why the hell did they want to talk to him anyway? He sidestepped and parried but wasn't quick enough. The prince himself, metaphoric rapier raised for combat, stepped into Jack's path.

"Ah, Lord Blackthorne. You have been a naughty boy." The prince winked and his fleshy face jiggled with laughter.

Jack bowed. "Your Royal Highness. How kind of you to extend this invitation to my wife."

Prinny waved the lace handkerchief in his hand. "Castleigh's such an incredible bore. Apparently his daughter takes after another side of the family. Found yourself a wild one, have you?"

Jack clenched his hand, resisting the urge to punch the prince in the nose. "Our meeting was somewhat unconventional, but the lady—"

"Unconventional!" The prince gazed at the lackeys standing near him, and all burst into laughter. "Now, Blackthorne, I have heard stories about carriage chases, duels, and a muck-up at Gretna Green. You simply won't get away without revealing some details. The juicy ones, Blackthorne."

The prince's hand came down hard on Jack's

shoulder, his muscles taut with apprehension. Where the devil was Maddie? He ground his teeth, "Your Royal Highness, I would love to regale you, but my wife—"

"Will wait." Prinny snapped his fingers, and the group surrounding him parted, revealing two thronelike chairs. Smiling, the prince squashed his considerable bulk into one and gestured to the other. His expression was resolute.

Jack gave one last fleeting look in the direction Maddie had fled, blew out a breath, and took his seat.

"Now," the prince began, "tell me everything."

"Catie! Josie!" Maddie rushed into her cousins' arms and the three spun around in happiness.

"Where have you been?" Josie cried.

"I was so worried about you!" Catie chided.

"Where's your husband?" Josie asked, looking about on tiptoes.

"And how dare you marry without us?"

Maddie, deluged by their questions, only laughed. It was so good to hear their voices again. It was so good to be wrapped in the flood of their friendship.

"How dare you marry at all," Josie added, giving the laughing Maddie a dubious look. "Poor Ashley will be the only one of our club left."

"Oh, I think it's safe to say that our little club is now quite defunct."

Catie and Josie stared at her. "Then all the rumors are true?" Josie asked. "I don't believe it."

Maddie glanced about her, decided there were too many people milling about, hoping to overhear, and grabbed her cousins' hands. She pulled them through the ornate room, through the French doors, and out onto the deserted balcony. After checking behind a potted plant nearby, she turned to them. "It's true. Ashley's married."

"Who?" Josie asked. "To Lord Nicholas?"

"Oh, Lord, what will Aunt Imogen say?" Catie asked.

Maddie sobered then, thinking about the conversation that afternoon with Ashley's mother. She'd sent a note to Imogen Brittany as soon as she'd arrived home, and this morning, after Jack retired with his man of affairs, Ashley's mother had called.

Understandably, her aunt was distraught over her daughter's absence. And when Maddie informed her of Ashley's marriage, the poor woman had gone pale. Almost as pale as Maddie's own mother, who called an hour later. Maddie had been forced to sit through a long lecture and then promise never to elope again. She was certain Ashley would have to do the same when her mother saw her.

If her mother saw her.

Maddie sighed and began filling her cousins in on the details of the elopement.

At the end of the story, Josie was laughing, but

Catie's expression was strained. "The anvil priest really married the wrong couples?"

"Yes, and that was the last I saw of Ashley and Lord Nicholas."

"Oh, Ashley can take care of herself," Josie said confidently.

"I know, but I worry. Lord Blackthorne has hired investigators to locate them. We should have word of their whereabouts any day."

"I simply cannot fathom this," Catie said. "Don't misunderstand, I think the elopement worked out well for you, you obviously love Lord Blackthorne."

"Love Lord Blackthorne!" Maddie took a step back. "What are you talking about? I can barely stand the man."

Josie snorted. "That's a sure sign you love him. I want to kill Stephen almost daily. I'll probably do it one of these days."

Catie rolled her eyes.

"I saw that," Josie protested. "And don't pretend that Lord Valentine is perfect. Just last week you were railing because he hadn't moved from his desk and that stack of work for two days."

"Well, at least neither of your husbands tries to control you," Maddie said, crossing her arms over her chest. "Lord Blackthorne told me this morning that I'm only allowed to be actively involved with one charity." She held up a single finger to illustrate. "One."

Her cousins exchanged looks. "Actually, Maddie," Catie said carefully, "that's not such a bad idea."

"You really were trying to do too much," Josie said.

"Oh I was, was I? And what have you two done? Is that a new gown, Josie? Are those new diamond earrings, Catie? What about all the orphans who could have used that money?"

"You're right," Catie said. "We probably should try to help more."

"We should." Josie was trying hard to look contrite, but Maddie wasn't fooled. Her cousins were always attempting to escape from aiding with charitable endeavors. Josie said it was dull, and Catie could be shy with new people.

"I'm glad to hear you say that," Maddie said.

Catie narrowed her eyes at Maddie. "Why?"

"Because I've finally decided on my charity."

"What's that?" Josie stepped back and craned her neck, peering through the French doors. "I think Lord Westman needs me."

"Well, then he'll have to get in line behind His Royal Highness's Society for Invalid Veterans of Overseas Conflicts."

"Maddie, is that even a real organization?" Catie asked.

Maddie nodded. "Their founder sent me a heartbreaking note a week ago, and my mother brought it with the rest of my mail today. They need help with their annual fund-raiser and auction. I agreed to chair the event, and I need two co-chairs. You two have just been appointed."

While the prince laughed at one of his own jokes, Jack slipped behind an earl and a baron. Finally free, he glanced about for his wife. Every moment he was away from her, his chest grew tighter and his shoulders felt like they were being drawn together by a large fishhook.

He arrowed straight for the last place he'd seen Maddie, shooting a menacing look at anyone who stepped in his way.

"Damn," he swore when he reached the spot where he'd seen her standing and it was empty. The prince's ball was turning into a bloody inconvenient crush. He would never find her in the throng of bodies.

"Looking for someone?" The high-pitched voice came from behind him.

Whipping around, Jack found himself eye-to-eye with the Duke of Bleven.

"I know *I* am." The handsome man smiled, though no warmth penetrated his cold eyes.

Automatically, Jack allowed a mask of indifference to settle over his features. "If you're asking about my brother, I last saw him in Scotland several days ago. He could be anywhere by now."

"Ah, yes, Lord Nicholas," Bleven said, stroking the cleft in his chin. "I suppose I will have to deal with him later. But, of course, you know the person I was speaking of is your lovely wife. She and I have some unfinished business."

Jack clenched his jaw and forced himself to speak quietly. "If you have any business with my wife, you can take that up with me. I'll be more than happy to oblige you."

"Oh, but that wouldn't be any fun," Bleven said. His face twisted into an expression of exaggerated solicitousness. "I'd much rather spend my time with the lovely Madeleine."

Jack couldn't stop his rage from boiling over. He grabbed Bleven by the collar and hauled him up against the wall. The crowd surrounding them took a united step back, and Jack heard the hissing speculation.

"Blackthorne has Bleven by the neck."

"The duke will kill him."

"My money's on Blackthorne."

Bleven's eyes bulged out and his cheeks were red with indignation. Jack's face was inches from Bleven's, his voice little more than a whisper. "If you so much as touch her, you sadistic bastard, I'll kill you."

"Like you killed those men who had their fun with your mother?" Bleven's hoarse voice carried past Jack. There was a gasp from the crowd behind them, which made Bleven smile. He lowered his voice, speaking only to Jack. "They were my men, Blackthorne. Like you, I stood in the shadows and watched. I'd waited a long time for my revenge. I plotted and planned, and in the end it was sweet. So sweet."

Jack felt the bile rise in his throat, and his fist itched to smash into Bleven's face. "I'm going to kill you for what you did," he spat.

"Oh, promises, promises. Now allow me to make you one. You and your brother have insulted me for the last time, and you will pay. And I know just the currency—that pretty new marchioness."

Jack slammed the duke back hard against the wall again. "Goddamn it, Bleven. Stay away from my wife."

Bleven sneered. "Keep looking over your shoulder, Blackthorne, if it makes you feel better. But when I come for her, you won't be able to stop me."

"Step outside with me," Jack said between clenched teeth. "I'll stop you."

"How? Are you going to cry again, little coward boy?"

Jack knew what Bleven was doing, knew the other man was trying to goad him into making a scene or—worse—make him so angry that he forgot what was truly important: Maddie.

Exercising all of his willpower, Jack unclenched his fists from around Bleven's collar and lowered the duke to the floor. "I will protect what's mine," he hissed. "I'll come for you, Bleven. Don't ever doubt that."

He stepped back and swung toward the crowd,

scanning it for Maddie. Instead, he felt a hundred eyes on him.

"That's it, then!" A tall, dark-haired man stepped out from the sea of faces. "Nothing to see here. I think I heard his Royal Highness announce dinner was being served in the Circular Room. Right through there."

The crowd reluctantly began to disperse, and the man, who looked somewhat familiar, held his hand out to Jack. "Quint Childers, the Earl of Valentine."

Jack took his hand absently, still looking for Maddie. He had to find her. "John Martingale, Marquess—"

"I know who you are, my lord. And I suppose I have the advantage because I also know where your wife is."

Jack gripped Valentine's hand hard. "Where is she? Is she safe?"

"She's fine. She's with her cousins on the balcony."

Jack nodded, starting in that direction. "And how do you know this?"

"I'm married to Lady Madeleine's cousin—excuse me, she's Lady Blackthorne's cousin now. I'm married to Catherine, Lady Valentine."

"I see."

"You don't have to rush. Lord Westman is keeping an eye on them."

"Westman?" Jack gave Valentine a skeptical look.

"He's married to your wife's other cousin, Josephine. When Castleigh told us you'd rubbed Bleven the wrong way, we decided we'd better keep an eye on all the girls. You never know when or how the Black Duke will attack."

They'd reached the French doors, and through the glass Jack could see Maddie laughing with the two women from before. He felt the pinch in his shoulders lessen and the constriction around his chest give way. He turned back to Valentine. "It sounds like you've dealt with Bleven before."

"Only in Parliament. But I've heard what he's capable of."

Jack reached for the French doors, but Valentine's hand on his shoulder stopped him.

"Blackthorne, just in case you need it spelled out, we love Maddie, too. You don't have to protect her alone."

Jack nodded his assent, but he knew, in the end, saving her would fall to him.

And this time he wouldn't fail.

Chapter 20

"Jack," Maddie said, smiling. "I have to get out of bed. My cousins will be here soon."

"What is this aversion to beds?" Jack asked, rolling her over, settling his weight comfortably on top of her.

She sighed, finding him even more difficult to resist than usual. Outside the bedclothes, the air was so cold, and inside, Jack was so wonderfully hot. She could have stayed wrapped around him all day . . . if her cousins weren't due any moment.

"I don't have an aversion to beds," she said. "After all the time I've spent recently in carriages and on the ground, I rather appreciate beds."

"And I'd like to appreciate you in one," Jack said, smiling his wicked smile. His dark eyes were filled with desire for her, and it made her own blood heat. "Do you know that I've never had you in a bed?"

Maddie blinked. She hadn't realized. She and Jack had made love so many times now. How could they have never done so in a bed? What kind of wanton woman was she?

She smiled. Very wanton. Jack had always made her feel wild and uninhibited, and she loved that sense of freedom. If only he would stop trying to control her outside the bedroom.

She kissed his nose. "I promise to rectify the situation soon, but right now isn't the time. Catie and Josie will be here shortly." She pushed against Jack, but he didn't release his hold. Instead, he bent to her ear and whispered a very sinful alternative to her charity meeting.

Maddie blushed all the way to her toes, and if pressed, she would have admitted that she was very tempted by the suggestion. But she couldn't justify neglecting her work today. After all, today's meeting would not wait. And she had so much to do.

She just hoped she could concentrate. Jack and his creative diversions had a way of invading her thoughts at the most inopportune moments.

"Jack," she said regretfully, moving away from him. "I must go. We're starting plans for the fundraiser for His Royal Highness's Society for Invalid Veterans of Overseas Conflicts today."

Maddie rose from the bed, and Jack propped his head on a stack of pillows, watching her. "The Society for Invalid Overseas— What is this cause?"

"Why don't you come to our meeting and find out?"

He frowned. "I have a bear enclosure to design. The beast managed to break out of the last one."

She pulled on her dressing robe and brushed her hair back. "Is that what you do, locked in the library all day? I cannot imagine a bear enclosure takes that much thought. What are you really plotting?"

His face darkened for a moment, as though he were thinking of that very thing, and Maddie shivered. His grim expression worried her. She'd seen that expression on his face several times in the past two days, but each time she'd asked him about it, he'd said it was nothing.

She'd heard rumors about an altercation between Jack and Bleven at the prince's ball, but when she asked Jack, he told her not to worry, he wasn't going to allow anything to happen to her.

Apparently, he wasn't going to allow her to know anything either. Since their conversation about his mother, he'd been even more closed than usual. Maddie wanted to find a way to reach him, to assuage his guilt over his mother's death, but she didn't know how.

"Well," she said, walking to him now and kissing his forehead. "You're welcome to join us if you want."

Two hours later she prayed Jack wouldn't take her up on her offer. She could just imagine his reaction if he happened to glimpse the chaos reigning in the drawing room.

But it wasn't her fault! In fact, the more she thought about it, the chaos was his fault. If Jack wouldn't let her go to the needy, she had to bring them to her. It was that simple.

Though, had she the choice, she might have brought fewer.

When she told Laura Millingham, the society president, that she'd like to meet some of the invalid veterans of overseas conflicts, she hadn't expected Miss Millingham to respond quite so enthusiastically.

At present there were eight invalid veterans crowding in the drawing room. Even Maddie had to admit they were a motley bunch. A few resembled pirates more than decorated officers. Perhaps it was Captain Roberts's peg leg or First Lieutenant Finch's eye patch and gold hoop earrings, but something about the men made her pray that Jack stay ensconced in his library.

She had hoped to solicit the men's opinion on the decorations and food to be served at the fund-raiser, but the conversation had rapidly degenerated into a heated argument as to who had suffered more in the Colonial Wars.

"Ha! You think having a finger shot off is bad?" a Colonel Shivers shouted at a Lieutenant Beebe. "Try having your toes frozen off. Lost three of them. See here."

Maddie rubbed her temple as the bearded colonel removed his boot and wiggled the mutilated

toes at the room as a whole. Poor Miss Millingham was white as a ghost.

The colonel swung the foot in Maddie's cousins'
direction, and Catie shrunk back to avoid having
the limb smack her in the face. "Oh, very, ah . . .
nice." She set her tea on the table and pushed it
away.

Josie, seated beside her, craned her neck to get
a better look. "Whoever the surgeon was, he did a
good job sewing it up."

"What surgeon?" Colonel Shivers said. "By
that time the Colonials had so overrun us, it were
every man for himself. Why, I remember one time
a friend of mine had the green rot on his—"

"Sir!" Maddie stood abruptly, jostling her own
teacup and spilling the liquid. "I know all of us
are fascinated by your campaigns under Corn-
wallis, but perhaps you could save a few stories
for later. We wouldn't want you to have to repeat
yourself."

The colonel chuckled. "Oh, no chance of that. I
have a thousand stories, but of course some aren't
suitable for ladies."

Maddie could only imagine what those might
involve.

"In the meantime, we need to discuss"—she
consulted her notes—"the refreshments."

Catie nodded at her eagerly. "Good idea. I
have the list of possibilities we compiled right
here."

Maddie took it and perused the selections. Behind her, the drawing room door opened, and Maddie stifled a frustrated groan. She finally had everyone's attention, and now the staff needed her. She'd told them she didn't wish to be disturbed. The servant—whoever it was—would simply have to wait.

"One moment," she said over her shoulder, not bothering to see which member of her staff had intruded. "I'll be with you shortly."

She turned back to her audience and noticed they were all sitting quite a bit straighter. Despite his peg leg, Captain Roberts had even risen from his chair. Maddie sighed. It must be Ridgeley behind her. He was the only intimidating member of the staff.

"Captain Roberts, do not worry about Ridgeley. Please sit and make yourself comfortable."

The captain opened his mouth to speak, but no words came out. Maddie shrugged. If he wanted to stand on one leg, she wouldn't argue. At least everyone had stopped quarreling. The room was silent.

She cleared her throat and was surprised when several veterans jumped.

"I was thinking that we might keep the refreshments simple—" she began.

"Maddie?" Josie interrupted. "You might—"

Maddie gave Josie a sharp look. "Just a moment, Lady Westman, let me finish."

"But—"

"We could serve tea, chocolate, and coffee."

The room as a whole gasped, and several other men rose, backing away from her.

Maddie raised her hands. "Very well. No coffee, then. What if we had punch instead?"

Several veterans began scrambling over one another, trying to get behind the chairs and couches farther away from her. Maddie, desperate, held up a hand. "Fine! No punch. We could have—"

Behind her she heard a distinctive grunting sound and turned on her heel to find Blackjack pushing his nose into her dress.

Maddie smiled. "Oh, this is what you were afraid of. I thought it was the coffee."

Without thinking, she reached down and patted the bear's wet nose, and the room erupted into pandemonium. Soldiers were rushing to get away from her and Blackjack, but all their canes and crutches had hooked together and Lieutenant Beebe fell over Colonel Shivers, knocking a lamp down in the process. Captain Roberts hopped on his peg leg, and another man, who did not seem to be an invalid and who Maddie speculated had joined the society only for the tea and biscuits, made loud gasping noises.

Meanwhile Miss Millingham, the society's fearless leader, was cowering in a corner, and Josie and Catie were laughing and shaking their heads. Maddie frowned at them.

"You needn't be afraid," she shouted, trying to calm everyone. "He probably escaped his enclosure again."

"Oh, I'm not afraid, ma'am," Lieutenant Beebe told her. "I just remembered an appointment."

Blackjack grunted.

"A pressing appointment!"

Someone threw open the door and Beebe and Roberts fought each other to be the first to exit.

"No fighting!" Maddie cried when a vase teetered on the edge of a table. "Please don't scare Blackjack."

Colonel Shivers hobbled past her. She hadn't realized a man missing so many toes could move that quickly. She caught his sleeve. "So coffee, then, Colonel, or punch?"

Suddenly, the door swung wide, and Maddie knew without looking who had arrived.

"What the devil is going on?"

Jack took a quick survey of the room. There were three old men trying desperately to escape; a lamp and two chairs were overturned; his wife's cousins were sitting on the couch, dissolved in a fit of giggles; and Maddie was pushing the bear behind her. No doubt trying to protect the beast.

From him.

Wise woman. He was in a mood to murder someone.

But it wasn't going to be the bear.

"Who the devil are all these men? Where the hell did they come from?"

Maddie frowned at him. "Don't talk to me like that in front of our guests."

"Guests?" Jack saw three men who looked like they'd just come in off a pirate ship. He'd be damned if one of them didn't have an eye patch and gold hoop earrings. What next? Would he be forced to walk the plank?

"Lord Blackthorne," Maddie said, "please calm down."

"Calm down?" How the hell was he supposed to calm down? His wife was driving him mad. First bears, then street urchins, now pirates, and . . .

Jack frowned. Was that a woman hiding under the side table?

"I can see you're upset," Maddie was saying.

He cocked an eyebrow at her.

She inclined her head. "Very well. I can see you're angry."

He advanced on her. "Oh, angry doesn't begin to describe what I'm feeling right now, madam."

"And that's your own fault," she told him, standing her ground, the bear now snuffling a potted fern.

"*My* fault?"

"That's right. You won't let me leave the house, so I had no choice but to bring everyone here."

"Everyone?"

She nodded. "The veterans."

Jack paused, glanced at the remaining men. "You're veterans?"

"Sergeant Timms, my lord," one of the veterans said, doffing his ragged cap. "If you'll excuse me, there's a bear . . . "

Jack sighed, moving out of the doorway so the remaining soldiers could escape. He wished he could do the same. "Who is that?" he asked, pointing to the woman cowering under the table.

Maddie bent down and peered under the table. "Oh, Miss Millingham! Lord Blackthorne, this is Miss Millingham, president of His Royal Highness's Society for Invalid Veterans of Overseas Conflicts."

"Of course it is. And I suppose she brought the, ah"—pirates — "veterans."

"I asked her to," Maddie said, instantly on the defensive. "I wanted to consult with the men on the decor and refreshments for the fund-raiser."

Grizzled veterans decorating a society fund-raiser. Jack wanted to laugh.

But Maddie didn't look like she was laughing. In fact, her eyes looked decidedly watery.

Oh, bloody hell. He closed the remaining distance between them and pulled her into his arms. "Don't start crying."

"I can't help it," she blubbered. "I'm just working so hard on this fund-raiser, and nothing is going right."

From the corner of his eye Jack saw Maddie's cousins and Miss Millingham slip away. Blackjack lumbered after them. Jack held his wife tighter. "It will all work out, Maddie."

"But we still haven't made any decisions. Should I serve coffee or punch? And what about red and blue for the color scheme? And we don't even have a location. Josie is supposed to make some inquiries, but she'll probably forget."

"We can have the fund-raiser here. In the ball-room," Jack said.

Maddie arched her back and stared at him.

"I know it's a bit small," he conceded, "but—"

"No! Jack, I—" She sniffed. "Jack, do you really mean it?"

No, he didn't. He would rather shove a knife in his gut than allow a bunch of hoity-toity females and bedraggled pirates in his house to whisper and sip tea. But at least if the event was here, he'd have some control over his wife.

Some was the operative word because, obviously, he had no control over her. All morning he'd been sitting in his library, imagining her upstairs, innocently sipping tea with her two cousins. In reality . . . well, he didn't want to think about the reality. But if the fund-raiser were here, he could arrange extra security to keep Maddie safe.

"I really mean it," he forced himself to say.

She beamed and threw her arms around him. "Oh, Jack! Thank you." She kissed him. "I love you."

His arms suddenly felt heavy. His whole body felt overburdened, so weighted down that he could barely stand. He couldn't have heard her correctly. Had Maddie just said she loved him?

His head was ringing, and the words seemed to reverberate through his entire body. *I love you. I love you. I love—*

No one loved him. No one since . . .

Losing his mother had almost killed him. The guilt, like a parasite, still ate at him. He couldn't face that kind of anguish again. Even all the vaunted glories of love weren't worth the pain.

Jack pulled back, quickly extricating himself from his wife. "Look, Maddie. That's a nice . . . sentiment, but it's not necessary."

She was staring at him, her eyes wide. He swore she looked as surprised as he. "But, I think—I mean, I really do love you. I—I don't know when it happened, Jack, but I—"

He put a finger over her lips. "Don't say it again. Don't even think it. You're feeling emotional."

"I know. I'm trying to tell you about my emotions."

"You're overwrought. You're not thinking straight. In fact, I want you to take a nap. I think it would be good for you."

He took her hand and dragged her out of the room, up the stairs, and into her bedchamber. Once there, he pulled down the covers and hoisted her into them.

She gave him an incredulous look. "But I'm not tired, and it's the middle of the day."

"It's been a trying afternoon. You could use the rest. Sleep, Maddie."

And he was out of the room, down the stairs, and locking the library door behind him in record time. With an unsteady hand, he poured three fingers of brandy and drank it down.

What the hell had just happened? One moment everything was going fine. Well, not fine. His wife was aggravating him to the point of madness, but other than that everything was fine. Marriage wasn't half as bad as he'd assumed. Maddie was intelligent, amusing, a good conversationalist. She pleased him in bed, and he knew he pleased her.

Why did she have to throw love in and ruin everything? Now she was going to expect him to reciprocate and blather on about his feelings.

The thing was, he didn't have any feelings. Not that kind anyway. He liked Maddie. He was fond of her. But he didn't love her.

Love was a noose—pleasant at first. Pleasant until it squeezed all the life out of a man. He wasn't going to let that happen. He wasn't going to stick his neck in the noose for anyone.

Maddie lay in bed and stared at the ceiling. What had just happened? She'd told Jack she loved him, and he ran away. He couldn't be rid of her quickly enough.

There was a quick tap on the door, and then Josie and Catie popped their heads inside. "The butler said you'd come up here," Catie told her. "Can we come in?"

Josie squeezed onto the bed beside Maddie, and Catie took the chair across from them.

"What's wrong?" Catie asked. "You look like Atlas trying to carry the world."

"I feel like him," Maddie said. "There's so much to worry about. This fund-raiser, Ashley—"

"Still no word from the investigator as to Ashley's whereabouts?" Catie asked.

Maddie shook her head, and Josie frowned. "Drat. Even I'm beginning to worry."

Catie smiled encouragingly. "You know Ashley. When she returns, she'll be brimming with stories of adventure. Speaking of which, that meeting today was quite an adventure, Maddie."

"Maybe it's better if we leave the adventure to Ashley. Everytime I try to do something impulsive it goes awry. Look at my elopement."

"What's there to look at?" Josie argued. "You and Blackthorne are perfect for one another. Maddie, anyone could see that he's mad for you."

Tears stung Maddie's eyes before she could dash them away.

"What's wrong?" Catie said, coming to sit on the edge of the bed opposite Josie.

"He isn't mad for me," Maddie said, accepting Josie's handkerchief when the tears wouldn't stop. "He doesn't love me."

"Of course he does," Josie said. Maddie wished she had her cousin's conviction.

Maddie shook her head. "I made a huge mistake. I accidentally told him I loved him. He said we could have the fund-raiser here, and I was so excited that I just blurted it out." She looked at her cousins. Their faces were blurry. "I didn't even know I loved him, and then, when I said it, it wasn't just a slip—something you say because you're happy and don't really mean it. I really meant it." She shook her head. "I think I was more surprised than he was. I really do love him."

"Of course you do," Catie told her.

"But I don't want to love him. He makes me so angry, and he's always trying to protect me. Most of the time I feel like strangling him."

Josie patted her hand. "But you don't because you can't live without him. We know, Maddie. You can deny it all you want, but you do love him."

"And he doesn't love me."

"But he does," Catie said. "He just can't admit it."

"Why?"

Catie shrugged. "I don't know, Maddie, but I have a feeling that you do."

His mother. The thought came to her unbidden. His mother might have been the only other woman he'd ever loved, and he lost her so violently and so young. Jack was afraid to hazard his heart again. Just as he was afraid to risk her own safety.

Maddie sighed. How could she overcome something like that? What could she do to make Jack risk his heart again?

She looked at her cousins. "It's hopeless."

Catie raised her eyebrows. "What happened

to all your optimism? You're always saying we should think positively."

"I know, but this time it really is hopeless. He'll never jeopardize his heart again."

"He already has," Josie told her. "You only have to make him realize it."

Chapter 21

⁓⸺♋⸺⁓

Maddie stood back, surveying the ballroom one last time. It was draped in red and blue silk, colors she'd chosen to pay homage to the British military uniform. In one corner was a long table filled with the items for auction. Beside it there was a raised dais, where the auction would take place, with a group of chairs facing it.

In little less than an hour the guests would arrive, and she would hand each a program. Footmen would circulate through the room, carrying silver trays laden with tea cakes, sandwiches, crumpets, and assorted delicacies. More footmen would circulate with coffee, tea, and punch.

"It looks perfect," Catie said, coming to stand beside her.

"It *is* perfect," Maddie said. "For the first time, I've done everything exactly the way I wanted. I had time to oversee every detail, no flitting from this society to that and another. All my attention was focused here."

"I thought you'd hate that."

"I did too, but I realized that all these years I've been trying to do too much. In the end, I accomplished very little. It's so much better to do one thing really well than a hundred things poorly."

"Don't let Blackthorne hear you say that."

Maddie bit her lip.

"He's still not speaking to you?"

"Oh, he speaks to me, but not about anything of consequence. We talk of the weather, Parliament, rising taxes. We don't talk about love. I'm afraid to mention the word in conversation. Yesterday I started to say, 'I love apricots,' and ended up saying, 'I lo-like apricots so very much.' I hate this."

Catie put a hand on her arm. "Give it time."

Maddie nodded, her throat too tight to speak. She wanted to give Jack time, knew he needed time, but she needed to hear him tell her that he loved her. She knew he cared, knew he would do anything to protect her, keep her safe. But she wanted the words of love.

Catie squeezed her arm. "Don't look now, but I think our veterans have arrived."

Maddie didn't need to look. She could hear Captain Roberts's peg leg click on the marble floor in the vestibule and Colonel Shivers and Lieutenant Beebe quarreling about whose joints ached the most.

"They're early," Maddie hissed at Catie. "How am I supposed to keep them away from the tea cakes?"

"You'd better think of something."

* * *

Jack stood in the corner of the bustling ballroom and watched Maddie glide from one group to another. Sometimes when he watched her from a distance he couldn't believe she actually belonged to him. She was so beautiful with her chestnut curls and sapphire eyes, her teasing smile and creamy skin.

He had the urge to touch her, to kiss her each time he saw her. Today she wore a light blue muslin gown that made her waist look tiny and showed a great deal of her rounded shoulders. The color brought out her already amazing eyes. He couldn't help but imagine that gown crumpled on the floor of their bedroom, and Maddie naked in bed beside him.

Smiling, she left one assemblage and flitted to the next. As soon as she joined the trio of ladies, the women burst into laughter. She had that effect on people. He admired the effortless way she charmed and set them at ease. People genuinely liked her, and she seemed to feel the same.

He, on the other hand, had always felt awkward at social events. He didn't dance, didn't flirt, didn't chitchat. Though he'd done a lot of chitchat lately. The comfortable conversation between Maddie and him had suddenly dried up, and he'd been forced to talk of banalities.

He knew it was his fault. Every time he saw his wife, he worried she'd repeat her declaration. He worried she'd press him to make one. Just one more way love ruined everything.

As he watched, the last of the guests took their seats in the cluster of chairs and the auction began. If the number of people in attendance at the fundraiser was any indication—about a hundred, by his estimation—it should be a rousing success.

Of course, most of those people had come to gawk at the newlyweds. That or to see the bear. Last night he had learned that one item up for auction was an afternoon with Blackjack the Bear. Maddie apparently thought the opportunity to pet a wild animal would be a popular attraction. Little did she know, he intended to bid on the afternoon with Blackjack.

And win him.

He'd already begun construction on a large outdoor enclosure at his country house, and he intended to move the animal there at the earliest opportunity.

Thus far, Blackjack had been tame and well-behaved, but Jack wasn't taking any chances that some idiot buck would bid on the afternoon with the bear, tease the beast, and get his intestines ripped out for the effort.

And if Maddie didn't like that he was bidding on her prize item, she couldn't complain. All the money went to help the pirates—er, veterans.

Jack watched Maddie's skirts swirl as she went to stand beside her cousins. She whispered something to Lady Westman, and the trio erupted in smiles. Despite the added security at the house today, he was keeping a close eye on his wife. So far the task had been easy, but now Maddie whispered something to Lady Valentine and then disappeared into the crowd and exited the ballroom. When she didn't return a moment later, he moved to follow her. He didn't like having her out of his sight.

Unfortunately, the auctioneer chose that moment to place the afternoon with Blackjack up for bid.

With a low curse, Jack stepped forward and placed the initial bid. It was far higher than what was being asked, and he didn't expect any resistance. He intended to win, and win quickly. But before he could claim victory, he was countered first by Lady Wiggleswade and then by Lord Addison.

Normally, Jack loved a good fight, but he didn't have time for it today. His next bid was, once again, exorbitantly high, but his competitors weren't deterred. Lady Wiggleswade offered ten pounds more, and Addison offered twenty.

With a last glance at the door Maddie had passed through, Jack bid again.

Maddie slipped out of the ballroom, smiling to herself. The auction was going splendidly. Soon, His Royal Highness's Society for Invalid Veterans of Overseas Conflicts would be able to afford a new hospital and better medical care. Perhaps they might even be able to provide housing for those veterans and their families who needed it.

She skipped along the passage outside the ball-room, on her way to the stairs leading to the kitch-ens. As she'd feared, the veterans had partaken in more than their share of tea cakes, and she hoped Cook had thought to hold some in reserve.

"Lady Blackthorne." She heard a weak voice calling her, and turned in a slow circle, searching for the source.

At the end of the passageway, she noticed Jack's library door was open and moved closer. Hadn't they locked all the rooms not being used on this floor? She neared the open door and it swung in-ward, revealing Sergeant Timms inside, beckon-ing her.

"Sergeant?"

His face was pale, and he clenched the door as though unsteady on his feet.

"What's wrong? Are you well?"

"My lady, I need your help." He released the door and stumbled back.

Alarmed, Maddie rushed inside. Timms was leaning against the bookshelf to the left of the door, and she went to him immediately. "Sir, what is the matter?"

He looked up at her, his blue eyes filled with sad-ness. "I'm sorry, my lady. I didn't want to, but—"

"Oh, shut up already," barked a high-pitched voice.

Maddie turned toward the door, but it slammed shut, revealing the Duke of Bleven and two of his men.

Her heart lurched into her throat and she backed away from the Black Duke. She wondered briefly if anyone would hear her scream.

"Your Grace." She tried to keep her voice from wavering, while her mind raced for an escape plan. The inside door, leading to the dining room, was locked, and she didn't have the keys with her. The window to the garden? "How kind of you to attend my fund-raiser," she continued in a light voice. "The auction is in the ballroom." She bumped into Jack's desk and reached a hand back to steady herself.

Bleven sneered at her. "I didn't come for the auction, Lady Blackthorne."

Maddie swallowed. Her hand closed on something cold and metallic—Jack's letter opener—and she palmed it, hiding it in her skirts.

"What did you come for?"

"You."

He signaled his two men, and the thugs advanced on her. One carried a large sack and the other a gag and rope.

Maddie slipped the letter opener into the inside pocket of her dress just before the men grabbed her.

"One hundred pounds! Going, going . . . sold to the Marquess of Blackthorne."

The room erupted in applause, and Jack, smiling, bowed. Lady Wiggleswade glowered at him.

Old bat. As though he wanted to wager a hundred pounds for an afternoon with his own bear. He should have let her win. She probably would have fainted at the first sight of Blackjack.

Lord Addison approached, holding out a hand in congratulations. The baron was saying something about making other arrangements for his young son to meet the bear, but though Jack accepted the man's hand, he barely heard Lord Addison. He glanced around for Maddie, wanting to see her sweet smile, her approving gaze.

He saw her cousins, but the spot Maddie had occupied earlier beside Lady Valentine was still empty.

Jack scowled.

"Excuse me, my lord." Knowing he was being rude to Lord Addison, and not caring, he turned his back on the baron and stalked toward Maddie's cousins.

"Congratulations," Lady Westman said when he neared. "Maddie will be pleased her item raised so much."

"Where is she?"

Lady Westman's brow furrowed. "She said she was going to the kitchen to request more tea cakes. I'm sure she'll return in a moment."

"I'll go check on her."

But Maddie wasn't in the kitchens. And his cook hadn't seen her. Jack climbed the stairs and strode quickly back to the ballroom, scanning the room for Maddie. The auction was over now, and the guests were standing about, making it difficult for him to find his petite wife.

He saw Lady Valentine, looking equally anxious. As soon as she spotted him, she rushed over. "My lord, did you find her?"

"No. She hasn't returned?"

"No."

"Fire!" a shrill voice carried over the din of voices.

"What the devil?" He'd just been in the kitchens. There was no fire. But panic had overtaken the guests and it was too late to soothe them.

"Fire! Run!"

There was a screech and then a momentous clatter as the hundred or so guests stumbled over one another to reach the exit doors.

"Devil take it!" Jack grabbed Lady Valentine's hand and yanked her to his side. He bent to help an elderly lady, who'd been knocked to the floor, back to her feet and handed the woman to Lady Valentine. "This way."

Pulling Lady Valentine behind him, Jack carved a path to the doors, slamming them open and pushing Lady Valentine through. There were only two sets of double doors, the doors to the dining room having been locked, so he ran to the sash windows that overlooked the side garden. One by one he threw them up, opening the house. One set of windows was stuck, and he kicked the glass, breaking it in an effort to provide more escape routes.

"Slow down!" Jack ordered, grabbing a man elbowing his way through. "Go slowly."

Next he headed back toward the inside doors. As he moved, he scanned the crowd for Maddie, stopping several women with hair the color of hers to peer at their faces as they rushed by. Where the hell was she?

And that's when he smelled the smoke. Dear God, there really was a fire. The crowd seemed to realize it as well, and their pushing and shoving became more frenzied and vicious. Torn between keeping order and finding the source of the fire, he chose the latter, ducking out of the ballroom and into the crowded passageway.

Smoke burned his eyes and nose. Disregarding instinct, he turned toward the source of it. The smoke billowed from the back of the house, from his library.

"Maddie!" he yelled. "Maddie!"

Past the ballroom there was no crowd, and he only had to fight the smoke to find his library. But the damn door was closed and locked, and he had to jam his shoulder into it. "Maddie!"

The door was warm. He felt its heat even through the thick material of his tailcoat.

Please God, don't let her be inside. Please don't let me be too late.

Jack moved back and ran at the door, ramming his shoulder into it. The door shuddered but the thick wood held. Swearing, he rammed it again. This time he heard a crunch and the door gave way. Flames, bursts of searing red and orange, licked at him. Coughing, he stumbled forward.

"Maddie?"

No answer. He bent low, groping blindly along the floor. His hands grazed the edge of his bookshelf and then something else.

A foot?

"Maddie?"

He fell to his knees, forcing his eyes to open in the smoke, to peer more closely.

"Oh, God."

Maddie had given up fighting.

In the library, Bleven's lackeys had bound her hands, gagged her, and thrown her in the canvas sack. Then they'd opened the library window and handed her out of the house.

At least she thought that was what they'd done. She couldn't see anything through the thick canvas, and the heat inside was stifling. Better to remain still, she thought. Fighting made it hard to breathe.

Now she was inside a carriage, tossed on one of the seats as the conveyance wound its way leisurely through London's streets. Someone was across from her—Bleven, she supposed—and he didn't appear to be in a hurry or even to be worried that his treachery would be discovered.

Jack would come after him. Of that, Maddie had no doubt. She only hoped it wouldn't be too late.

Jiminy! What was wrong with her? If ever there was a time to think positively, now was it.

Concentrating hard, she felt the edge of the letter opener prick her thigh. All she had to do was convince Bleven to untie her and then get close enough. She knew the letter opener would slide cleanly into Bleven's pale skin.

She only needed the opportunity. And the courage.

"You're awfully quiet over there, Lady Blackthorne." Bleven's high-pitched voice floated across the carriage. "I hope you haven't tired yourself out. I have big plans for you, and I shall find my games so much more enjoyable if you have a bit of spirit left."

If she hadn't been gagged, she would have cursed him.

And then, as though he had read her mind and was granting her wish, the bottom of the sack was loosened and removed. As it whooshed over her head, cool air rushed over her. Maddie took deep breaths.

When she'd had her fill, her gaze found Bleven. He was seated across from her, and even in the dimness of the carriage she could see he was smiling. But she took solace in the knowledge that he'd taken the precaution of closing the coach's drapes. He wasn't as confident as he appeared if he showed some measure of concern at being caught.

"Oh, I'm not going to be caught," Bleven said.

Maddie could only blink at him. Did the man read minds, too?

"I don't imagine you're much of a card player, are you, Lady Blackthorne? Your face gives all away."

Maddie glared at him, hoping he could read exactly what she was thinking at that moment. Bleven chuckled.

"There's the spirit I was hoping for."

And that was as much as he was going to see of it. Jack would find them any moment, and then Bleven was going to be very, very sorry.

"Your husband won't be coming after us," Bleven told her, his tone blasé. "Not right away, at any rate. By the time he realizes you're gone, it will be too late. He'll never find where I've taken you."

Maddie shook her head. Let Bleven believe what he would. She knew Jack would come for her.

"Oh, you think so, do you? Do you not agree that a fire can be a powerful distraction? Surely, your husband will have to deal with that small inconvenience before coming after you. If he's even realized you're gone."

Maddie stared hard at Bleven. Hating him, yet needing the drips of information he gave.

Fire? What on earth was he talking about?

Bleven grinned. His teeth were small and even. He reminded her of a small spaniel that growled and barked to make a show but ran away at the first sign of danger.

"Oh, that's right," Bleven said, baring his puppy teeth. "You didn't see us start the fire in the library, did you?" His face was overcome with mock sadness. "I do hope none of your guests was injured in the blaze."

Maddie didn't want to believe what she was hearing, but looking at the duke's face, she knew it was true. How dare he? How dare he come into her home and—

With a scream of anger, she launched herself at Bleven. Her hands were bound, but her feet were free, and she kicked at him. One foot landed in his soft belly before he wrestled her to the floor, pinning her legs.

With the duke's considerable weight on her, Maddie struggled to breathe, and her own gasps and the noise from the carriage wheels just below her were so loud at first that she couldn't hear the duke.

He was laughing.

Jack pulled Sergeant Timms out of the library and dropped him on the back steps. Lord Valentine was standing nearby with his wife.

"Don't let him move," Jack demanded. "Hold him. I'll be back for the bastard."

Without waiting for a response, Jack turned away and gathered his servants. "Grab every pail and container you can find," he ordered. "Dip them in water from the water butt and make a chain to extinguish the fire."

When the men and women rushed to do his bidding, he sent other servants to the nearby houses to warn his neighbors of the fire danger and to solicit more aid.

And then he went back inside. The library was now engulfed in flames, and he forced himself to rush by it. Instead he searched the ballroom, the dining room, and the upper floors. He heard Blackjack bellowing behind Maddie's bedroom door, and he flung the door open, hoping that Maddie was with her bear.

But the beast was alone, panicked by the fire. Jack threw a blanket over the animal's head and led it downstairs and out the front.

He handed the animal over to a wary Ridgeley and scanned the milling crowd for Maddie again.

She wasn't there. Damn it.

Rushing to the back of the house again, he saw that the fire in the library was receding, falling victim to the chain of servants and their full water buckets.

Valentine raised a hand and motioned him over. "Did you find Maddie?"

Jack shook his head. "She's not inside."

"You'd better talk to him." Valentine gestured to Sergeant Timms. The man's face was blackened with soot, making his blue eyes appear brighter. Jack was reminded of another pair of blue eyes, and his anger surged.

He grabbed the sergeant by his collar and hauled him up. The man weighed practically nothing, and Jack easily dragged him over to one of the outer walls. "Where the hell is my wife? If you know anything, speak now, or I swear on all that's holy that I'll kill you where you stand."

"I didn't want to do it," the man blubbered, refusing to meet his gaze.

"Didn't want to do what?"

"Forgive. Forgive. Forgive."

"He's been saying that for the past ten minutes," Valentine said from behind Jack.

"What did you do?" Jack tightened his grip. "Where is Lady Blackthorne?"

The sergeant shook his head. "The Black Duke has her now."

Jack's heart stopped and everything around him seemed to lose color and sound. He swayed on his feet for a moment, then let out a howl, slamming the sergeant hard against the brick. Once. Twice.

Valentine grabbed Jack's shoulder and jerked him back. Jack's grip on the sergeant's neck loosened, but he turned on Valentine, rage roiling through him.

But Valentine held his gaze steady. "Kill him now and we'll never get any more information."

Jack was breathing hard and murder pulsed in his blood. But he knew Valentine was right. He turned back to the sergeant, now slumped against the wall. "If you want to save yourself, speak now. Where is my wife?"

The sergeant shook his head. "You might as well kill me. I don't know."

"Goddamn it, you tell me something!" Jack demanded.

"My job was to lure her into the library. I didn't want to do it, but he would have killed me otherwise. I don't know what they were going to do with her afterward. I was supposed to go along, but one of Bleven's men hit me hard, left me for dead." His gaze finally met Jack's. "That's all I know, I swear."

Valentine pulled Jack aside. "I think he's telling the truth. He'd served his purpose. What use would Bleven have for an old man?"

Jack nodded. But if the sergeant didn't know where Bleven had taken Maddie, then the trail was cold. He would never find her.

"You could try his town house," Valentine suggested. "It's unlikely, but one of the servants might know something."

Jack nodded. "Fetch my horse!" he ordered one of his footmen. The man jumped to attention and rushed toward the mews.

"Give me a moment," Valentine said. "I'll come with you."

Jack shook his head. "You have a promising political career ahead of you, my lord. You don't want your name mixed up in this."

"My career be damned. This is Maddie we're talking about, not to mention arson and the kidnapping of an innocent woman."

"No," Jack said, striding toward his mews, where the footman was helping a groom saddle his best horse. "When I find Bleven, this will be murder."

He mounted the horse, yelled for the gate to be opened, and rode away.

Chapter 22

When the carriage stopped, the door flew open and one of Bleven's thugs grabbed Maddie by the hair, pulling her out. Her feet tangled in her skirts and she fell hard to her knees. The other thug yanked her to her feet and dragged her through the warehouse door.

It was dark and smelled moldy inside. Maddie's heart kicked in her chest. This was it. Whatever Bleven had planned would happen here. And with her hands tied, she was completely helpless. The letter opener secreted in her pocket might as well still be on Jack's desk.

Jack.

Oh, please God. Please let him be safe, she prayed. But she knew that if anything happened to her, he would never recover. He'd never forgive himself, though this was no more his fault than his mother's death had been. She knew she had to stay alive, not just for herself, but for Jack.

Resolution making her strong, she twisted away from Bleven's man and swung around to face the

Black Duke. He was standing in the doorway, the sunlight shining around him in a deceptive halo. Maddie hoped he could see her face. She willed him to see the contempt and the challenge in her eyes. Was he so much of a coward that he kept her, a defenseless woman, bound and gagged?

"You do have spirit left, don't you?" Bleven said. He entered the warehouse, and the door closed with a loud thud behind him. One of the men lit a candle, and Maddie took a quick inventory of her surroundings. There wasn't much to see: a few crates, a scarred table where the candle burned, and an old mattress in one corner of the room.

Maddie's belly lurched violently when she saw the mattress. It was dirty and stained with something that looked very much like blood. She swallowed the rising nausea.

Everything was going to work out. Everything would be fine. Jack would find her.

"Free her," Bleven ordered his thug, and Maddie quickly ducked her head. She didn't want Bleven to see how pleased she was.

The lackey, a blond man with light brown eyes and a large forehead, yanked the rope hard, and Maddie stifled a gasp. A few more tugs and her hands were free.

Pushing the man away, she loosened her gag and pulled it down.

"There, isn't this much more civilized?" Bleven motioned his men toward the door. "Out."

"But you said we could watch," the blond thug complained. "And we could have her when you were done."

Bleven rounded on them, and both men stepped back. "Get out."

The men obeyed, and when the door thudded closed, Bleven turned to face her. "Now, Lady Blackthorne, shall we do this the painful way or the more painful way? I want to hear you scream."

Jack smashed his fist into the butler's face. The servant's nose broke this time, splattering blood on Jack's tailcoat. The man howled and tried to crawl away, but Jack hauled him back, clutching him by the throat. Jack tried to ignore the river of viscous liquid pouring from the man's nose and coating his hand with crimson.

"Now, I'm going to ask you one more time," Jack said quietly to the butler. "And I'm going to ask you nicely. But if you don't answer me, you give me no choice but to show you my nasty side. I don't think you'll like it."

The man whimpered.

"Where is your master?"

The servant opened his mouth, and Jack held a finger up. "Do not tell me you don't know."

He tightened his hand on the man's throat, the blood making their contact slick and sticky.

"But he'll kill me, sir," the butler whined.

Jack leaned close to him, the metallic smell of blood flooding his nostrils. "Not if I kill him first. Do you think I can do it?"

The servant nodded, eyes wide.

"Tell me," Jack demanded.

The butler gurgled, then spoke.

Maddie took a step back, trying to put more distance between her and Bleven. He was advancing on her one small step at a time, and the leer on his face left little doubt as to what he planned.

Her hand itched to retrieve the letter opener, brandish it and ward him off, but she knew if she acted now, it would be too soon. Besides, she was trembling so much she would probably drop it.

She had to be brave. She had to forget she was Lady Madeleine—Lady Blackthorne—Lady anything. She had to become the kind of woman who could slide a steel blade into a man's chest and twist it until he coughed, choked, and died.

And if any man deserved to die that way, it was Bleven.

He moved toward her again, and she took another step back.

"My husband is going to find you, Duke," she told him. "And when he does, he'll kill you slowly."

Bleven laughed. "I'd like to see him try. I have plans for Jack Martingale. Yes, I do."

Maddie stepped back again.

"But first I want to deal with you. Now, my lady, stop scurrying about. There's no place to hide." He crooked a finger at her. "Come here."

She shook her head. "I don't think so."

Bleven's smile never faltered as he reached in his coat and withdrew a slim small pistol.

Well, that changed things a bit.

Maddie bit the inside of her cheek. Hard. She had to still her body's shaking.

"Let me phrase that another way. Get over there." He waved the gun at the mattress. "And take your clothes off. I'm done playing cat and mouse."

Jack rode as fast as he could into the shipyard, reining his mount hard before jumping off and running for the warehouse. He recognized the dingy blue building immediately as the one Bleven's butler had described. If the man had lied to him, he swore there would be hell to pay.

The warehouse looked deserted, but Jack wasn't taking any chances. He kept scanning and listening for Bleven's men. But nothing moved and all was silent. The men must be inside with Bleven and Maddie.

An image from his youth—of three men pinning a woman down in an alley—flashed through his mind.

No. It wouldn't end that way. Not this time.

Jack reached into his pocket and withdrew the Manton pistol. He'd had enough foresight to grab it from his desk before dragging Sergeant Timms outside the burning library. Now, he hefted the familiar weight in his hand and reached for the warehouse door.

It was locked, and he realized there would be no way to make a surprise entrance. So he stepped back and rammed his foot into the door handle, splintering the wood and jarring the passage halfway open.

With a yell, he raised the pistol. "Let her go, Bleven, or I kill you now!"

His voice echoed, but nothing in the warehouse moved. Nothing breathed.

Cautiously, Jack moved forward, nudging the door fully open with his boot. He moved aside, allowing the light to stream over his shoulder. What he saw made him slam his fist hard into the door, ripping it off its hinges.

The warehouse was empty, deserted.

"Bloody hell!"

"Looking for 'is Grace?" someone behind him asked.

Jack rounded on the small man and aimed his pistol at the stranger's chest. The man was short, his face dark and weathered. He was obviously a former sailor.

"Don't shoot me, gov." "I can't 'elp you if I'm dead."

"Who are you?"

"Work for 'is Grace, I do. Looks like you got a quarrel with 'im."

"Do you know where he is?"

The man shrugged. "I might. Wot's it to me? Maybe I don't know. Maybe I don't rightly remember."

Jack reached into his pocket and withdrew a handful of coins. "How's this for incentive?"

The man stuck his grubby hand out. "Me memory just improved."

Maddie was running out of options. She didn't believe Bleven would shoot her, but she'd backed herself up against the wall, and he was coming closer. Her hand hovered near the opening to her dress pocket, but she didn't dare grab the letter opener yet.

Bleven closed the distance between them until she could see the bead of sweat on his temple. He was too close. She scooted to one side, then heard a scraping sound.

Jack?

She glanced toward the door to the warehouse, and when she took her eyes off Bleven, he pounced. He slammed into her, one hand grabbing her around the throat and thrusting her back hard against the wall. Her head thudded on the wood and she tasted blood.

Bleven's hand tightened on her neck, and she was forced to gasp for air. Forgetting the letter opener, she clawed at his hand and struggled for breath. She was able to loosen one of his fingers, but then he pocketed the gun and his other hand came up.

His face was close, the small teeth bared in an expression halfway between a smile and a grimace. Maddie wheezed as black dots flitted across her vision. Her feet were sliding out from under her, and she struggled to keep her footing. She dropped her hand, fumbling in her skirts for the letter opener.

"Let . . . go," she managed to hiss, but his hands closed harder, and the room began to dim. She kicked at him, tore at his fingers with one hand while her other closed on the warm metal hidden in her skirts.

She struggled for one last breath, even the smallest particle of air to keep her going.

But blackness descended and her grip relaxed.

Jack knew he was running out of time. If what the compact sailor had told him was correct, Bleven's other warehouse was clear across town. He didn't know if he'd make it in time.

And if the sailor was wrong . . . He did not want to even think about that.

He rode through the back streets, hoping to avoid the traffic and make quicker time. The wind whipped around him, making a screaming sound in his ears.

Or perhaps the screaming was within him.

He pushed his horse faster and harder, and finally turned into a lane leading toward a row of ramshackle warehouses. At the far end, Jack caught sight of two men. They loitered outside a warehouse, one with his ear pressed to the wooden door.

Jack's breath came quicker; the screaming in his head muted.

He'd found her.

Maddie was jarred back to her senses as she fell on the mattress. It was thin and did little to cushion the hard floor beneath.

Above her, Bleven was yanking his cravat loose. The white linen fell down his chest like a snowy bird.

She took a shaky breath. Blinking, she tried to dispel the black dots still floating before her eyes.

"I've been looking forward to this," Bleven said, unbuttoning his collar. "I've been waiting to put my hands on you, to see Jack Martingale's face when he realizes what I've done to you."

Maddie swallowed. Her throat was too raw to allow her to speak, and she knew it would be a wasted effort anyway.

"The Martingale family has insulted me for the last time. First the mother . . . " Bleven paused. "Did your husband tell you what I had done to his mother?"

Maddie's hand was still in her pocket, and at his words, she closed her fist around the handle of the letter opener. It was Bleven? He had been responsible for the death of Jack's mother?

"This time I won't be in the back watching.

That wasn't as fulfilling as I'd hoped. This time I'll do the honors."

Maddie felt her belly churn with nausea, but she pushed it down. As Bleven removed his tail-coat, she slowly drew the blade free of her pocket, keeping it hidden behind her skirts.

Her hand closed tight. *Come and get me.*

Bleven dropped his tailcoat, and then, with ·a leer, he was on top of her. Maddie's arm was pinned and she could feel the dull blade dig into her hip. Bleven ripped at her bodice, and she brought her knee up sharply, hoping to dislodge him and free her hand.

He grunted and moved slightly, but it was enough. The letter opener free, she slid it from her skirts. Bleven had torn the material of her dress, and she could feel him fumbling with his panta-loons. One minute more and he would rise up. That was her chance.

Outside, she heard something bang against the door. Her head whipped in that direction and her hand froze.

Jack.

She closed her eyes, and could all but feel his presence.

Jack.

It had to be. *Please God, let it be.*

There was a sound like a grunt or the thump of a man falling, and her heart stopped. If Bleven heard . . .

He glanced that way, then reached a hand under her skirts. He flipped them up and, to her shock, arched up to free himself from his pantaloons.

His throat was bare, his neck at the perfect angle. One quick thrust and she could kill him. She knew it. She saw it so clearly.

She heard the door slam open, heard Jack call her name, and using the distraction, thrust the blade up hard. But Bleven must have seen the movement. With a roar, he knocked it out of her hand.

The letter opener clattered to the floor. It tumbled away, and with it, her perfect strike was gone.

Bleven rolled off her, rising to face Jack.

Maddie turned her head and her heart swelled at the sight of her husband standing in the doorway. His dark eyes blazed, and his black hair fell over his forehead. His face was sooty and his clothes were covered in ash and blood, but in that moment he was the most beautiful man she had ever seen.

She opened her mouth, tried to warn Jack that Bleven had a pistol, but no sound emerged from her bruised throat. It didn't matter anyway.

Jack had already raised his own pistol. "This is for my mother."

The warehouse reverberated from the loud burst of gunpowder, and Bleven's body jerked back.

As Blevin spun around, Maddie caught the duke's expression. He looked surprised as he fell. There was a soft thud as he hit the floor, and then Jack was beside her.

His warm strong arms came around her and he gathered her close. She clung to him, tears streaming down her cheeks. "I love you, Jack," she croaked. "I love you."

Chapter 23

He'd almost lost her. That one thought dominated his mind, making it impossible to think of anything else.

It was Maddie, in her raspy voice, who had suggested they go to Lord and Lady Valentine's town house. It was Maddie who told him they should hire the first hack they saw, and Maddie who gave the jarvey directions.

All Jack could do was hold her, stroke her glossy hair, touch the soft skin of her neck, now marred by the red imprints of Bleven's fingers.

"I'm fine," she told him over and over. "You saved me."

But Jack couldn't believe it. He needed to hold her, to kiss her, to have her beside him, and then maybe, in a dozen years, he would believe she was actually safe.

When they reached the Valentine town house, Maddie's cousin took one look at them and whisked them out of sight. Jack found himself in a moderately sized bedchamber with clean linen and a small bathtub.

But he refused to be separated from Maddie so that she might bathe as well. Instead, he ordered another tub and more water, and when he finished washing himself, he assisted with her bath.

An hour later they were both clean and fed and naked. He tucked her snuggly under the covers in the tester bed.

"I'm anxious to see how much damage the town house sustained," Maddie was saying.

Her voice sounded better, and Jack rose on his elbow to look at her neck. The red welts from Bleven's fingers were fading.

"You said you thought the fire was contained to the library?" she asked.

Jack watched her mouth move, watched her red lips part, listened to the sweet sound of her voice.

"Jack?" She touched his shoulder. "I asked you—"

"I almost lost you," he said. He was looking down at her, his hand fanning her damp chestnut hair out over the pillow. He touched her pale cheeks and then her swollen lips. He'd kissed her so much that her lips were red and slightly puffy.

"I'm fine," she said, smiling at him. "I told you." She lowered her eyes. "Why didn't you tell me, Jack? Why didn't you tell me Bleven was the one who had your mother killed?"

He closed his eyes. "I wasn't certain until the night of the prince's ball. And I didn't want you to worry. I'll always protect you."

"I know you will, Jack. I knew you would come for me today."

He shook his head, marveling at her trust in him. He hadn't been at all sure if he would make it in time. And if he hadn't . . .

"Maddie, if I'd lost you without telling you how I felt, I would have regretted it the rest of my life."

"I know how you feel, Jack." She twined her fingers with his. "I know how much you care."

He shook his head. "You don't, sweetheart. I've never told you." He clutched her hand tighter. "Madeleine, I love you. I think I loved you the first time I saw you, but since then my feelings have grown . . . immeasurably. I adore you. I can't live without you. I love you so much." He buried his head in her lavender-scented hair. "I love you so much."

He felt her arms come around him, wrapping him in the warmth of her body. "I love you, too." She pulled back, met his gaze. "So much."

He lowered his head, kissing her softly, tasting her and memorizing her sweetness. He'd slipped his head in the noose now, and his new vulnerability was almost a relief. He'd fought it for so long, so hard. Surrender was inevitable—

With a low moan, Maddie arched under him.

—and gratifying.

"I want you, love," he murmured in her ear.

"Please." Her fingernails dug into his back as her legs opened to cradle his erection. She was burning up, and he could feel her wetness.

And still he made no move to enter her, wanting to prolong and heighten the tension. The exquisite torture.

He lowered his head, taking one of her hard nipples in his mouth. His tongue rolled over it as his hand palmed her lush breast. "Sweetheart," he murmured against her flesh. "Have you noticed anything?"

He looked down at her flushed face and misty eyes. She looped her arms around his neck and pulled him in for a kiss. Arching her hips invitingly, she whispered, "You feel wonderful. Make love to me, Jack."

"Patience, love. Have you noticed where we are?"

She frowned at him, once again wiggling beneath him. "In bed?"

He smiled and bent to kiss her. "Finally."

Maddie shuddered as the pounding underneath her reached a crescendo. The tea service clattered on the tray beside her, the lamp on the table shook, and, across from her, Catie closed her eyes and tried to hold her teacup steady.

The pounding ceased for a moment, and Maddie took a breath. "As I was saying, Jack's new library should be completed in a matter of weeks. And then we'll begin work on the dining room. It sustained minor damage from the fire's heat."

Catie nodded. "You're fortunate no one was hurt. If Lord Blackthorne hadn't acted so quickly, the whole house might have gone up in flames—and taken several others with it."

"Jack's amazing. I don't know how he was able to think so clearly, considering everything else that was going on."

Catie frowned as a low pounding started up once again. "Did you see the *Post* this morning?" she asked over the din.

Maddie nodded. "They're calling Bleven's death the work of thieves."

"Didn't the investigator find it strange that Bleven's butler had disappeared? There was no mention of it in the papers."

Maddie shrugged. "Apparently, the investigator came to the conclusion that the duke was killed during an attempt by thieves to burgle his warehouse. I'm not certain what the investigator thinks the thieves were trying to steal in that rancid place. There was nothing of value." She paused, wondering what the investigator had made of the silver letter opener.

"They're also calling Bleven's death a horrible tragedy," Catie said. "He's to have a state funeral. Do not tell me that doesn't anger you. If they knew—"

"It would only cause more scandal. Jack and I would have to prove our case by sullying a dead man's name. When all was said and done, there'd be more questions than answers. I'll gladly make Bleven a national hero if it means Jack and I will be left alone."

"And I'm sure this forgiving attitude has nothing to do with His Royal Highness's Society for Invalid Veterans of Overseas Conflicts."

Below Maddie, a second hammer joined the first, and the house shook. "What was that sound?"

Catie shook her head and laughed. Maddie smiled too, because, of course, her cousin was correct. It wouldn't help His Royal Highness's Society for Invalid Veterans of Overseas Conflicts one bit if its new president were embroiled in a notorious scandal. And she had the most wonderful charity ball planned for the end of the Season.

She'd even started the preparations, though she hadn't told Jack quite yet. He was still overprotective toward her. But Maddie had noticed that since the incident with Bleven, he'd relaxed a bit.

It seemed he was coming to realize that he couldn't protect her all the time. She'd said as much to him last night, mentioning that life, with all its risks, was meant to be lived to the fullest.

Jack had nodded. "My mother used to say the

same thing, and despite what happened to her, I don't think she would have been happy living any other way."

"Her death wasn't your fault, Jack," Maddie had said again, looking into his eyes and willing him to believe her.

He'd smiled and kissed her, but she thought she saw a flicker of acceptance in his eyes. A flicker of forgiveness for the boy that he had been.

She felt hopeful that, given time, Jack would pardon that little boy.

She also hoped that, given time, he would worry less about her. He would love her more and guard her less.

And then maybe she could convince him that the Orphan's Munificent Society could use her efforts to help build a new foundling house. After all, by the time the renovations on their town house were done and Blackjack's large enclosure at Jack's country house was completed, she would know more about construction than most women. Who better to oversee a construction project for the orphans?

"What time is it?" Catie yelled over the noise.

"Five-thirty!"

"Wasn't—" The banging ceased, and Catie lowered her voice. "Wasn't Josie supposed to have tea with us?"

Lord, not another missing cousin. Maddie stood.

"I'll go see if she has sent a note."

Maddie left the drawing room and met Jack on his way up the stairs. With a smile, she moved aside to let him pass, but he snagged her around the waist at the last moment, pulling her up the stairs and into an alcove beside the drawing room.

He put his arms around her, holding her close. "Mmm, you smell good. Come up to the bedroom with me. I want to forget about all the hammers and workmen for an hour."

Maddie tried to disentangle herself, without success. "Jack, Catie is in the drawing room, and we're waiting for Josie. I was just going to see if she'd sent a note."

Jack nuzzled her neck. "Aren't your cousins married?"

"Yes." She felt a delicious warmth spreading through her body.

"Why don't they go home to their husbands?"

"Because we're having a meeting. Their husbands are going to have to wait. Just like you."

His expression was fierce, and she smiled, tracing his frown with one finger. "There's nothing wrong with a little anticipation," she whispered. "You don't want life to get tedious."

He raised a brow. "I have a feeling life with you will never be tedious."

"Maddie! Catie! Where are you?"

Jack sighed. "See what I mean?"

Maddie peered over his shoulder and saw Josie rushing up the stairs, Ridgeley hard on her heels. "Madam, allow me to introduce you!"

Josie shook her head. "There's no time for that!"

Jack released Maddie, and she stepped out of the alcove.

"There you are!" Josie said, pausing at the top of the stairs and panting. Her color was high, her red curls in complete disarray, and her gown stained.

"What on earth is the matter?" Maddie asked. Jack moved protectively closer, and his arm came about her waist.

"I ran all the way here," Josie wheezed, still trying to catch her breath.

Maddie's heart began to pound. "What's wrong?"

But instead of answering, Josie said, "Where's Catie? Is she here?"

"In the drawing room."

"Good. She won't believe this."

"Believe what?"

"It's Ashley," Josie said, moving toward the drawing room door. "She's back."

"With Lord Nicholas?" Maddie asked.

Josie nodded. "Oh, yes. And they've been back for"—she fumbled with the doorknob—"three days."

"Three days?" Maddie called after her. "Why hasn't she come to see us?"

"Good question. You'll have to ask her, and

when you do, ask just how long she's been involved with Lord Nicholas."

Maddie frowned. "What does that mean?"

"According to my source, they were seen together numerous times *before* your elopement."

Maddie exchanged a glance with Jack. They
had both suspected Ashley and Lord Nicholas
had a previous relationship. The nature of that relationship, however, was unclear.

"I don't know what is going on, but I intend to
find out." Josie finally turned the doorknob and
stumbled into the drawing room. Catie, already
on her feet, rushed to hear the news.

Maddie stood outside, still holding Jack's
hand.

Finally, he said, "I suppose we had better call
on them."

She nodded. "I suppose. But it's bound to be a
horrible muddle."

He considered. "Or perhaps it's like you always
say. Everything works out in the end." He bent to
kiss her, and Maddie, her heart full of love, kissed
him back.

Epilogue

"**A**ren't you going to tell me anything?" Maddie asked.

Ashley pursed her lips, and the sunlight glinted off the long golden curls tumbling down her shoulders. They were strolling in Hyde Park, their white parasols bumping into one another. A few yards ahead of them, Jack and Lord Nicholas stood facing one another.

Poor Jack. He looked frustrated. As usual, Lord Nicholas looked amused.

"What else do you want to know?" Ashley finally said. "I told you what happened."

Maddie shook her head. "But I don't believe it."

"Then you won't believe the rest." Ashley's sea green eyes stared back at her levelly.

"So I am supposed to believe that you and Lord Nicholas actually conspired—"

"I wouldn't have said we *conspired*. We collaborated."

Maddie sighed. "Fine. You collaborated to ensure that Lord Blackthorne and I married. I find that difficult to accept."

"That's how I felt when I realized you were eloping with a dog breeder. Really, Maddie! Someone had to save you!"

Maddie frowned at her. "How did Lord Nicholas become involved?"

Ashley bit her lip. "That's a rather long story."

"I have time."

"Suffice it to say that Lord Nicholas wanted to do his brother a favor. He felt guilty for all the trouble he'd caused over the years."

"And I was the favor?"

"You needed to be saved and Lord Nicholas thought his brother needed a wife. I thought you two would be perfect together."

"But that doesn't explain the innkeeper who chased us or the Duke of Bleven or the drunk priest. You cannot possibly have orchestrated all of that!"

Ashley raised her brows. "You underestimate us. A little bribery goes a long way."

"You bribed the Duke of Bleven!"

"No. That was one factor we hadn't counted on. I'm sorry he hurt you, Maddie. He was never part of the plan."

They walked in silence for a moment. Up ahead, Lord Nicholas slung his arm about Jack's shoulder. Jack looked like he wanted to shrug it off, but he didn't.

"And what exactly was your relationship with Lord Nicholas?" Maddie asked.

"He's an old family friend," Ashley said quickly. Too quickly.

"I see. I find it hard to imagine the two of you consp—collaborating together. You don't seem to like each other very much."

"We've had a few . . . minor difficulties.

"And now?"

"Now?"

"Ashley, stop being so evasive! What are your feelings for Lord Nicholas? You said before that you had trouble resisting him. Are you in love with him?"

"No!" Ashley cleared her throat. "I mean, no. It's a marriage of convenience. A marriage that worked out rather well for you."

"I don't believe any of this. I *know* you feel something for Lord Nicholas, Ashley, and he for you. I can see it—"

"Maddie!" Ashley rounded on her. "Stop trying to help."

"I can't," she protested quietly.

"Think of something else."

"Very well. Where have you been all this time?"

"Would you believe kidnapped by pirates?"

"No."

"I didn't think so."

In front of them, Jack turned and motioned for her to join him. Maddie gave Ashley one last look.

"You know, as much as I love Jack, I do miss our Spinster's Club."

"We were its last members."

"Perhaps we can form a new club."

Ashley laughed. "Why am I not surprised? Very well, then." She linked her arm with Maddie's and they started toward Jack and Lord Nicholas. "What shall we call it?"

Maddie smiled. "How about Misadventures in Matrimony?"

Author's Note

I first heard the story of Joseph Paisley several years ago on a writer's workshop tape about runaway marriages. Paisley was one of many men who went to Gretna after the English Parliament passed the Hardwicke Marriage Act in 1754. The act made it illegal for couples under the age of twenty-one to marry without parental consent, but the law only applied on English soil. In Scotland the law was more lenient. Couples only needed to be sixteen and in the presence of two witnesses to marry. As Gretna Green is the first town over the Scottish border, it became a popular spot for eloping English couples.

Paisley was one of the first anvil priests. One of his original occupations was smuggling, and most reports of him call attention to his fondness for drink. But what struck my fancy was a story about how he was called upon to marry two couples at the same time and accidentally married the wrong brides to the wrong grooms. Accounts of the event report that he shrugged off what he called a "trifling mistake" and told the newlyweds, "Ah weel, juist sort yersels oot."

I don't know what the real-life couples did, but the story gave me a kernel of an idea for a book—this book. As is the case with most books, I started with a question: What if two brides were accidentally married to the wrong grooms? And what if the mistake couldn't be readily corrected? What if the mistake was actually the best thing that could have happened? And so the story of Maddie and Jack was born.

Bear-baiting also plays an integral role in this novel. As cruel as it seems, it was a popular pastime in England until it was finally outlawed in 1835. The "sport" is very much how I have described it, with the exception that the event usually took place in an arena that was built like a theater. These bear-gardens were numerous and the favorite amusement for kings and queens. Unfortunately, the cruel practice of bear-baiting continues today in isolated areas of the world.

Maddie's sympathy for the animals would have been quite unusual in her time, but I don't believe it is unrealistic. There have always been people who fight cruelty, whether toward people or animals. Maddie is modeled after these courageous, unsung heroes and heroines.